RACHANEE LUMAYNO

HEIR OF
MAGIC
AND
MISCHANCE

KINGDOM LEGACY BOOK THREE

Editing and proofreading by Tom Loveman

Cover art by Fiona Jayde Media

Thank you for reading, I hope you enjoy Heir of Magic and Mischance!
If you have the time, please leave an honest review on Goodreads or wherever you purchased this book! Thanks!

ALSO BY RACHANEE LUMAYNO

CONTENTS

Join the Newsletter

Hello Dear Reader!

Here's a fun fact for you—the first book in the Kingdom Legacy series, Heir of Amber and Fire, was inspired by a character in a Dungeons and Dragons campaign that I never got to play. Even though the game never happened, the character's backstory stayed with me, and became the basis of Jennica's story.

Since the first book had such strong ties to tabletop gaming, a friend suggested I create a campaign set in the world of the Kingdom Legacy series. And so *The Mysterious Magical Emporium* was born, and I'd love to send you a FREE copy! Just sign up for my newsletter at www.rachanee.net/newsletter, and your new campaign will be sent to you right away.

So grab your friends, grab some dice, and grab a copy of *The Mysterious Magical Emporium*, and get ready to spend some time in the kingdom of Calia with your new friends, Jennica, Beyan, and Taryn!

PROLOGUE

THERE WAS A STORY I had grown up knowing, for most of my entire life, without knowing how I knew it. You know how you know a song, or a random item of information, but you don't remember where you first heard it? It could be a rumor, some sort of folklore passed on from person to person. A cautionary tale, meant to scare you into obedience.

This was one of those stories.

Years ago, the tale went, a young man had joined the Rothschan army as soon as he was of age. Joining him was his childhood friend and sweetheart—and right before they started their training, she became his betrothed as well. They were to be wed after their training was completed, and before they started their military service in earnest.

But the girl guarded a dangerous secret: she could wield magic.

Somehow she had been able to suppress it and keep her ability hidden for most of her life. Which, in the rational country of Rothschan, was a necessity. Here, magic is regarded as suspect and practically evil.

Did her intended know? If he did, he must have been too in love with her to care. If he had known, but hadn't turned her into the authorities—or at the very least shunned her and cut off all contact with her—then he would have faced a steep fine, or worse, if his transgression had been discovered.

In the final week of their training, it was announced that a person of great importance would be visiting their company. All were expected to be on their best behavior and acquit themselves well. Not just because their behavior would be a reflection on their superiors, but also because the visitor would be looking for the best and brightest talent that could potentially be pulled for special assignment.

But their superiors needn't have worried. The visitor, the Lord High Seneschal, arrived with the royal secretary, and both men were extremely impressed.

The Seneschal requested private, one-on-one meetings with each member of the company, for just a few minutes each, in one of the tents in the center of the company's camp. Nothing seemed amiss as each person went in for their private meeting.

Now it was time for the young woman's interview. Her betrothed patiently waited outside for his turn. The midday heat bore down on him, and he stifled a yawn. Time dripped by.

Until a scream from inside the tent pierced the air.

Although the Lord High Seneschal had given strict orders that no one was to interrupt his interviews—indeed, even the royal secretary who had traveled with him was not allowed to be present during these meetings—the young man burst into the tent, protocol be damned.

What happened inside the tent, no one knows for sure. Men's voices, raised in the heat of anger, could be heard. The poor young woman, already under duress, may have screamed again. Witnesses later swore that the tent glowed a strange, bright white, brighter even than the noon sun that was shining overhead.

Then the world grew unnaturally still.

As the white glow faded, the young man emerged from the tent, looking a little dazed. In his hand he held a peculiar silver rod studded with colored jewels that blinked in the sunlight. The man stumbled a few steps away.

The Lord High Seneschal threw back the tent flap, ignoring the gasps and cries from the waiting crowd outside. Some murmured about his strange disfigurement, wondering aloud what had happened. Others ran forward, asking, "Sir, are you all right?" The Seneschal waved them all away, leaning heavily on the tent frame as he pointed directly at the retreating young man.

The Seneschal screamed, "Arrest that man!"

The young man broke into a run.

Some of the man's comrades gave chase, but soon found they couldn't move, caught in place by fast-growing vines that had snaked up from the ground to wrap around their bodies. Certainly not natural flora, but the other possibility—that these vines were magical constructs—was, obviously, ludicrous and untrue.

Others came to cut them free from the plants, but the vines resisted the sharp blades. It would take hours to free them. Anyone else who tried to pursue the man found themselves unable to cross an invisible barrier, as if the air had solidified around their camp and wouldn't let anyone out.

Meanwhile, the young man kept running and running, until he was out of sight and well away from his would-be pursuers.

People later speculated that the young man must have possessed illegal magic—the silver rod, perhaps?—and used it against his former friends and the Lord High Seneschal. Although the Seneschal ordered a kingdom-wide search, the man was never captured, and no one ever saw him again. Perhaps he perished in his reckless escape from the camp.

But, if by some miracle he lived, I'm sure that no matter how much he ran, or how far he went, he would never truly be safe from himself.

1

CHAPTER ONE

"ADALYNN. ADALYNN!"

My father's voice broke through my musings. "Huh?"

"Is everything all right, Adalynn?" Father asked me. He followed my gaze to where I had been staring. "You looked like you were far away. Or is the peeling wallpaper really that interesting?"

"Oh." I flushed, laughing weakly. "The wallpaper's fine, Father. Although I think that shade of green went out of style when I was five years old."

"Well, maybe that can be the first thing we spruce up around here," Father laughed. "It can be your birthday present—to us!"

Now I laughed in earnest. "I'll be happy to fix up this house with my earnings. But I don't think the first thing I'd pick will be the wallpaper!"

We all laughed—Mother, Father, and I. There were so many things wrong with our house, it would be hard to pick which one to fix first. The leaking roof? The warped wooden floorboards? Not to mention the threadbare, faded furniture that graced each room.

But even though our little house was old, and falling apart, it was ours. It was where I grew up, just my parents and me, in our home in a village on the outskirts of the kingdom of Rothschan. A cozy little home for a cozy little family.

Father beamed at me as Mother placed a small, homemade raisin spice cake in front of me. The two of them spoke in unison. "Happy birthday, Adalynn."

"Thank you! It looks delicious," I said. Father passed me a knife. The handle was a little wobbly, but it was our sharpest blade. I took it from him and began cutting little slices for each of us, passing them around the table.

Even though it was my birthday celebration, it was just the three of us, as it usually was. Growing up as an only child, I was very close to my parents, and didn't mind our small, family-only gatherings for special occasions.

This was an important birthday, though. I turned twenty-one today. Which meant that I was now eligible to enlist in the Rothschan military for my mandatory three-year term, after which I would have the option to either continue serving the kingdom, or could leave the military and pursue a different vocation.

"I'm sorry it's not fancier." Mother fretted at me as I accepted the slice of cake.

"Nonsense," I said. "It's perfect."

While I'd miss my parents, there were certain things about living at home that I wouldn't miss. Like my mother's constant need for reassurance. She often expressed sadness that we couldn't afford more than the most basic of necessities. It didn't matter to me that our neighbors and my schoolmates were better off than my family was, but for some reason, it mattered a lot to my parents. My mother especially.

It wasn't that Mother wanted fancy things to show off our nonexistent wealth. Honestly, I had never been able to figure out exactly why she cared so much about it. Of course, having more money would have made things easier growing up, but we got by. We had an—admittedly leaky—roof over our heads, and food enough to not be starving. Perhaps if we had been a bit wealthier, Mother and Father would have had more friends amongst our neighbors, and I would have had an easier time in school. But I had my family, and I tended to keep to myself anyway, so I didn't feel the lack of close friends too much. Usually.

Which was why this birthday was so momentous. Being in Rothschan's military meant my parents wouldn't have to worry about my wellbeing for the three years I was gone, and I would also be earning a regular salary and could send every coin home. I'd tried to help my family over the years by taking various odd jobs, mostly running errands. But I was never allowed to hire myself out as a servant to any households, even to our nearby neighbors—my mother didn't like the idea of me being away from home for more than a few hours. The idea of working as a live-in servant to another household, even if it was with the wealthiest and most secure residence in all of Rothschan, upset Mother so greatly that, after seeing her reaction to the first time I suggested it, made me reluctant to ever bring it up again.

So, even though I loved my parents dearly, I was also secretly excited at the prospect of going. Not necessarily because I thought I'd make a good soldier, although the idea of attaining knighthood someday was a bit appealing. But mandatory was mandatory, after all, and Mother and Father would have to let me go.

And after my three years were done, who knew what could happen? I'd most likely stay in the military, as I didn't have many prospects here in Rothschan that I could come back to. Being poor wouldn't have necessarily deterred potential suitors. But, when I had started growing old enough to notice such things, I realized that many of our neighbors were polite, but distant. Coupled with my parents' fierce protectiveness of me and their reluctance to talk about our lives before

I was three—the age that I could recall my earliest memories—and I often felt like I was carrying the weight of their unspoken worry.

But—if I was lucky, and smart, and saved enough money—perhaps I could leave the army after the three years and go see the rest of the Gifted Lands. I'd have the skills to hire myself out as a guard, or maybe even a mercenary. Although I didn't think I could ever have the mindset of a mercenary. Still, there would be more possibilities and opportunities after my service was done than I had now.

As if he read my mind, Father asked, "Will you be enrolling tomorrow?"

I nodded, even as I caught the slight frown on Mother's face. She pushed back a tendril of grey-and-brown hair behind her ear, a sure sign that she was upset. Mother always grew fidgety when she was uncomfortable. It was her tendency, whenever anyone talked about the Rothschan military, for her to grow quiet. And now that I was at the age of enrollment, she hated hearing me talk about it. I didn't understand why. She knew it was inevitable. I figured it was just because she was afraid of losing her only child. But she needn't worry. The kingdom of Rothschan hadn't been involved in anything that could even be remotely considered a skirmish in years. Our kingdom's reputation was too fearsome; no one would dare go against us. I was confident I would be just fine.

As was my father, who smiled at me. The crinkles around his eyes, a testament to his years of hard work filled with equal parts worry and laughter, deepened. "We'll miss you. But it can't be helped. And it can only mean better times, for all of us." He looked at my mother, who was still and silent. Gently, he said, "Let's all go together. To keep today's celebration going. It will be a defining moment, for our whole family."

Mother met his gaze, and I was surprised to see tears glistening in her eyes. Before I could say anything, Father gave me a warning glance. *Don't acknowledge it.*

In an effort to lighten the mood, Father asked, "What were you thinking about earlier, Adalynn?"

"Oh. It was nothing, really. Just ... do you remember that story that was going around a few years back, about how some crazed person attacked a Seneschal at one of the training camps with forbidden magic, and then escaped? The story just came to mind and I wondered ... whatever happened to the Seneschal? And did they ever find his attacker?"

Both Mother and Father froze at my words. It was like a veil had dropped over their faces, shuttering them completely from any emotion.

"What made you think of that?" Father's voice was flat and harsh.

Surprised at my father's tone, I stammered, "I—I don't know. Probably because I'll be enrolling tomorrow, and then that made me think of that story. It just got me curious, is all. I'm sure it's nothing more than rumor. Mettie Shamplen was the one who told me, and you know what a gossip she—"

"Don't speak of that story ever again," Father said. His face was flushed—from anger?—but his hands, gripping the sides of his chair, were deathly white. "Even if you think it's nothing but rumor, don't talk of it outside these walls."

"But why—"

"Eat your cake." Following his own instructions, Father tucked into his slice of cake, barely finishing one bite before shoveling another into his mouth. As if he didn't want to be engaged in any more conversation.

"It's just a story, anyway, dear. Pay it no mind." Mother picked up her fork and began eating as well, but slowly, lost in her thoughts. Even her chewing seemed subdued.

Unsure of how to respond—or even *if* I should respond—I picked up my own fork and took a bite of my birthday cake. The sweetness of the raisins and brown sugar burst over my tongue. Finishing my bite, I smiled at my mother. "Honors to the cook. It's delicious. Perfect, as always, Mother."

Her answering smile was tinged with sadness. "Thank you."

After that uncomfortable moment, the rest of my birthday celebration passed pleasantly and without any other incidents. As if by unspoken agreement, my father and I avoided talking about my upcoming military enrollment and instead just conversed about everyday, innocuous topics. Mother relaxed as the night wore on, but I could sense that undercurrent of unhappiness behind all her words and actions.

When we had our fill of cake and conversation, I stood up, intending to grab all the dishes from the table and start cleaning up.

Mother gently took my dish from my hand. "It's your birthday, you shouldn't have to do any cleaning," she said. She paused, putting her hand on my cheek as she regarded me. "You have a big day tomorrow." She shooed me away.

I laughed and gave her a big hug, then turned to hug my father. "All right, then. See you both in the morning."

I headed to my room at the back of the house, where my parents' bedroom was just across the hall.

Once inside my room, I approached the plain wooden dresser on the far side of the wall and grabbed the pale blue ceramic pitcher that sat atop it, intending to pour some water into the nearby matching bowl so I could wash my face. The pitcher was surprisingly light;

looking inside, I realized I forgot to refill it after using the last of the water this morning. No matter—I could refill it from the communal bucket of water in the kitchen. I grabbed the pitcher and headed back there.

As I approached, I heard my parents talking in low voices. Something about their discussion made me slow my footsteps and approach quietly. They didn't seem to be arguing, but whatever they were talking about definitely had them agitated.

"... You don't know that," Mother was saying as I crept up slowly to the doorway.

"And *you* don't know that anything will happen, Pella," Father retorted. "Just because it happened once, doesn't mean it will happen again."

"But if it does ... I'd rather Adalynn is safe at home. If something should happen during her three years away, we'll never know. And we won't be able to help her."

What does Mother mean, they'll never know? I thought. Was she talking about me being injured, or killed? Of course if that happened, my parents would be informed.

But recalling Father's statement, I didn't think my parents were discussing the possibility of me getting hurt. They were talking about something else entirely. *Just because it happened once, doesn't mean it will happen again.* But what did they mean?

I was so busy mulling over this, I nearly missed the next part of their conversation.

"She's made it to her twenty-first birthday, and so far nothing untoward has occurred. She should be in the clear, now," Father said.

"But look at what happened to Laydon," Mother said. "Do we really want to risk—"

There was a rustling sound, as if someone had moved quickly. From somewhere closer, Father said urgently, "Do *not* say his name."

"It's been long enough, surely—"

"You never know who might be listening. Don't tempt fate. Best to leave the past where it belongs."

A choked sob escaped from my mother's lips. The rustling sounded again; I surmised my father was holding my mother.

I could hear my mother sniffling quietly, but she quickly got her crying under control. "You're right," she said. "I'm fretting over nothing. Everything will be fine tomorrow, and beyond that."

"That's the way to think about it," my father said encouragingly.

There was more rustling of fabric, followed by footsteps and the clinking of dishes as my parents walked around the kitchen, tidying it. Under the cover of all their noise, I crept back to my room, where I placed the still-empty ceramic pitcher back on top of the dresser. I quietly closed the door behind me and leaned against it, thinking furiously.

What was it that my parents were so worried about occurring?

And who was Laydon?

2

Chapter Two

My mother held a letter in one hand. She was crying, and the wrinkled piece of paper was streaked with her tears. Her other hand was clutched tightly around something, but I couldn't make out what it was she was holding.

Her hands trembled as she addressed my father. "But they told us he was killed."

Father shook his head. "That's what they want us to believe, so we won't raise a fuss. But my contact told me that the incident happened several months ago. It was well hidden—I don't think anyone suspected. Least of all him. But it got to a point where it couldn't be hidden anymore."

"How will we find him?" Mother asked.

Father's head drooped. When he looked up again, there were tears in his eyes. "We can't. Or maybe I should say, we shouldn't."

"Then what can we do?" Mother's voice broke.

Father sounded choked up as well. "Keep Adalynn safe. It's the only thing left that we can do."

I opened my eyes, the remnants of last night's dream teasing the edges of my waking consciousness.

I had mulled over my parents' whispered exchange late into the night, trying to piece together what it was was they had been discussing. Finally I had fallen into a fitful sleep, dreaming about a cryptic conversation between my parents.

It was so vivid, almost like I had been there to witness their discussion. In my slowly wakening haze, I realized that Mother and Father had looked different in my dream. The gray that feathered my mother's hair was completely missing, and the lines in Father's face were nonexistent. It kind of felt like ... a memory.

But that couldn't be right. I had no idea who the "he" was that my parents kept referring to in my dream, and their discussion about a missing person wasn't one I had ever witnessed in my waking life.

I lay in bed a few moments longer, thinking about the dream. I finally dismissed it as some odd mix of what I had overheard the night before and my anticipation over enrolling in the Rothschan military later today. Certainly my dream wasn't prophetic or held some hidden meaning. Like the other citizens of Rothschan, I was extremely pragmatic and didn't hold with silly superstitions like that. Some of the other kingdoms in the Gifted Lands, such as Calia, our neighbor to the northeast, believed in such delusions wholeheartedly. No wonder the twenty-some year match between Calia's queen and her first husband, Sir Hendon of Rothschan, had come to such a bad end. Poor Sir Hendon. Living so long in a kingdom that condoned the use of magic would drive anyone insane. Superstitious nonsense, attracting only fools, or the easily deluded. To think there was a whole kingdom of people like that! It was a wonder Calia hadn't been taken over years ago.

Now fully awake, I sat up and put my feet on the patchwork rug that lay on the floor by my bed. I curled my toes, relishing the feel of the soft fabric beneath my feet. It had been rewoven so many times that I could no longer remember the original color, but Mother's deft hand for weaving made the old rug feel practically new.

My face felt grimy from not washing it last night, and I stepped over to the dresser to pick up the pitcher before I remembered I hadn't refilled it.

No matter, I thought. *At least this morning I won't accidentally come across any awkward conversations.*

I reached out for the ceramic pitcher, and nearly dropped it in surprise. It was heavy, and I could hear liquid sloshing around inside. I steadied it with both hands and placed it carefully back down on top of the dresser. Peering inside, I could see the pitcher was filled to the brim with clean, clear water.

Confused, I picked the pitcher up again and poured some of the water into the matching ceramic basin nearby. I cautiously touched my finger to the liquid and tasted it. It was, indeed, water. Cool, and as fresh as if I had just drawn it from the well near our house.

I paused, thinking furiously. The pitcher was completely empty last night when I walked into my room after my birthday celebration. I had intended to fill it, but I hadn't. Had I? No. No, I knew for sure I hadn't refilled it. I had gone straight back to my room after sneaking away from eavesdropping on my parents, and I had fallen asleep instead of leaving my room a second time to try to get some water. From the bucket in the kitchen, which would have been a little musty and stale from sitting out for several hours.

Maybe I had walked in my sleep and refilled the pitcher at the well? But that made no sense. Aside from how impossible it seemed to me to do all that activity in the dark and while sleeping, my parents would have heard me. I would have had to pass by their room on my way out of our house. And as I had never done anything like that before, it was highly unlikely that I would start doing that now.

I had no idea how this had happened—perhaps Mother had refilled it? Although I hadn't heard her come into my room.

Oh well. The mystery of the water-filled pitcher would have to wait. I had more important matters to attend to.

Like starting the next part of my life.

My spirits buoyed, I washed my face and turned to my wardrobe to pick out an outfit for the day. I wanted to look smart in every sense of the word.

I sorted through a few items, not fully satisfied with my options. Not that I had many. Rummaging around, I searched for my favorite burgundy trousers and cream linen shirt. The outfit would look smart against the deep red fitted coat I had seen other knights wear, although—I had to laugh at my daydream—I'd probably start out as a squire or man-at-arms first.

I plucked the clothes from where they were stuffed in the back of the wardrobe and shook them out, dismayed. My pants were ripped down one leg, and my shirt had a huge stain on the front. I sighed. No wonder I had put these items in the back of the wardrobe. If only I had time to repair and clean them.

Well, it couldn't be helped. I would have to find something else to wear.

I threw the ruined clothes on the bed and rummaged through my wardrobe again, choosing a brown slit skirt and matching top. I turned to the bed to lay out the outfit, picking up the cream linen shirt to move it aside.

And stopped short.

The cream shirt looked as fresh and new as if I had just walked out of the tailor's shop with it. There were no wrinkles from having been crumpled in the back of my closet for so long.

And the hideous, large stain was gone.

Amazed, I put the shirt down and picked up my burgundy pants.

The tear that had run the length of the right leg was gone. Not even mended, but vanished as if it had never been.

My hands shook as I slowly put the pants on. While I was glad I could now wear my favorite outfit, I couldn't make sense of what was happening around me.

I finished getting dressed, tying my auburn hair back with a cream-colored ribbon, and left my room. I nearly ran into my mother, who was standing just outside my door in the narrow hallway.

"You're awake!" Mother said. "I was just about to knock on your door to see if you were up. I wanted to let you sleep in, but the day's also going by."

"Thanks for coming to check on me," I said. "And thank you for refilling my water pitcher last night. Oh, and for mending and cleaning my outfit." I indicated where the stain had been on my blouse, and the now-invisible tear in my pants. "You can't even tell that my clothes were ruined."

Mother gave me a funny look. "I didn't do any of those things, dear. Now, come and eat some breakfast before you head into the city."

She turned and walked down the hallway, leaving me to gape at her retreating back.

3

— · —

CHAPTER THREE

MY PARENTS AND I gathered around the table as we had last night. Only this time it was for breakfast, instead of my birthday.

Mother and Father kept up a steady stream of conversation that washed over my confused thoughts. As I listened to them talk while I ate, I slowly started to feel a sense of normalcy again.

"Adalynn. Adalynn!"

I realized Mother was calling my name.

"Oh, I'm sorry, Mother," I said. "What were you saying?"

Mother chuckled. "Maybe you *should* have slept in a bit longer. I was saying that if you and your father decide to go shopping after you enlist, I can come meet you. That will give me time to get some chores done around the house, but I wouldn't mind going into the city for a bit."

"Shopping?" I repeated stupidly.

"For supplies," my father said. "The military will provide most of the items you need, but just basic things. There will be some things you'll want that they won't consider essential, I'm sure."

"Oh. That's a good idea." I added hesitantly, "But do we have the extra money?"

Mother smiled gently. "Don't you worry about that. Your father and I have it well in hand."

"But—"

"Great." She nodded, as if I hadn't spoken. "It's settled. You two get going to the city, and I'll be along shortly."

"But what about—?" I stood up, holding my empty plate.

Mother plucked the dirty dish out of my hand and kissed me on the forehead. "Don't worry about that either, I'll take care of it. You two should get going before it gets much later."

"All right."

With a cheerful wave to my mother, Father and I set off on the road that would lead us into Rothschan's capital. As we lived in a small village just outside the city, we could reach the city's gates in about a half hour traveling on foot.

As we headed toward the capital, I took the time to really take in our surroundings. We had walked this road countless times, of course. But I realized that, after today, things would completely change. And move fast. After I enrolled, I would only have a week left at home, and most of that week would be filled with preparations to leave.

In spite of my excitement, I felt a slight sense of anxiety. I had never left home for any length of time. I'd miss my mother and father immensely. Would they be lonely without me, too, or were they just putting up a good front?

Beside me, Father filled the silence with random advice, seemingly oblivious to my inner turmoil. "Do well, and I wouldn't be surprised if you're not knighted by the end of your second year. They move up exceptional people, regardless of lineage."

I smiled as my father's pride in me chased away any lingering shadows of the odd conversation I had overheard between him and Mother last night. And the weird happenings of this morning.

We reached the gates of Rothschan just as the sun began to burn off the morning chill.

As we waited in line to gain entry to the city, Father asked me, "Is there anywhere you want to go first? Or do you want to go straight away to enroll?"

I shook my head instantly, not bothering to entertain the thought for a moment. "Let's get it out of the way. It's why we're here, after all. I wouldn't be able to concentrate if we went anywhere else first."

Father laughed. "Come on, then."

Once inside, we headed straight toward the Merchants' District, where the conscription office was situated at the outskirts. Beyond the Merchants' District was the Nobles' District, where the Rothschan palace rose up in the center of the city. Made of sturdy gray stone and proudly displaying the red banners of the kingdom, the Rothschan palace wasn't ostentatious in any way. Unlike other kingdoms in the Gifted Lands. In fact, if you didn't know that Rothschan was ruled by a royal family, you might think that the palace was just another fine mansion, although perhaps a little grander than the other buildings in the area. The reason behind the relative simplicity of Rothschan's royal palace was twofold: my country prided itself on practicality of design over aesthetics; and if our palace didn't look like a "normal" palace, then it was less likely to be a target for invaders.

We traversed the sidewalks, passing by the neat, orderly rows of shops and street vendors, where the citizens of Rothschan were conducting business in similar neat and orderly fashion. Everything about Rothschan—from the austere storefronts to the modest clothing in subdued colors that we favored—could be described as "neat and orderly." You learned, early on, that to stand out in Rothschan was to invite trouble. It was easy to tell who the visitors were to our kingdom by how foreign they were to our customs. Not that Rothschan had many visitors; we weren't usually considered a travelers' destination. But I didn't mind. I liked knowing my place in society. Every part of my life had its place and its purpose, and I wouldn't have wanted it any differently.

Just ahead of my father and me was a fruit cart parked on the side of the cobblestone street, piled high with red and green apples, apricots, pears and cherries. As we walked by, a small hand shot out and grabbed a plump red apple from among the piles of fruit. The slight figure that owned the hand darted away, even as the cart's owner noticed the fruit pilfering and yelled, "Stop! Thief!"

The thief dashed across the sidewalk a few feet in front of us, heading toward a dark alley just ahead and to our right. Other shoppers in the area looked up when they heard the fruit seller's cry, but they were either too far away or too slow and laden with packages to be of much help.

Behind me, I heard the fruit seller yelling, alerting any guards in the area to come to his aid.

Reflexively, I sprinted forward, grabbing the thief just before they could disappear into the alley. The thief squirmed in my grasp, but I only tightened my hold on their arm. I'm a petite woman, but up close, I was surprised to realize the person I was holding was shorter than me—actually, just a child. With their close-cropped hair and gaunt figure, I couldn't be sure if they were a boy or a girl, but I could tell they couldn't have been more than seven- or eight-years-old. Perhaps ten, if I was being generous.

"What's your name?" I asked the child. The child didn't answer me. Instead they just stared at me, wide-eyed, and began thrashing about even harder, testing my grip as they tried to break free. The apple they had been clutching fell from their hand.

Father reached us at the same time as the fruit seller huffed over. The fruit seller, who had hastily given a neighboring merchant temporary control of his cart after our brief scuffle, was a heavyset, middle-aged man. His lip curled up in a sneer as he looked down at the young thief.

"Thought you could steal from my cart, did you?" he scoffed. "I'll make sure you never think of doing that again."

By now, two guards had arrived on the scene and, following the pointing fingers and vocal exclamations of other merchants and shoppers in the area, approached our little group. Quickly assessing the situation, they didn't even bother to ask for an account of what had occurred, instead asking, "First offense, do you know?"

The fruit seller immediately replied, "Yes, they've stolen from me before, and other merchants as well. I've seen them often in the market."

The child screamed, "No! He's lying! I've never seen him before in my life! And I've never stolen anything at all before today."

The fruit seller sniffed. "A thief would say that, to save their skin."

One of the guards reached out to take my prisoner, but I instinctively stepped in front of the child. "Wait," I said. "What are you going to do?"

The guard shrugged. "If this man—" he indicated the fruit seller, who was openly smirking "—says it's a second offense, then we'll have to treat it as such."

"But they're just a child!" Somehow my grip on the child had changed to them clinging to me, instead of the other way around. As I shifted my weight, shielding the child further, the guards stiffened, ready to take action against me. Next to me, my father shook his head ever so slightly. *Don't make trouble, Adalynn!*

"Doesn't matter, even children know the laws. Should have thought of that before they decided to steal something."

The guard pried the child's fingers from my arm and, along with his colleague, began dragging the child away. Their wails of, "But I swear, it was the first time! I won't do it again!" seemed to echo around the Merchants' District as the guards walked through the market with their diminutive prisoner.

The gawkers in the area quickly looked away as they passed, and soon the area was filled with the usual noise and bustle of the market. The fruit seller gave a satisfied sniff as he watched the trio disappear.

"Merchant," I said, before he could head back to his stand. "Tell me truly, *was* it that child's second offense?"

The man's smirk deepened, and he sniffed a second time, even more smugly than before. "What does it matter? I promised that ruffian they'd never think of stealing again, and so they won't."

With a self-satisfied air, the merchant went back to his cart.

My father touched my arm. "Adalynn ..."

"The guards didn't even question anyone else in the market. Maybe that child was telling the truth, and the other merchants could have vouched for them. If they truly had never taken anything before—"

"Adalynn, please. Keep your voice down. And just leave it be." Father put his arm around my shoulders and began gently steering me down the street.

"But they'll kill that little child! All on the word of only one witness! And a biased one, at that."

In a low voice, Father said. "You know the laws. If it's a second offense, then there's no leniency. The laws keep us safe, and we should be grateful."

It was a statement I had heard all my life—in school, at home, around our village. It was a statement I had always staunchly agreed with and believed in.

In regards to thievery, Rothschan law stated that, depending on the severity of the theft, a first offense could be worked off for a set period of time in the king's mines. The work was dangerous, but at least it was honest.

A second offense, regardless of age or circumstances, was an instant death sentence.

In theory, I thought the law was just. After all, if someone committed a crime a second time, it meant they were beyond redemption. Or at least, that's what we'd always been told.

But this was the first time I had witnessed the laws being carried out in such a way that didn't seem fair. And it made me uneasy. Not just because the guards hadn't taken the time to prove or disprove the child's claim that it was their first time stealing. But also because the fruit seller had all but admitted that he had exploited the law to his advantage, just for a bit of petty revenge.

As Father and I hurried away from the malicious merchant and the scene of the child thief's downfall, I spared one last glance back at the fruit cart. The hateful seller's smug grin made me want to hit something, to scream about the unfairness of it all.

The cart suddenly collapsed, the wheels popping off in all directions, scattering the large piles of colored fruit all over the cobblestones. The fruit seller started yelling in dismay. "My fruit! My beautiful fruit!"

He angrily kicked at the damaged cart. "Stupid thing! How could it break like this? This is a brand new cart! When I talk to Heyan the woodworker about this...."

The seller tried in vain to gather up his now-damaged merchandise as it all rolled every-which-way down the street. The laughter from his fellow merchants didn't improve his bad temper any.

I laughed as well, feeling rather satisfied. And a little unsettled. I knew of Heyan—his work was impeccable. If, as the merchant had said, it was a new cart, it shouldn't have fallen apart like that.

My foot kicked something round, small and firm. It skittered down the street, stopping only when it hit a nearby wall. I sobered as I got a good look at the object I had kicked. The now bruised apple shone in the sun, bright red as blood.

4

— · —

CHAPTER FOUR

FATHER AND I HURRIED to our destination. After the incident in the market, we weren't in the mood for happy chatter, and our playful mood was now gone.

Seeing the austere gray rock façade of the Rothschan conscription office was a relief. I practically tore open the door in my haste to get into the safety of the building. Even though everyone else had done as my father and I had—walked away quickly, heads down, studiously and obviously minding their own business—I had still felt like everyone was watching us.

I stepped inside and to the side, allowing Father to enter right behind me. I heard a soft click as he gently closed the door.

I blinked as my eyes adjusted to the dimness of the office. Even though the office door was flanked by two large windows, the heavy black curtains were drawn across them, effectively blocking any of the bright sunlight outside. Instead, several lamps placed at precise intervals along the wall provided the room's illumination. I sniffed experimentally, noting that the candles in the lamps didn't give off any smoke. A closer look at the walls showed they were pristine, lacking the heavy black soot streaks usually found in other homes and businesses. My musings turned to wonder. Whoever ran this office was obviously used to the finer things in life. Sootless candles were expensive, and had to be imported from other kingdoms, notably the magic-rich ones like Calia or Shonn. The office's occupant might serve Rothschan, but they apparently didn't mind bending the rules a bit if it made their life easier.

My pondering was cut short by a deep voice. "May I help you?"

The steady glow of candlelight illuminated a broad-shouldered man with a shock of silver hair sitting behind a gleaming mahogany desk. He looked up from his paperwork, and I stifled a gasp as I got a good look at him.

The left side of his face was horribly disfigured, as if it had been singed away. The skin was rippled, raw and red, as if whatever had caused his injury had just occurred, although I didn't think the accident had been recent. The corner of his left eye drooped a little, the eyelid permanently swollen and heavy. The mottled skin continued down his neck and disappeared under the collar of his shirt, making me wonder if that entire side of his body had been affected by whatever had mutilated his face.

As I hesitated, my father put an encouraging hand on my shoulder and slightly nudged me forward.

I approached the desk and the imposing figure behind it.

"Yes, Sir ...?" My voice squeaked out.

The man snorted. "Just Renton. There's no need for titles here."

He didn't want me to use his title? It seemed like an odd thing to say, but I plowed bravely on. I coughed slightly, clearing my throat. In a louder voice, I said, "I'm here to enlist."

The man gave me an assessing look. "How old are you?"

"I just turned twenty-one yesterday."

He sat back, appraising me. "I thought you looked rather young." While it was mandatory that every Rothschan citizen had to serve in the military at some point, we had several years to actually carry through on that obligation. Even though you could join at twenty-one, most people waited a few years before doing so. Among my friends and classmates, I was the only one I knew of who was going to sign up immediately once I was eligible. Then again, none of my friends needed the money so desperately, either.

"I may be young, but I'm eager to serve my kingdom, sir."

He nodded and then shrugged. He reached over, pulling a leather-bound book that was lying on the table toward him, and reached for a quill and bottle of ink that was nearby. As he did so, I thought I heard him mutter something like, "Stupid kids ..."

He opened the leather tome and uncapped the bottle, dipping the quill in the ink. He looked up at me. "Name?"

"Adalynn Taethen."

The man's indifferent expression suddenly sharpened. "Taethen. That's an unusual family name."

I blinked, unsure of how to respond to that. Renton looked behind me, seemingly noticing my father for the first time standing just outside the lamps' glow.

"I thought you looked familiar." The man crossed his arms as he addressed my father.

"It's been awhile, Renton," Father said, keeping his voice carefully neutral. He stepped up behind me and placed a casual hand on my left shoulder, but I could feel the tension in his body. And between the two men.

"Show some respect," Renton growled.

"There's no need for titles here." Father parroted Renton's earlier statement with a slight quirk to his lips. Was he mocking the man? Renton ground his teeth, staring with unbridled hatred at my father.

"I'm surprised after what happened that you would even dare to show your face here," Renton said. "If you think that by bringing your daughter here, you could make up for—"

"It has nothing to do with Adalynn," my father said firmly. "Surely enough time has passed for you to forgive and forget any transgressions that happened."

Renton snorted. "Forgive? Hardly. Forget? Never."

I listened to this exchange between Father and Renton, my mind whirling. *What could they be talking about?* Renton looked to be about the same age as my father, maybe a few years older. Perhaps they had served in the Rothschan military together, and Renton held a grudge against my father? All my life, Father had peppered my childhood with stories of his time in the military, and I thought he had told me all of his adventures—and misadventures. He hadn't held anything back, or so I thought. As I rapidly flipped through my mental catalog of Father's stories, I didn't recall him mentioning a person named Renton, or a grudge that spanned decades. If Father had known Renton personally, I was sure he would have mentioned it.

So *did* he know Renton personally? And if so, why *hadn't* he mentioned it?

My attention snapped back to the conversation at hand. "Please, Renton, let's just put the past behind us," Father was saying. He put his other hand on my right shoulder and tightened his grip, pulling me closer to him. "You made sure my family would never forget, either. I'd say we're even."

Renton was looking at both of us with unconcealed loathing. "And how do I know your daughter won't be a problem? It's not worth the risk."

"Adalynn is ready to serve Rothschan. Shouldn't she be praised for that decision, not shamed? Please don't take this away from her." My father's voice cracked, and I was shocked to hear that he sounded close to crying.

Renton's expression suddenly changed, from hatred to calculating. "You're right. A decision like that should be lauded. Of course, my dear, you'll be enrolled right away. If you would just come with me for processing ..."

"Processing?" Father sounded horrified. "I thought that practice had been stopped years ago."

"Processing?" I echoed. "Father, what's he talking about?"

Renton spoke first. "The only thing that stopped was making it optional. Now, it's mandatory for any new conscript." He gave my father an oily smile. "Unless you wanted to pay for the option to make it optional. After administrative fees, labor costs, the price of testing ... it would be a rather handsome amount."

Father stiffened. "You know I can't afford to pay something like that."

Renton shrugged. "Then your daughter goes through processing." He turned that ugly smile on me. "Don't worry, my dear. If you've nothing to hide, then you've nothing to fear. It will be my pleasure to personally oversee your testing."

I didn't like the way he said that last sentence. It might be his pleasure, but it wouldn't be mine.

Father moved in front of me, shielding me. "Whatever you're getting at, Renton, I don't like it. So, no. Absolutely not."

Renton didn't say anything for a long moment. Then, surprisingly, he shrugged. "Fine."

My father blinked, astonished. I hadn't expected Renton to give in so easily. Father moved his head slightly toward me. "Come, Adalynn, let's get going."

I nodded, turning toward the doorway. I couldn't get out of there fast enough. Behind me, Father turned completely as well to exit, his back to Renton.

The sound of a wooden drawer opening was the only warning we had. As Father, then I, looked back to see what was happening behind us, a knife came whistling from Renton's hand down the center of the room.

Straight toward my father.

There was no time to react. If Father ducked to avoid the dagger, it would have left me vulnerable. But the attack was so sudden and so swift that Father could only stare in shock as the knife came hurtling toward him.

I screamed.

And just before the knife would have pierced my father's heart, the room exploded.

5

— · —

Chapter Five

THE CANDLELIT SCONCES AROUND the room all bloomed into blazing torches, their unnatural brilliance spilling over and over-powering the room. And my eyes.

For some reason, I couldn't hear anything either. It was like all sound had been sucked out of the room. I reached my arms out blindly.

"Father?"

No answer. All my senses seemed to have deserted me. I called out again, louder. As if that would somehow help. "Father?"

My outstretched hands didn't find anything. Could that mean ...? I dropped to my knees, feeling the area around me, hoping to find my father yet scared to at the same time.

Slowly, sensation began to return. The smell of smoke wafted on the air, and a constant crackling sound assaulted my ears. Sweat was pouring down my face, and I felt overheated. Blinking rapidly as my sight returned, I saw the entire office was ablaze.

Fire licked at the curtains along the walls, threatening to devour the decor entirely. Bits of flame littered the bookcase at the end of the room and along the carpet. Soon it would reach the large wooden desk in the center of the office, and the overhead beams that held up the roof. And if that happened, the entire room would easily collapse.

At the foot of the desk lay Renton, unmoving.

My father was on the floor, just an arm's length from where I was kneeling. Even as I crawled toward him, he rolled on his side, coughed, and sat up. Relieved, I saw the knife hadn't reached him.

To my left, a glint caught my eye. Curiously, the unbloodied blade was embedded in a thick tome on one of the bookshelves, surrounded by fire. Even as I watched, several books turned to ash. The unnatural blaze would soon be out of control.

"What happened?" Father asked me.

"I don't know," I said. "Can you get up? We need to get out of here."

"Where is—?"

I looked over Father's shoulder. He turned slightly, paling when he saw Renton lying on the floor nearby. He reached over, taking the other man's wrist in his fingers. Frowning, he moved closer and touched Renton's neck.

"Is he ...?" I couldn't bring myself to finish my thought.

Father shook his head. "I don't think so. But we shouldn't linger. Come on."

He quickly stood up, reaching a hand down to help me off the floor. Together we stumbled to the door, trying to shield our faces from the smoke and flames. We opened the door just enough to slip through, shutting it firmly behind us. Coughing, we hurried away from the office, heading toward the gates, hoping to get home as fast as we could.

I risked a glance behind us. Curiously, from the outside, the conscription office looked completely ... normal. Perhaps it was because the curtains had been drawn when we entered, but the building's façade didn't betray the fire burning within. But I knew it was only a matter of time before the fire consumed the office entirely, and then our secret would be revealed.

We slowed our pace, only slightly, enough to look like we were purposefully walking somewhere but not fast enough to raise suspicion. We hadn't gone far when we came across Mother in the market, a bag slung over her arm.

"Oh, you're done already?" she remarked as we approached. "I didn't expect—"

Father gently grabbed Mother by the elbow and steered her away from the bustling market.

"But I'm not done shopping—"

"We need to go," Father said in an undertone.

Mother caught the urgency in Father's voice. "What's happened?" She sounded just as worried as he did.

"It's Laydon, all over again," was his cryptic response.

Cryptic to me, at least. Mother understood whatever it was Father was trying to say, and gasped. Even as we rushed along, she turned her head sharply to look at me.

"Father, do you know what happened back there?" I panted, trying to get answers while keeping pace with my parents.

But if I was hoping my father would enlighten me, I was to be disappointed. He just shook his head, putting his finger to his lips to signal that we shouldn't talk about this—whatever *this* was—right now.

We had nearly made it to the city gates when alarm bells sounded.

My parents and I stopped and looked around. At first all I noted were the other citizens, equally arrested by the furious peal of the alarm bells. Then I saw several guards running back the way we had come, some holding empty buckets as they headed toward the fountain in the city center.

"Fire! There's a fire at the conscription office!"

Father, Mother, and I exchanged a three-way glance. While everyone else in the area stood and stared at the commotion, or rushed to the other end of the city to help, we began edging our way to the gates.

We kept our heads down and our pace unhurried, trying not to appear suspicious in any way.

"Just keep calm, and let me do the talking," Father said in a low voice.

I wiped my palms, slick with sweat, against my burgundy pants. I was sure we would get detained, questioned ... or worse.

The guard at the gate was watching the disturbance as well. When we approached, he looked us over and frowned. "You're not going to stay and assist?"

I eyed Father from under my lashes. I was amazed at how calmly he answered the guard. "No, my wife has a weak constitution. She can't handle stressful situations very well. If she faints, she'll hinder the others."

The guard eyed my mother, who did her best to look like she was going to faint any minute. Then he turned to me. "But you're young, and able-bodied. At the very least, you should stay. Your father can take your mother home while you help back here."

My mouth felt dry, my throat scratchy. From nerves, though, not from the fire from which we had just escaped. I opened my mouth to respond to the guard, who was looking at me expectantly, but nothing came out.

What should I say? What should I do?

The sound of a loud explosion in the distance distracted all of us. As one, we all turned toward the source. Even from where we stood at the front gates of Rothschan, I could see the flames licking the roof of the former conscription office, dancing across to other buildings in the area.

"The castle! We must make sure to save the castle!" Another guard ran by, thrusting an empty bucket into the arms of the guard who had detained us. Our guard ran after him, abandoning our conversation in his haste to go help put out the flames.

Over his shoulder, he called, "Grab a bucket, and come along!"

Father called back, "Yes, we'll be right there!"

Thankfully, the guard didn't turn around to make sure we were behind him.

Now that the guard's post was vacant, my family and I rushed through the gate and out of Rothchan's capital city, hurrying down the road that would take us home. We didn't run, but our pace was brisk enough that we may as well have been. We made it home in a third of the time it normally would have taken us, and I didn't have enough extra breath to question Father about the strange events that had occurred in the office, nor about the cryptic exchange between him and Renton.

Once we reached our home, Father quickly unlocked the front door and flung it wide open, practically pushing me toward my bedroom. Mother disappeared into the kitchen, where I heard a lot of banging about.

"Hurry, hurry!" My father opened up my wardrobe and began rummaging through my clothes, throwing pants and shoes and stockings onto the bed in a reckless fashion. He reached into a dark corner and pulled out an object triumphantly. It was my knapsack. Tossing it toward me, he said, "Quickly, pack your things! Not too much that would be a burden, but enough to help you get by."

I gaped at my father, who continued to pile clothes onto my bed. "Father, what's going on? What happened back at the conscription office, and with that hateful man, Renton?"

Father pulled out a crumpled pair of linen trousers, and then plucked a matching tunic and dark jacket from where they hung in my closet. He tossed them at me. "These should be good to take with you. Now, what else would you need?" He crossed the room to my dresser, and frantically pulled open the top drawer. Heedless of my embarrassment, he flung various undergarments on the bed.

When he saw that I was simply standing there, watching him open-mouthed, he growled at me, "Adalynn, there's no time to waste! Start packing!"

My hands started folding the trousers automatically. "But why, Father? What's happening?"

Having emptied the contents of one drawer completely onto my bed, Father paused to look at me. "You don't know what you did, do you?"

I shook my head as I stuffed the now-folded pants into the knapsack. "No, I don't. One minute Renton intended to stab you in the back, and I screamed. The next thing I knew, the place was on fire."

Father drew in a ragged breath. "When you screamed ... it wasn't just a cry of fear. Something more primal, more instinctual, came from you. You didn't want Renton to hurt me, and so you stopped him from doing just that."

"How?"

Father shook his head. "I don't know, exactly. I don't understand it myself ... because I don't understand magic."

"*Magic*?"

What Father was telling me didn't make any sense. The kingdom of Rothschan had no need of magic, which we regarded as silly superstition anyway. Everything that occurred under the sun could be explained in some rational, logical way. We had no magicians in this country, and as I came from a decidedly non-magical family, there would be no reason I would have this ability.

Father studied me carefully. When he spoke, he picked his words just as carefully. "Adalynn, have you ever … experienced anything unusual? Something you couldn't explain, no matter how much you analyzed it? Perhaps you willed something to occur, and then it did?"

I started to shake my head, then stopped, remembering the strange occurrences that had happened this morning, in this very bedroom. Hesitantly, I said, "Ye-yes."

Father met my gaze gravely. "That was magic."

My head spun, my breath coming fast. I sat down heavily on the bed, trying to regain my composure. *Magic? Me?* It couldn't be.

And yet, deep down, Father's words rang true, stirring something in me that felt akin to relief. I wasn't crazy. Whatever had happened today, I now had a name for it.

Magic.

I looked up at Father, who shook his head at me and resumed pulling things out of my dresser. "I don't know how, Adalynn. I certainly don't have that ability, nor does your mother. But—"

As if summoned, Mother suddenly appeared in the doorway. Her arms were full with various items she had grabbed from the kitchen: a waterskin, two small loaves of bread, some fruit. "There's no more time!" she cried, rushing over to the bed and hurriedly throwing her items into my bag. "Adalynn needs to go, *now*!"

While I sat there dumbly, Mother grabbed some of my underthings from off the bed and crammed them into my knapsack, then followed suit with the shirt and jacket I hadn't finished folding. She pulled me into the hallway and toward the front door of our house. Father followed, holding my stuffed bag.

"What are you talking about, Mother?" I asked as she peered through the window. Looking over her shoulder, I could see a cloud of dust rising in the distance, steadily getting larger.

"Riders. Coming from the capital," she announced. "Go out the back door."

The three of us rushed into the kitchen, where the back entrance opened onto our small garden and the fields beyond. Father opened the door and peered around quickly, satisfied that no one was around.

Mother gave me a quick hug and kissed me on the forehead. Father followed suit, pushing my knapsack into my arms. "Go, Adalynn. Hurry!"

"But where am I going?" I asked, even as I started backing away from the house.

"To Calia," Father said. "To their capital city. Perhaps there you can find some help. Now, go!"

I turned, not even bothering to shoulder my bag properly, just clutching it in my arms, and began running across the field. Behind me, the door of my childhood home closed with a decisive click, leaving my parents to face whatever fate was coming to them from the implacable justice of Rothschan.

6

CHAPTER SIX

I RAN.

I ran through the field, through the trees that bordered it, through the eventual scrub that lined the main thoroughfare that led north to Calia. Eventually my adrenaline flagged, and I sat down on a convenient rock just off the road to catch my breath. And my thoughts.

Although I had known for quite some time that I would be leaving my parents' home, this wasn't the way I had imagined it happening. An uneasy feeling settled in my stomach, a mix of fear and regret over leaving my parents behind ... and an anxious anticipation over where they had instructed me to go.

So, Mother and Father wanted me to travel to the kingdom of Calia. I frowned, wondering what their reasoning could be.

Calia, one of our northern neighbors, was supposedly the strongest seat of magic in the Gifted Lands. Superstitious nonsense. It seemed to me that Calia had poor priorities; instead of building up their citizens with sound, rational thought, they were filling their heads with silly ideas that would only cripple their kingdom.

Still, it would be interesting to visit, and see how an entire country functioned believing in such absurdity.

I sighed. Even though my parents had said, *Go to the capital city*, it was still bound to be a big place. I wished they had given me some sort of direction: a name, a shop, *anything*.

I stood up and started walking. I was eager to put as much distance between Rothschan and me as possible. I had no idea if those riders would be satisfied with whatever excuses my parents gave them, or if they would start coming north in pursuit of me. On foot, and alone, I had little hope of escaping them.

To turn my anxious thoughts away from the idea of capture, I instead puzzled over the things I had learned so far. I thought back to my birthday celebration, when all this began—had it really been just a day ago?

I could will things into existence, although I didn't seem to have much control over what I created or how to temper it when I did. Whatever was happening to me had apparently happened before, with a person that my parents knew named Laydon. There must have been an incident with this Laydon person as well, since Renton at the conscription office had alluded to it.

And whatever ability Laydon and I possessed, the kingdom of Rothschan didn't like it. It made me ineligible to serve in the military; instead people like me were rumored to go somewhere else, for some other purpose. But what? And why?

My ruminations occupied me for the next several hours as I traveled north. It wasn't until I noticed the shadows getting longer that I realized the sun was setting. My hasty departure meant I only had a little bit of money on me, not enough to hire a room at an inn. But as a lone traveler, it didn't seem wise to just camp out somewhere by myself, either.

My weary footsteps brought me to a crossroads where a country inn was situated. Even though I knew I couldn't afford it, my steps slowed as I stared longingly at the cheery, well-lit building.

While I debated whether or not I should move on, the door to the inn opened and a heavyset, middle-aged woman came into the yard. Her brown hair was tied back with a kerchief, and I could see the streaks of gray at her roots in the glow of sunset.

"Narren! Narren!" After she loudly called out, she waited for a few moments, but no one appeared. Frowning, she looked around, muttering to herself. "Where is that boy? Lazy good-for-nothing. If he wasn't my nephew …"

She then noticed me, and, smoothing the annoyance from her face, pasted on a smile. "Hello, dearie! Come on in! Are you looking for a room for the night?"

An idea came to me. "Actually, if you need any help around the place, I'd be happy to work in exchange for a night's lodging."

The innkeeper's brows drew together as she thought, frowning. "Well, I don't really—"

A cloaked rider came charging down from the western road. The person stopped their dapple gray horse in front of the inn, pushing back the cloak's hood to reveal a dark-haired man with emerald green eyes, somewhat near my age. He addressed the innkeeper.

"Evening, my good woman." The man's rich baritone floated through the golden air toward us. "I'd like a room, a meal, and stabling for my horse, if you have them."

"Of course," the innkeeper said. "Come on inside, sir, and let's get you settled."

"Thank you." The man dismounted and looked around. Not seeing anyone that looked like a stablehand, he gave the innkeeper a confused look.

She pointed toward me. "She'll take care of your horse, sir."

The man nodded. He handed me the reins, patting his horse briefly. "Be good, King." The horse whickered in response. The man smiled, then strode into the inn.

The innkeeper turned to me and said, "Do you know your way around a stable?"

I nodded. I had helped out in the Rothschan public stables a time or two, anticipating that I might be part of the mounted cavalry when I joined the kingdom's military.

"Consider yourself hired, then," the woman said. "Take care of this man's horse, then come inside and grab a meal when you've finished."

I smiled gratefully. "Of course. Thank you, Mistress ...?"

"Cataluna. And you are?"

"Adalynn."

"Well met, Adalynn. You have remarkably good timing. For that, *I* thank *you*."

She bustled back into the inn, leaving me alone with King. *Pretty fancy name for a horse*, I thought. In the fading sunlight, I led the gray around the side of the building, to a small stable just behind it. Once inside, I noticed the place was a mess. Cataluna's nephew obviously hadn't taken care of the stable for quite some time.

Flies buzzed around the dirty hay that was in each of the three stalls. Although there were pegs on the wall to hang tools and other items, they were empty; buckets lay haphazardly on the dusty floor, as well as several brushes, a shovel, a pitchfork, a rope, and a broom.

Shaking my head in disgust, I hung my knapsack on the wall to keep it out of the filth, then led the horse into one of the stalls and tied it to a ring on one of the walls. I then grabbed the pitchfork from the floor and began mucking out the stall, creating a pile of dirty hay a few feet away from the stable. As I was already cleaning out one area, I figured I might as well clean the whole stable as much as possible, and proceeded to muck out the other two stalls. It was a sweaty, thankless task, but fortunately it didn't take long. While I worked, the dapple gray regarded me calmly.

After I had removed the dirty hay, replacing it with the clean hay piled outside the stable, and swept the stalls out as best I could, I picked up two buckets and went in search of a well. I was in luck; there was one nearby. In the deepening twilight, I filled up both buckets and brought them back to the stable. I put one down next to the gray and the other one just outside the stall. As King started to drink, I eyed him enviously. I was so parched from all that heavy labor that I was tempted to drink from the other bucket, but caution held me back.

After returning the tools to their hooks on the wall, I patted the horse and said, "I'm going to go get something to eat, and hopefully find *you* something to eat. I'll return soon."

King just snorted at me and then continued drinking.

I trudged inside the inn, looking forward to the prospect of a hot meal. At least it would give me the energy to finish the rest of my stable chores.

The inn's interior was rather quiet, with just a few patrons finishing their meals around the room. I didn't see King's owner; he must have retired for the night. I walked over to the kitchen, where I saw Mistress Cataluna stirring a pot of something over a fire. The smell of a hearty beef stew hit my nose, and my stomach growled loudly. When she heard that, she turned, saw me, and straightened.

"That took longer than I expected," she said, wiping her hands on her apron. "I figured you would have been in here hours ago to claim your meal."

"Well, ah ..." I hedged. I couldn't figure out a polite way to say that her stable was a mess, without insulting her or her nephew.

Mistress Cataluna snorted, sounding a bit like the horse I had just left. "If you were going to say that the stable is atrocious, you needn't bother. I already know that." She gave me a measuring look. "Don't say that you cleaned the whole place?"

I shrugged. "It could use a more thorough scrub down, but I did the best I could."

Mistress Cataluna raised an eyebrow. "Will wonders never cease! That's the best news I've heard all day. If it's true."

She bustled past me and out the door toward the stable. I stood in the quiet kitchen awkwardly, waiting for her to return. Fortunately, I didn't have long to wait. Catching movement through the window, I could see Mistress Cataluna practically running back to the inn.

Upon seeing me, a big smile spread over her face. "My dear, you've more than earned your meal." She crossed over to the hearth. Scooping some stew from the pot, she handed me the bowl. It was filled so high I was amazed she hadn't spilled anything. "If you want more, you just let me know. As much as you want."

I grabbed a clean wooden spoon from where it lay drying on a towel and started eating. The stew, normally passable traveler's fare, tasted like the finest of the king's dishes to me. I didn't even care that the hot meal burned my tongue as I wolfed it down.

I was halfway through the bowl when I remembered. "Mistress Cataluna, is there any grain for the horse?"

She pointed to a full bucket of oats in the corner. "You can take that back with you when you go. My nephew Narren was supposed to bring it out this morning, but he never showed up. Won't my sister get an earful when I see her next!"

I nodded politely, more intent on refilling my bowl. As I tucked into my second helping, Mistress Cataluna said, "I wish I could reward you better for your hard work, but that man whose horse you're taking care of took my last open room." She looked around the kitchen doubtfully. "I suppose you could bed down here, or maybe—"

"There's fresh hay in the stable, I can sleep in there," I said. "There's plenty of room. But—" I looked down at my soiled clothes, wrinkling my nose at the smell in my hair. "I don't suppose there's a way I could clean myself up?"

Mistress Cataluna pursed her lips and nodded. "There's an old tub out back behind the kitchen. Might be a little rusty, it's so old, but it's still decent enough. You can use that. But you'll have to fill it from the well, and it's dark out now."

"That's fine." The light from the inn should be enough to illuminate my way; I would be more worried about any random onlookers.

As if reading my thoughts, Mistress Cataluna said, "You should be fine, dearie. All the rooms face the road; there are no windows that open to the back, except for the one here in the kitchen. And I'll be in here most of the time, so you don't need to worry about any strangers watching you."

"Perfect." I ate the rest of my stew quickly, eager to finish my work in the stable so I could wash up and get to sleep.

When I was done, Mistress Cataluna plucked my dirty bowl out of my hands and shooed me out the back of the inn with a linen towel and the bucket of oats for the horse. "Sleep well, dearie. I'll have a nice hot breakfast ready for you in the morning."

Standing in the cool night air, my excitement over having a bath waned. I'd have to haul bucket after bucket to fill the tub, then drain the tub after I was finished. And the water would be cold, unless I wanted to take the time to heat all that water in the kitchen hearth.

I sighed and looked around for the tub. At least I could see how big it was and estimate how many trips to the well and back I'd have to make.

Just as Mistress Cataluna had promised, there was a medium-sized metal tub just a few feet away from the back door of the inn. It was just outside of the candlelight spilling from the kitchen window, affording a bit of privacy for a bather. A quick glance told me it was large enough to accommodate most guests; a man of just over average size could easily fit in it with room to spare.

I walked closer, wondering if it was dirty and if I'd have to clean it before using it. If that were true, I would probably just give up on the entire endeavor.

But when I reached the tub, I noticed two things about it. One, it was sparkling clean, looking practically brand new; and two, it was filled to the brim with water already. Hot water. I could see the steam rising in the chill air.

I stared in surprise as I carefully set the towel on the side of the tub. Hadn't Mistress Cataluna said the tub was old? "A little rusty, it's so old" was what she had said. And yet this tub looked like it had just been purchased today. And it was impossible for it to be filled with hot water; I would have seen someone heating water for it, as the only fire for doing so was in the kitchen. The small main room of the inn had no fireplace.

My skin prickled. More of this magic stuff then. That was the only way I could explain it, yet I didn't like it.

But then again, if magic could do things like draw a hot bath for me with ease, then it might not be so bad after all.

Cheerfully, I hauled the bucket of oats back to the stable so I could feed the horse before grabbing my things to come back to the kitchen, where a nice, hot bath awaited me.

7

CHAPTER SEVEN

TAKING A HOT BATH under the stars gave me a momentary respite from the craziness that had dogged me for the last day. For a brief hour or so, I let myself relax, and firmly quieted my fears about my parents and about my journey to Calia.

Surprisingly, the water stayed hot even while I took the time to feed the horse and fetch my bag, and its temperature remained steady while I soaked both myself and my smelly, dirty clothes. And by the time I reluctantly left the warmth of the bathtub, I noticed the water looked and smelled as pristine as it had when I first discovered the full tub.

I dried myself off as fast as possible, shivering in the cool air. I turned back to dump the contents of the bathtub, figuring if I got wet again at least I wouldn't have soaked my only dry set of clothes. When I looked at the tub again, though, it was empty, clean and dry as if it had remain unused.

Despite myself, I grinned. Maybe magic wasn't so silly after all. If this was what life was like with magic, then I could really get used to having it.

With that chore taken care of, I got dressed and grabbed my wet but clean outfit to hang in the stable. The rope I had spied earlier would be a good makeshift drying line.

King had finished his dinner by the time I returned to him. I strung up the rope and hung my clothes over it, then looked around for a place to sleep. The dappled grey snuffed at me.

"Okay then, boy," I said, walking over to him. He nudged me with his nose and snorted. "You don't want to sleep alone? I completely understand."

I grabbed my knapsack and entered the empty stall next to him. Putting my bag under my head like a pillow, I settled into the straw. The horse's head peeked over the short wall, into my stall.

"Good night."

King snuffed again, and I imagined him saying back to me, *Good night.*

I woke up to the feel of something coarse scratching at my cheek. Turning on my side, I opened my eyes and found myself nose to big gray nose with King, while his big brown limpid eyes seemed to bore into my soul.

I sat up abruptly and sneezed.

Startled, the dappled gray sneezed back.

"Ah, she's awake." The melodious voice I had heard the night before from the gray's owner came to me over the stall door. I twisted my neck to see a young man with a shock of dark hair looking down at where I lay on my makeshift bed. Those emerald eyes twinkled. Feeling a bit on display, I grabbed my knapsack and hastily placed it on my lap, as if it could completely cover me from his gaze.

"I'm impressed. King doesn't take to just anyone," the man continued, as the horse nosed his owner for a treat. The man pulled an apple from under his cloak, but instead of giving it to King, he tossed it my way. I caught it, holding it out to King, who eagerly took it from my hand.

As King munched happily, the man assessed me with his piercing green eyes. "Well, you and King seem to have become fast friends. Any friend of King's is a friend of mine. What's your name?"

"Adalynn." Caution kept me from giving my family name as well, but the man didn't seem to notice my omission.

"Well met, Adalynn. I'm Enlar Edson, of Bomora."

Bomora was in the westernmost part of the Gifted Lands, well beyond my home country of Rothschan. My surprise must have shown on my face, for Enlar laughed. "Yes, I know I'm rather far from home. But at least my journey is nearly done."

"Where are you headed?" I asked.

"Calia." He looked me up and down pointedly. "Funny. I could have sworn Mistress Cataluna was complaining last night about her good-for-nothing nephew who was supposed to work in the stables and the kitchen, but you don't look like a nephew. Unless she was mistaken?"

I blushed. "Ah, no. I'm traveling through, like you. I just offered to help out last night. A more affordable option for me...."

I realized I was babbling and abruptly shut my mouth.

Enlar chuckled. "That explains that, then. Where are you traveling, Adalynn?"

"Same as you," I said. "Calia."

"Well, that's something! We should travel together, it would be nice to have the company. And it would be good to have someone to help me with the horse."

It was an odd comment, but Enlar's smile was so infectious, I couldn't help smiling back, my fleeting thoughts quickly forgotten. But then I quickly sobered.

"I'm afraid I might slow you down," I said. "I'm traveling on foot." I didn't tell him that I unfortunately did not have the time to stop to hire a horse while I was busy running for my life, and all that.

Enlar shrugged, that smile still teasing his lips. "I don't mind, I'd rather have the company. We can take turns riding King until we get to a town where we can hire a horse for you. Meira's near here, or we could even stop at Orchwell." Meira was a town about halfway between the kingdom of Rothschan and Orchwell, another kingdom in the Gifted Lands.

Hope flared in my heart. Traveling with Enlar would neatly accomplish two things: it would get me to Calia quicker, once I had a mount for myself, and it would put distance between me and my pursuers from Rothschan much faster. Plus, anyone looking for me would be searching for a lone female, not a pair of travelers.

Now, I just had to hope that Enlar was trustworthy.

I did some quick calculations in my head. On horseback, it would take about two days to get from where we were just outside of Rothschan to Orchwell. From there it was about another day or so from Orchwell to Calia. On foot, of course, it would take twice as long, perhaps more.

That meant Enlar and I would be together for at least two or three overnights. The only weapon I carried was a small eating knife.

The desire to travel fast warred with the need to stay safe. I shook my head slowly, knowing that it wasn't wise to trade a known danger for an unknown one.

Enlar caught the expression on my face. He held both of his hands out toward me, palms up, in the gesture widely accepted throughout the Gifted Lands as signifying *peace* or *no ill intent*. "I completely understand your hesitation. I promise I will do you no harm during our travels together."

A blue light flared up from the center of his palms. I watched, entranced, as the light enveloped his hands, and his fingertips glowed.

"Place your fingers to mine."

Mutely, I touched my fingertips to his.

The light spilled from his fingers to mine. The blue glow crept its way up my fingers, into my hands, and then gradually grew lighter as it reached my wrists and beyond. Soon, there was no blue light left, just an odd tingling in my fingers. I looked at Enlar inquisitively.

"You may remove your hands now," he said.

I took my hands back and gingerly shook them, flexing my fingers experimentally. Within a few seconds the tingling sensation had dissipated.

"What *was* that?" I asked Enlar.

"A spell of binding," he said. "Binding me to my word, and binding you to me as the one that oath was intended for. As I declared in the spell, you have nothing to fear from me. I cannot harm you, physically or magically, without bringing harm to myself."

Without warning, Enlar reached over and pinched my arm. I let out an instinctive, "Ow!"

There was a small red spot on my upper arm where Enlar had pinched me. He pointed at a spot on his arm. In the same spot was an identical angry red dot where the skin puckered slightly. Even as both spots faded, Enlar said, "See?"

I rubbed at my arm, trying to get the pain to fade faster. "Uh, thanks for the demonstration, I guess?"

He chuckled. "You're welcome."

What Enlar had said earlier came back to me, and I asked in wonder, "You can do magic?"

"Yes, it's why I'm going to Calia," he said. "Now, what do you say?"

"To traveling together?"

Knowing he couldn't hurt me greatly eased my mind. That, along with my other reasons, decided me. And perhaps he could teach me about magic along the way.

"Yes, let's do it."

"Great!" Enlar flashed that engaging grin again. He opened the stall door and began untying King. "I'll get King ready if you want to eat a quick breakfast before we leave."

I nodded, giving King another pat before heading into the inn.

Inside, Mistress Cataluna was wiping down a wooden table with a rag. A stack of dirty dishes was piled on the corner of the table. She looked up when I approached, smiling when she saw me.

"Adalynn! I figured you'd come in soon, when I saw that the young man was up and about. There's a bit of porridge in the pot over the fire, and some leftover bread, if you're hungry. Help yourself."

"Thank you." I picked up the pile of dishes over Mistress Cataluna's protests, and brought them into the kitchen, carefully placing them in a basin of soapy water to soak. Then I grabbed a clean bowl and spooned some porridge into it, grabbing a bread roll before heading back to the main room to eat.

Even though Enlar was waiting for me, I ate slowly, since the food was rather hot from simmering over the fire. The room was empty save for Mistress Cataluna and me, and we chatted about mundane topics while she cleaned and I ate. After a few minutes of idle conversation, I felt comfortable enough to bring up the topic I really wanted to discuss.

"That man whose horse I took care of—Enlar, I think he said his name was—what's he like? Did you have a chance to talk to him at all last night?"

Mistress Cataluna frowned, her movements slowing as she thought. "No more than any other patron," she admitted. "The inn was fairly busy when he arrived. He was polite, paid promptly, didn't cause any problems. To me, that's the best kind of customer." She gave me a sharp look. "Why do you ask?"

"He asked me to travel with him to Calia," I said. As her eyes narrowed, I added quickly, "It's all right, though, he did some magic spell that ensured he can't harm me in any way."

A thoughtful look replaced the look of concern on Mistress Cataluna's face. "Did he, now? But he's traveling to Calia? Where's he from, originally?"

"Bomora."

"Interesting."

"Why interesting?"

"Bomora's not known for magic. That's Calia's speciality. I'm not saying that someone from that far out west couldn't have any magic, but it's rare. Plus, Rothschan's ... shall I say, extreme *pragmatism* ... has somehow blocked magical talent from moving beyond its kingdom."

This was the first I had ever heard of my country's staunch disbelief in magic affecting the other kingdoms in the Gifted Lands, and it intrigued me.

"What do you mean?" I asked Mistress Cataluna.

Her face instantly shuttered. "Even if it's just the two of us here, and you seem like a trustworthy enough sort, I won't go into it." Her mouth puckered in a frown, and a worry line appeared between her brows. "We're too close to Rothschan, and you never know who's listening, or how." When I opened my mouth to question her further, she gave me a hard look and shook her head. "Let's just say, keep your mouth shut and your ears open. You might learn a lot while you're traveling."

I took her advice and didn't speak. Instead, I finished my breakfast while Mistress Cataluna changed the conversation back to safer subjects, such as funny stories about some of her regular patrons.

Mistress Cataluna took my empty bowl, waving away my offer to help clean. "You've done more than enough for me, Adalynn, and I'm sure that young man is ready to get on the road by now. But before you go ..."

She hurried into the kitchen, returning with a few cold bread rolls and a small hunk of cheese tied up in a napkin for me. She handed me the bundle, then said, "Hold out your other hand."

Mistress Cataluna poured several coins into my outstretched palm. I gasped and tried to give them back to her, but she refused. "You did more in that stable in one night than my good-for-nothing nephew has done in four months. You deserve every coin I'm giving you, and don't offend me by not accepting them."

I placed the money in my pocket, then embraced Mistress Cataluna. "Thank you."

"Thank *you*," she responded. "Now, get going while the day is good. Safe travels, dear, and if you come back this way do stop here."

"I will." I gave her a cheerful wave goodbye as I opened the inn's door and stepped into the bright sunshine.

8

---·---

CHAPTER EIGHT

TRUE TO HIS WORD, Enlar and I switched off riding King throughout the day, although I suspected he let me ride the horse more than he did. I'm not sure whether or not we made good time, but Enlar was right—it *was* pleasant to have company while traveling.

After our first hour on the road, spent in idle, polite chitchat, I turned the conversation to something deeper. "So, you're headed to Calia," I began.

"Yes, I am. As are you," Enlar pointed out cheerfully.

"Why? When you already know magic?" I asked. Enlar hesitated. Seeing that, I quickly added, "You don't have to tell me if you don't want to."

He shook his head, chuckling, as he walked beside me riding on King's back. "What else are we going to talk about? We'll be together for a while, so we may as well get to know each other."

King plodded along as I stayed silent, waiting for Enlar to elaborate.

"Well, as you already know, I hail from Bomora," he said. "Bomora's not known for magic, although it can randomly appear. If a person does manifest magic, it's a very small and limited ability. Perhaps the person is good at minor charms, or can cast a slight spell of protection on a house. Just enough to ensure the inhabitants don't have too many accidents and are, for the most part, happy."

I frowned, thinking of Mistress Cataluna's assertion that something about my home kingdom prevented magic from going into the western part of the Gifted Lands.

"I heard that magical ability didn't exist west of Rothschan," I said, wanting to test Mistress Cataluna's theory.

"It doesn't," Enlar agreed. "People like me are rare. Usually, if someone has magical ability, it manifests around fifteen or sixteen, and then peters out over a couple of years. In a very small number of cases, such as mine, rather than fading away until it's gone, it grows stronger."

"It did? But then, how old—"

"I'm twenty-five," Enlar said readily. "I've had magic much, much longer than anyone else in Bomora has ever had, or at least that anyone in Bomora can remember."

"You've had magic for ten years?" I marveled. After my disastrous encounters with my magic—so strange to start thinking of it as *mine*—I couldn't imagine living with it for ten years, let alone one week.

Enlar laughed. "You have to recall, my magic started off small and grew larger with time. Everything I've learned about magic so far has just been cobbled together from what other former magicians in Bomora were able to teach me. It's finally reached a point where I need to formally train, or it could get out of control and consume me.

"I have a cousin, Rhyss, who moved to Orchwell when we were about thirteen or so. He wrote me and told me about a magic school in Calia. Apparently his former employer's wife started the school, and I understand she still has an active hand in training future magicians."

Oh! Perhaps that was the reason my parents had instructed me to go to Calia. I hadn't heard of this magic school, but considering how my whole world had revolved around Rothschan and my now aborted future in the military, it wasn't surprising.

"Who did your cousin work for?"

"A dragon Seeker named Beyan."

"Dragons! Really?" When I was a child, I thought I had seen one of the magnificent beasts flying overhead. But, like magic, we in Rothschan had been told they were just old legends and superstitions, and that they had gone extinct ages ago.

Enlar laughed. "How have you not seen a dragon up to this point in your life? They're everywhere. Well, everywhere that has magic, which is pretty much any place in the Gifted Lands except magic-barren Rothschan."

"Do you think we'll encounter any on our travels?"

Enlar smiled, like he knew a secret. "It's possible. We can ask my cousin when we get to Calia."

"Oh, that's right! We were talking about your cousin. Continue, please."

"Beyan and Rhyss became friends when Rhyss moved to Orchwell. I believe they went to school together. When Beyan took over the family business, Rhyss and another friend of theirs, Farrah, accompanied Beyan on his seeking commissions, to help with the cooking and serve as protection if need be. But I believe Beyan retired once he got married."

"His wife must be pretty important, if she founded an entire school of magic."

"Oh, she is." Enlar smirked. "She's the Queen of Calia."

My eyes widened. I might get to learn magic from a queen!

I sobered. If, of course, I could afford it. And if my magic didn't go wild and hurt anyone. Or me.

"I suppose this school is rather expensive?" I ventured.

Enlar shrugged. "I'm not sure what it costs to attend, although most likely the students have to pay *something*. They've got to pay the teachers for their time, after all. But I'm not that worried about it."

I looked away awkwardly. Even if I had left Rothschan under normal circumstances instead of making my escape, my parents wouldn't have been able to afford a fancy magic school. But I guessed Enlar came from money, or at least that his family lived comfortably. His clothes were made of a fine fabric and cut, he owned a good horse, and had enough money in his purse to pay for services while traveling. So he had nothing to worry about when it came to attending Calia's magic school.

Enlar blushed. "I'm sure there are other people around who could tutor magic students ... if you can't afford the tuition."

I shrugged. While attending a magic school would certainly be interesting, it wasn't the reason I was headed to Calia. Definitely not. I would find someone who could help me tame my magic, and more importantly, help me save my parents. Anything else would just have to wait.

"How about you?"

"What?" I blinked, bringing my focus back to our conversation. "What *about* me?"

"What's your story?" Enlar asked. "Why are you headed to Calia?"

For a few minutes the only sound was the steady *clop, clop* of King's hooves as I thought furiously. What would be safe to tell him?

"My parents suggested it, most likely because we had no other options," I said slowly. "Like you, I have an unexpected magical talent. But mine came on me suddenly, and sometimes uncontrollably."

Enlar whistled. "Calia would be the best place for you to go, then. Where are you from originally?"

"Rothschan."

He laughed. "That explains why you didn't know dragons existed, then. But you have magic? How can that be?"

Now it was my turn to laugh. "Honestly, I have no idea. It was quite the surprise."

"How long have you had your magic?"

"Since yesterday."

Enlar turned wide green eyes up to me. "You've only come into your magic just one day ago?"

I grinned. "Well, at this point, one day and a few hours. At least, that's how long I've been aware of it."

He grinned back. "You said yours is uncontrollable, though. What sorts of things have you experienced?"

I detailed the incidents that had occurred: my suddenly full water pitcher, my clean and mended clothes. Of the event at the conscription office, I merely said, "And I found I was able to conjure fire." Enlar didn't need to know the *exact* details of what had happened.

"Wow," he commented when I finished. "Sounds like you had a busy day."

Thinking of everything that happened to me in just one crazy day, I smiled wryly. "That's one way of putting it."

Enlar laughed, and after a moment, I joined in.

Once our laughter died down, Enlar looked thoughtful. "I am surprised, though. From what I understand, magical talent is thoroughly suppressed in Rothschan, which is why it doesn't come west. At least in Bomora, we acknowledge the existence of magic, although we give it little thought since it's so rare and fleeting. And if magic does come west, it's a mere shadow of the magic that permeates the rest of the Gifted Lands."

"This is the second time I've heard of this supposed 'Rothschan suppressing magic' thing, and I'm rather curious what it entails," I said. "For all that I grew up in Rothschan, I'd never known about any of this before."

"I can't say I'm surprised," Enlar said. "Your kingdom guards its secrets well; it's probably not something they'd want the general public to know about."

He looked up at the sky, noting the sun nearly directly overhead. "I tell you what, I'll explain what little I know about it, but let's stop first for lunch and a brief rest. It will be good for King to rest as well. I'll tell you then."

I, of course, was itching to having my curiosity satisfied immediately, but I had to acquiesce to Enlar's plan. We had been on the road for a while, and it wouldn't be fair to either King or Enlar to not take a break.

And my stomach chose that moment to grumble loudly, cinching Enlar's decision to stop.

We found a spot just off the road that offered both shade and a fallen tree to use as a makeshift table. The sound of trickling water could be heard nearby. I brought out the cheese and bread that Mistress Cataluna had given me, spreading out the napkin on the log to create a little picnic, while Enlar tied King to a nearby tree. He patted the horse's neck. "I'll take you down to the stream after we've had our lunch," he promised King.

Enlar ripped off part of a roll while I munched on some cheese and looked at him expectantly. He chewed thoughtfully for a bit, then took a swig from his waterskin. He produced a second full waterskin and tossed it to me. "I promised you that explanation. I'll be honest, I don't quite understand all of it myself, but I'll do my best.

"As I'm sure you already know, each of the kingdoms in the Gifted Lands has a special ability. Calia, of course, is the preeminent kingdom in magic, but in general, there is much magic that permeates the Gifted Lands. It's just that, of all the kingdoms, those of Calia know best how to harness magic.

"Because magic is in the very weave of the Gifted Lands, in theory, all who live here should be able to access magic, to varying degrees. And I think, many years ago, this was true. But Rothschan is a very — *practical* — kingdom, and that mode of thinking has a way of suppressing magic. After so many generations, there is no magical ability in the kingdom of Rothschan."

I smirked. "I wouldn't say there's *none*."

He nodded in acknowledgement. "You're the first person from Rothschan I've heard of who has magic in over one hundred years. Most unusual."

"So you're saying that, just because Rothschan denied the existence of magic for years and years, it effectively killed magic in that part of the Gifted Lands?"

"In essence, yes," Enlar said. "I wouldn't have believed that just the power of thought alone would be enough to suppress something as ancient and grand as magic, but the evidence is plainly shown in both Rothschan's magicless citizens and the severely limited abilities of those in Bomora."

"But then why am I able to do magic, if it's been a century of stopping it?"

"That I don't know. Maybe we'll find the answer to that in Calia."

"I hope so."

We finished our lunch quickly. Enlar untied King, leading him to the nearby stream, while I refilled the waterskins.

In the distance I could hear the sound of hoofbeats on the road, moving fast. Enlar seemed unaffected, not caring about other travelers we might encounter, but I hurried back to our roadside camp.

From where I watched, hidden among the trees, I saw two soldiers galloping north, the same direction Enlar and I were headed. They were traveling too fast for me to see their faces, but I caught the colors their horses bore: the deep crimson and slate gray of Rothschan.

Enlar strolled back into camp with King. He offered to let me ride, but I declined. It was his turn to ride, after all, and I felt restless after everything I had just learned. Walking would help me get rid of some of this nervous energy.

Although, as we set off, I couldn't help but feel like something in me had changed irrevocably. I was walking away from the life—and apparently, the lies—I had always known, and into a future I couldn't even fathom.

9

CHAPTER NINE

THE NEXT FEW DAYS passed in a relatively uneventful blur. Enlar and I exchanged stories about our home kingdoms; as I had never traveled much beyond Rothschan, I found his tales about growing up in Bomora fascinating. He was equally intrigued about my life in Rothschan. I hadn't realized that our kingdom was regarded as somewhat of a mystery to the other countries in the Gifted Lands.

"So you're all conscripted into the military when you turn twenty-one?" It was Enlar's turn to ride King, and I shaded my eyes as I squinted up at him.

I laughed. "You make it sound like a bad thing."

"Well, yes. I suppose if you want to do it, that's one thing. But to have to do it ..."

"I *did* want to do it. Well, I did because it was the best option. For my family, I mean."

Enlar sensed my sadness, and didn't pursue the topic. Instead, he said, "How's that spell coming along?"

I scowled. "I don't know why, but now, when I actually *want* to use my magic, it won't cooperate." I held out my hands, muttering the spell's trigger words under my breath, and a cool blue light appeared above my palms. It was no bigger than a pinprick, and lasted all of three seconds before sputtering and flickering out. "But it worked when I wasn't thinking about it."

Enlar frowned down at me. "I think that's exactly the issue."

"What do you mean?"

"You're trying too hard," he explained patiently. "You're so focused on the outcome that you're not allowing yourself to feel the process. Which is just as important, if not more, than the end result of the spell you're casting."

My scowl deepened. "How can I feel the process when I don't even know what the process is?"

Enlar looked thoughtful as we traveled in silence for a few moments. Then: "You said you trained a bit in swordplay, yes?"

I nodded, trying to follow the sudden change in conversation. "My father and I used to spar every so often. I was fairly decent at it, but I was looking forward to honing my skills once I joined the military."

"When you have a sword in your hand, what goes through your mind?" At my confused look, he said, "I realize at this point it's probably instinctive for you, but if you had to break it down moment by moment, what would you be thinking and feeling?"

I paused, speaking slowly as I gave Enlar's question some thought. "I suppose I ... well, first, I'd draw my sword and change my stance, readying myself for the fight. I would ... I would assess my opponent, figuring out what their strengths and weaknesses could be. They might have a longer reach, but move slower than I do. Perhaps they're already injured, and I could exploit that to my advantage. Then I ... I would ... probably bide my time, let them make the first move, so I could see if my instincts about their abilities were correct. Block their sword, and look for an opening in their guard so I can make my move."

Enlar nodded at my explanation. "And obviously you've practiced it so many times that those actions just come naturally to you, now."

"For the most part, yes."

"Try applying that knowledge of sword fighting to magic," Enlar suggested. "As you work on a spell, pause at each step and really absorb what it is you're doing. It's important that you understand what you are doing, and it will enhance the spell and show in the end result. The other thing you should learn to do is control your power. Right now it's just floating around inside you, unchecked. It's uncontrollable that way. Find your power, and imagine … putting it away, in a sense. Like if it was in a box that you opened to varying degrees, depending on how much of your magic you wanted to access."

I pondered Enlar's words as we continued walking, practicing the light spell he had taught me repeatedly, but stopping just short of actually completing the spell. I was very aware of each action, forcing myself to absorb each one as I went through the steps.

I also concentrated on becoming more aware of my internal source of magic. I could feel it permeating my entire being, and I tried to gather up the various tendrils of power that stretched throughout my body into one part of my self.

We were close to Meira, a town halfway between Rothschan and Orchwell. We would hire my mount there, but continue to make camp along the way to Calia instead of paying for an inn. I had enough money to get a horse and perhaps buy some food, but that was about all I could afford. Enlar had offered to pay for us to stay at an inn, and was willing to rent a room for me, but I had declined, not wanting to be indebted to him any more than I already was.

My musings took me all the way into Meira, and I'll admit I was a bit distracted while we looked at horses. I felt like I was just on the verge of a breakthrough, and was excited to stop for the night to see if my experimentation on the road had worked.

However, I snapped back to attention when we were in a general goods store, buying some rations. Enlar was on the far side of the store, still shopping, while I brought the food to the counter.

The shopkeep counted our order and idly asked, "Where are you two coming from?"

"The south," I said vaguely.

"Really?" The shopkeep leaned over the counter. "Did you see the riders from Rothschan?"

My blood ran cold. "No," I said, trying to keep my voice steady.

"They stopped in here a day or so ago," he said, eager to gossip. "A building exploded in their Merchants' District, near the royal residence. They think it was deliberate, and they're looking for the person responsible."

"Did they describe the person?" I asked, still striving for nonchalance. Inside, however, I was shaking.

"No, they didn't," the shopkeep said. "The soldiers didn't know if it was a man or a woman, how old the person is, or what he or she looks like. They just know that the person was traveling north. And they'll pay handsomely for any information."

"Is that so?" I said noncommittally as Enlar came up to the counter with one more item in his hands. "Thank you for telling me, we'll be sure to keep an eye out."

Enlar paid for everything and we left, heading back to the stables so we could collect our horses.

I mounted my new horse, a black mare named Luna. Even though King had been walking the greater part of the day, he eagerly bounded forward when Enlar gave him his lead. The horses clipped along at a good pace, forcing me to concentrate on not falling off Luna instead of thinking about magic.

The sun was riding low in the sky when Enlar slowed King to a walk and suggested we stop for the night. I agreed, my relief plainly evident. It had been quite some time since I had ridden, and it had taken me a while to get used to it again. Fortunately, Luna seemed inclined to follow King's lead.

In our makeshift camp, Enlar lit a fire and handed me some food. He looked in his bag, assessing its contents. "We'll probably need to hunt again in a day or two."

"We should stop early then, so I can set a snare," I said.

"That's a good idea," Enlar said. He grinned at me. "Speaking of good ideas, I noticed you practicing while we were headed to Meira. Want to show me what you've learned?"

"Sure," I laughed. "If I've learned anything."

"I think you have," he said encouragingly. "Try that light spell now. Remember to really feel each action, every step of the way."

I propped my bag up on a nearby tree, settling my back against it as I made myself comfortable. I closed my eyes. My breathing slowed as I turned my focus inward, searching for that powerful spark inside me that I recognized as my magic. I imagined it as a golden ball of light concentrated in a plain wooden chest, one that spilled a bit of power for my use as I lifted the lid ever so slightly. When I closed the lid, the bit of golden light floated around, waiting for me to command it.

Now that I had just the right amount of magic for my light spell, I worked on holding on to that power with part of my mind.

The spell itself wasn't a lengthy one, just one word to command the ball of light to appear in my hand. But whereas before I had focused more on pushing the power through my hand, this time I relaxed into the spell. I willed the power to spread throughout my body, feeling it manifest as a dull but pleasant heat as it unfurled within me. I imagined my whole being as a conduit for light, as if the glow I wanted to create would come from my entire body instead of just my hand.

When I felt like every part of me was lit, I held my hands out in front of me and spoke the word that would bring the spell into being. "*Illumine.*"

I heard a gasp, and then light applause. I opened my eyes.

A cold ball of light was cupped in my outstretched hands, casting a steady glow that illuminated several feet all around me. The light touched Enlar's beaming face as he clapped his hands in delight.

"That was excellent! You really have learned a lot, and in such a short time."

I ducked my head modestly, pleased by Enlar's praise. "I had a good teacher."

He laughed. "Thank you. But it's easy to teach someone who's a fast learner. And now you're able to control your magic a little better. How do you feel?"

I thought about what had happened back in Rothschan, and what I was able to do now. Conjuring a small light was nothing to causing a building to explode, but being able to choose how I used my magic and how much of it I used actually made me feel more powerful than when my ability first started showing itself. A slow smile spread across my face.

"Like I can do anything."

10

— · —

Chapter Ten

We made good time to Calia, reaching it within a day and a half.

Just before midday, we stopped at the public stable just inside the kingdom's gates. The stable master called for his apprentice, a young boy no older than ten, who ran out to grab our horses' reins. King, Luna, and the boy disappeared into the stable.

"What brings you to Calia?" the stable master asked as Enlar counted out the coins for the stabling fee.

"We've heard about the new magic school your queen founded," Enlar said, handing over the money.

The stable master pocketed the coins with a satisfied air. "Ah, new students! It's exciting to see so many foreign visitors coming to our fair kingdom. Well, if you're looking for the school, it's quite close. Just off the Merchants' District, turn left at the glassmaker's, and you'll see it ahead of you. They built it there because it was easiest to expand in that area. Oh, and once you're settled, do take some time to visit the palace. It was designed by a water mage, you know. If you can get some time away—I hear the professors work the students pretty hard."

We thanked the man and headed further into Calia.

"Wow, he was so nice. I hope everyone in Calia is so friendly," I commented.

"Are people in Rothschan not as helpful?" Enlar wondered.

"We get so few visitors in Rothschan, we don't know how to treat them when they do show up," I admitted. "People generally would rather keep to themselves."

Enlar wisely didn't comment.

Now that we had reached Calia, my uncertainty came back in full force. I didn't have enough money to pay the tuition for *any* school, let alone one that taught magic. I could offer my services in the kitchens or elsewhere on the grounds, but maybe they wouldn't need that, or maybe I couldn't study and work at the same time.

Mentally, I laughed at myself. What was I thinking? I was on the run. If I attended a school right now, I'd be extremely easy for the Rothschan soldiers to find.

If they weren't here in Calia already....

I was so busy sorting through my jumbled thoughts that I just blindly followed Enlar, not paying attention to where he was headed. It wasn't until we approached a well-groomed rose garden that I started to ponder my surroundings.

"Enlar," I said. "Did we pass the school? The stable master said it wasn't far from the stables."

"Don't worry," he said. "We can head to the school later."

We passed through the garden into an ornate courtyard. Blue and green cobblestones shimmered in the sunlight, making me feel like we were floating underwater. The pleasant sound of falling water came from two stone fountains that flanked the front doors of a ...

"Enlar, we're at the palace!"

"Yes, we are. I'm surprised it took you this long to figure it out." His lopsided grin told me there was no malice behind his words, just snark.

I was so surprised I didn't think to smirk back at him. "But what are we doing *here*? Shouldn't we go and enroll in the school? Isn't that why we're in Calia?"

"We can do that, yes. Eventually. But our first order of business is to see the Queen and King."

I stopped, dumbfounded. Enlar continued striding confidently across the palace courtyard as if he could, indeed, just walk on into the palace and easily gain an audience with the rulers of the kingdom.

Enlar stopped, realizing I was no longer keeping pace with him. He turned around to see me standing still a few feet behind him, gaping at him.

"Are you coming, Adalynn?"

To clear my confusion, I blinked and shook my head, then I nodded vigorously.

Enlar laughed. "Is that a no? Or a yes?"

I ran up to him, closing the distance between us. "Yes! Of course, I'm coming."

"Good." He continued walking toward the front doors of the grey stone palace. Two guards in polished silver armor stood at attention on either side of the tall wooden doors.

I plucked at his sleeve, stopping him just before we reached the guards. "But how are we going to get in? How does my hair look? Do I smell like horse?"

"Woah! Just relax, Adalynn. Trust me. It will be fine." Enlar started forward again, and I darted after him.

The guards watched us approach, polite but wary. "State your business," one of them said.

"We humbly request an audience with Queen Jennica and King Beyan," Enlar said. I marveled at his confidence.

The guard raised an eyebrow. "Names?"

"I am Enlar Edson of Bomora, and my companion here is …"

"Adalynn Taethen of Rothschan," I quickly supplied.

The guard gave a curt nod. "Wait here."

He slipped inside the palace, leaving us standing outside with the other guard eyeing us impassively.

Enlar flashed a smile at the guard. "Tell me, does it get hot in that suit of armor?"

Embarrassed, I hissed, "Enlar!"

The guard smiled back at us. "You'd think so, but the queen recently commissioned charms for all of us that keeps air flowing around inside. It attaches to the back, and it's quite nice, actually."

I had been about to tell Enlar to *Be quiet, already,* but this exchange rendered me mute. If Enlar had been so casual at the doors of the Rothschan palace, he probably would have been clapped in chains. And speaking of casual, what kind of kingdom was Calia where the queen herself would care about the minute welfare of her guards?

Enlar said to the guard, "You don't say? That's fascinating. How long do—"

The first guard rejoined us, saying, "Your party has been granted an audience."

The guard opened the door wider to allow us to enter, and Enlar calmly strode in as if he visited royalty every day. Perhaps he did. For my part, it was all I could do not to act foolish. Eyes wide, I followed after Enlar.

Pointing straight ahead, the guard said, "Please proceed to the Great Hall."

He shut the door firmly behind us. At the end of a long corridor, we could see its entrance, although other stone hallways branched off of the main one. Every few paces, we passed gilt-framed paintings in various sizes and styles.

Just outside the Great Hall, another painting hung, featuring two golden dragons and a stately-looking dark-haired woman wearing a crown. The trio was fighting a sinister, red-eyed man, also sporting a crown—and, curiously, a red-and-grey tunic that was reminiscent of an old Rothschan clothing style. Just under the painting, atop a pedestal, stood a carving of a golden dragon, wings unfurled and ready for flight.

I wanted to stop and study the painting and the figurine closer, but the doors to the Great Hall were open, and we could see a group of people within. Knowing it was unwise to dawdle, I looked longingly at the artwork as I passed by, still on Enlar's heels.

The dais at the end of the room boasted two thrones. Seated on these thrones were a dark-haired woman and a man with a headful of unruly brown hair. The king and queen of Calia, I surmised. A curly-haired blonde woman sat on a low stool next to the queen's throne. As we entered the Great Hall, I could hear the queen say to her, "What do you think of that last case, Taryn? Should the woman have to compensate her neighbor for the loss of his chickens?"

"It is a bit of a quandary, Your Majesty," Taryn replied. "On one hand, the neighbor should have built better fencing. A coop, or something. On the other hand, the woman's son was supposed to have been watching them. But on the other hand ..."

The man on the throne laughed. "Taryn, how many hands do you have?"

Taryn laughed as well. "As many as are needed to solve the problem, Your Majesty."

The king laughed even harder. "I still don't know why I can't make a proclamation saying that everyone just calls me Beyan? I mean, I am the king, right? I tolerated the whole 'Lord Beyan' thing, but this constant 'Your Majesty' thing is just too—"

Queen Jennica patted his hand fondly. "Try growing up with it. If I have to deal with it, then so do you." She laughed. "It's more for our subjects than anything. Thank you for being so patient."

King Beyan squeezed her hand, then raised it to his lips. "The things I do for you."

Enlar and I were now at the dais. He bowed deeply while I curtsied. I hoped I didn't show how nervous I was; curtseying wasn't a skill I had occasion to practice often.

The trio on the dais turned their attention to us. "Well met, Enlar Edson of Bomora," King Beyan said. "When Rhyss wrote us and said you'd be coming, Jennica and I were excited to meet you. Hopefully you'll be able to see your cousin soon; he and Farrah are supposed to come to Calia for a visit within the month."

Cousin! Of course! I had forgotten that Enlar's cousin Rhyss was a longtime friend of King Beyan's. And Rhyss had told Enlar about the Calian magic school. I mentally kicked myself for not making the connection sooner.

"Thank you, Your Majesties, for agreeing to meet with me," Enlar said. "When my cousin told me to expect a warm welcome at the Calian palace, I couldn't believe it."

"We're happy to welcome any friend or relative of Rhyss or Farrah," Queen Jennica said. "They're two of our dearest friends."

The king and queen then turned their attention to me. I did my best not to fidget under their gazes.

"And what was your name again?" Queen Jennica politely asked me.

"Adalynn Taethen. I come from Rothschan."

Queen Jennica stiffened, and she and her husband exchanged glances. Next to the queen, I could see Taryn come alert as well.

"While our kingdoms have had some contention in the past, we recognize that the sins of one do not represent the people of a country as a whole. So you have nothing to fear from any Calian in that regard," the queen said.

My brow furrowed as I considered her words. And then I remembered a vague bit of recent history that had fueled gossip for several weeks, years ago. The former Calian king had originally hailed from Rothschan; one of our finest knights, if I remembered right. But he had also gone insane with power and magic—*magic*, of all things!—and had fallen in battle against two mighty beasts. Dragons.

Suddenly, the painting outside the Great Hall made sense to me.

The queen smiled grimly, noting the flash of recognition on my face. "I see you understand what I'm referring to. As I said, no one will harm you. Although," she leaned forward conspiratorially, "if anyone tries, you just let us know."

I grinned, finding I liked this spunky queen's spirit.

"But now, to the other matter. Your family name is Taethen, you said?"

"Y-Yes," I stammered, surprised at the abrupt change of subject.

The king, queen, and Taryn exchanged a three-way glance. I didn't think such a thing was possible, but it was obvious they had plenty of practice.

"What brings you to Calia, Adalynn Taethen of Rothschan?" The queen sounded more curious than threatening.

I hesitated, unsure of how much I should disclose. Yes, she ruled the kingdom I was currently seeking succor in, and yes, she would be able to help me with my magic. But we were unknown to each other, and I didn't know if I could fully trust her.

As I opened my mouth to speak, the guard from the palace door who had announced us earlier burst into the Great Hall. "Your

Majesties, forgive the intrusion. But soldiers from Rothschan have arrived, and they are demanding entry."

11

---·---

Chapter Eleven

Queen Jennica's eyes narrowed. "How many?"

"Two, Your Majesty."

"Messengers, then, and not an invasion," she muttered to herself. To the guard, she said, "We'll have to admit them, but delay them as much as possible before granting them entry."

"Yes, Your Majesty." The guard hurried away.

The queen turned to Taryn, who was already on her feet. With a barely perceptible nod, she communicated something, and Taryn turned to the wall and started running her hands over it.

I said, "What's happening?"

The queen chuckled. "Oh, sorry. Taryn is the best advisor I could ask for. I don't even need to tell her what I'm thinking."

"Is it some kind of magic mind reading?"

Taryn gave a satisfied grunt as she found what she was looking for. She pressed something on the wall, and a portion of the wall slid silently open. She winked at the queen. "It's just another typical day in Calia."

"Adalynn, go with Taryn," Queen Jennica instructed me. I nodded and hastily moved toward the wall and the open stone door. The queen looked at Enlar. "You should go with them as well. It's probably best if the soldiers don't know either of you were here."

Enlar looked confused, but obeyed the queen. Taryn stood to the side to allow both Enlar and me into the passage, then stepped inside the doorway.

"Bring them to my chambers," Queen Jennica said. "We'll come as soon as we can."

Taryn nodded and pressed another stone inside the passage. The heavy stone door slid closed, plunging us into complete darkness.

A soft scraping sound came from somewhere on the ground, and then a small glow emerged. The lit candle illuminated Taryn's face.

"How did—" I started to say, but Taryn put a finger to her lips.

I heard unintelligible voices just beyond the closed door. A male's deep voice—the visitor from my homeland, I guessed. And then a lighter, higher voice, most likely Queen Jennica's.

In a low voice barely above a whisper, Taryn said, "It's not wise to linger. Unusual sounds in the walls will be noticed. Come."

She motioned for Enlar and me to follow her down the passageway.

Moving as quietly as we could, we crept down the darkened hall. The oppressing dark and the various twists and turns confused me. We also went up a flight of stairs, perhaps two. It was hard to tell in the never-ending darkness. Eventually I gave up trying to get my bearings and just concentrated on following the singular light of Taryn's candle.

I'm not sure how long we were in that secret passage—far too long, to my mind—but finally Taryn stopped. Holding up the candle to the wall, she found the latch and sprung the door. The door opened to a large, ornately furnished bedchamber, well lit by the sunlight streaming through the large windows.

Taryn motioned us to the settee by the unlit fireplace. "You two can sit there, if you like, and rest a bit. We should be undisturbed until the king and queen get here."

Enlar and I did as Taryn suggested and took seats on the settee. Taryn blew out her candle, and then turned to the wall, flipping a hidden latch that closed the door to the secret passage so it became a recessed mahogany bookshelf once more. She joined us by the fireplace, sitting in a chair opposite the settee.

"My apologies for shushing you, but you can never be too careful," Taryn said. "The sound can echo something fierce in the stone hallways."

"I understand," I said. "But now that it's safe to talk ... it *is* safe to talk now, isn't it?" Taryn nodded. "Well, I was just wondering ... where did that candle come from?"

Enlar gave me a bemused look. "We just walked through a secret passage in a foreign castle, trying to get away from soldiers from your home country, and that's the first question you think to ask?"

I shrugged. I had the same questions as he did, but this mundane thought would ground me in normalcy. I hoped.

Taryn smiled. "We've had a lot of practice, Queen Jennica and I. Before I was the Queen's Advisor, I was her lady-in-waiting for many years. And during that time, I served her mother, Queen Melandria, on, shall we say, matters of political confidentiality."

"You were a spy," I stated in admiration.

Taryn shrugged modestly. "I've had to use the passages often. So I started carrying a candle at all times, and left tinderboxes at each entrance."

Enlar said, "That explains how you and the queen were so quick to act, then. But why did Adalynn and I have to leave? I thought the queen said relations between Calia and Rothschan were good, or decent enough. And why—"

Taryn interrupted Enlar's stream of interrogation. "I believe it would be best to wait until the king and queen are here, so we don't have to go over the same things repeatedly."

"But—"

Enlar was interrupted again by the bedchamber door opening. All three of us turned to see King Beyan and Queen Jennica entering, and we all scrambled to our feet to bow or curtsey.

The queen waved away the formality. "We're not in the Great Hall anymore, it's just silly to be bowing all over the place when there's more important things we need to do."

Behind her, the king chuckled. "It would be great if we could do away with the formality in public, as well."

"Ah, but then, how would people remember to respect our positions? It's an unfortunate evil, darling."

Taryn delicately cleared her throat, gaining the pair's attention. I got the impression this was a common topic of conversation for them.

The king and queen joined us, sitting on a second settee nearby. "I'm afraid we'll have to forgo refreshments," Queen Jennica said apologetically. "It would be hard to explain how the three of you slipped by the servants."

"If you like, I can go down to the kitchens and bring up a tray," Taryn offered. "No one will think that odd."

The queen nodded. "Thank you, Taryn." Taryn stood and slipped out of the bedchamber.

"Now, then," Queen Jennica said. "I'm sure you have some questions over what just happened."

Enlar and I looked at each other, then back at the queen, and nodded emphatically. If the situation wasn't so serious, I'm sure we would have laughed at how silly we looked with our heads bobbing in time together.

"I'll do my best to answer your questions." The queen leveled her shrewd gaze on me. "And then I think you might have the answers to some of mine."

What information would I have that she could possibly want?

The queen settled back in her seat. "Are you aware of the history between Calia and Rothschan?"

Enlar looked confused, but I nodded. "I recalled something when you mentioned it in the Great Hall, Your Majesty. If I remember right, one of our knights married into your country's royal family?"

"Yes, that's correct," Queen Jennica affirmed. "Years ago, Sir Hendon of Rothschan saved Princess Melandria of Calia from a dragon that had come to our kingdom." Next to her, King Beyan snorted. The queen smirked. "That's true, dear, but we won't get into that right now."

Enlar and I exchanged a look, wondering what the queen was omitting from her story. "Anyway," the queen continued, "Melandria is my mother. The short version is that Hendon had been experimenting on the people of Calia in an attempt to gain magic. Even though he was from Rothschan and, in public, denounced magic and anything to do with it. I learned of his intentions, and, with the help of Beyan and some others, was able to stop Hendon.

"Hendon died, which did not endear Calia to Rothschan. It also didn't help that I had been betrothed, albeit against my will, to the Rothschan prince, Anders. Due to ... certain circumstances ... our engagement was broken, and he returned to Rothschan, humiliated on his wedding day."

"It really wasn't your fault, though, it was Hendon's," the king interjected.

The queen snorted. "Yes, well, even if I *had* been willing to go through with the marriage, the Queen of Rothschan made it very clear I would not have been a suitable daughter-in-law." She and the king smiled at each other, enjoying their private joke.

Queen Jennica's story was sparking my memory. "You know, now that you say all this, I *do* remember hearing something about it. I remember the prince's wedding preparations and his send off to Calia. Everyone in Rothschan celebrated for a week, in his honor."

Enlar looked amazed. "We didn't hear anything about this in Bomora. But then again, news from the middle kingdoms is slow to reach us in the west." He turned to me. "Whatever happened to Prince Anders after the failed wedding?"

I frowned, thinking. "I believe he got married, quietly, to some minor noble from Shonn." Shonn was another kingdom in the Gifted Lands, to the east of Calia. "The wedding happened quickly; he was barely home for a month before leaving again. The street gossip was that the royal family wanted him far away and settled fast so they could save face over what had happened in Calia. The queen went into seclusion for a year—I remember we all thought it odd, since she often liked to give huge, lavish parties. There were always announcements about them. And then, for a year—nothing. And the king? He put more focus on the military, and there were rumors about special programs that were created to make our military even greater than it already was." A faint thought tugged at my memory, something about the king's special programs and something the unfortunate Renton had said when Father and I were in his office.

A burst of laughter from Queen Jennica caused my tenuous thought to completely flee my mind. "I'm sorry," she said in between giggles. "I really shouldn't laugh at another's misfortune. It's just ... the Rothschan royal family probably wanted their son with a 'normal' woman, which is why they were glad Anders and I didn't wed. And yet—Shonn has strong ties with the Fae. So Anders may have ended up with a magical being after all."

The king laughed along with his wife, and even Enlar chuckled. I wasn't sure how I should feel. Privately, most of us in Rothschan had regarded Anders as a pompous, arrogant fool. But Rothschan was still my home country, the one I had been willing to die to serve. Even if it no longer wanted me anymore.

Especially because I was now one of *those* people, the ones that possessed that most hated thing of all. Magic.

The queen caught my mood, and sobered instantly. "I truly am sorry," she said. "I meant no offense."

"It's all right," I shrugged, even though it wasn't, really.

She cleared her throat, trying to move past the awkward moment. "Anyway, Calia was fortunate Rothschan didn't try to retaliate with their full military power. We have a few mighty weapons at our disposal—" she smirked again "—but we're a country of scholars. We'd prefer not to have blood on our hands. Our two kingdoms have reached something of an unspoken truce between us, but we're still very cautious."

"That makes sense," Enlar said. "But if relations between the kingdoms are okay, then why hide Adalynn and me? We have nothing to do with the issues between Calia and Rothschan."

The queen turned to me. "I believe that would be Adalynn's story to tell."

12

CHAPTER TWELVE

ALL EYES TURNED TO me. I looked around at everyone's expectant faces, not sure what the queen wanted me to say.

Luckily for me, the door to the bedchamber opened and Taryn entered, balancing a large tray laden with a pale green teapot, matching porcelain cups, and some small cakes and sandwiches. Enlar stood up, rushing over to help Taryn with the tray.

My inquisition was paused while Taryn poured tea and handed out cups. Once we were all settled again, now with food and drink, Queen Jennica looked at me expectantly.

"I—I'm not sure what you would like me to say," I said hesitantly.

"Start with what brought you to Calia. I believe that question still remains unanswered from earlier."

"All right, then." I recounted my story, starting with my birthday, to the magical manifestations the following morning, the fire in the conscription office, and my flight from Rothschan. I told them how my parents had instructed me to head north to Calia, and what had happened at the inn when I was about to fill the bathtub.

When I got to the part about seeing the Rothschan soldiers on the road, and what the shopkeep in Meira had told me, Enlar stopped me.

"Wait. You knew that there were soldiers after you, and you didn't tell me?"

I flinched under his accusatory glare. "Well, I couldn't be sure it was me they were after ... and then after Meira we didn't run into them again ... and ... I—I'm sorry."

He sighed. "I guess I can't say I blame you for keeping quiet about it."

"Thank you."

"And we made it here safely, so I can't complain about it either."

"I really am sorry."

"I know."

The queen leaned forward. "Then it was truly fortunate that we sent you two with Taryn when those soldiers showed up. And in truth, they were looking for you, Adalynn. Even though they didn't have an exact description, they wanted us to look out for any newcomers from Rothschan. In addition to Meira, they stopped in Orchwell, and inquired at several towns and farms along the way. They said you were wanted for questioning in relation to an incident back in Rothschan. They didn't give any more detail beyond that."

Tentatively, I asked, "Did they ... did they say what the price upon my head was?"

King Beyan raised an eyebrow. "Trust us, you don't want to know."

He was right. I really didn't. I didn't want to know how badly the Rothschan military, the most feared in all the Gifted Lands, wanted me in their custody. Alive, or more likely, dead. In the eyes of Rothschan law, being wanted for questioning was as good as saying a person was guilty of an offense.

I shuddered.

"I'm more worried about my parents," I said. "Did the soldiers say what happened to them?"

The king shook his head. "No, they didn't say anything about your family. I'm sorry, Adalynn."

I sighed in frustration. But I wasn't truly surprised by the lack of information. I just had to hope that that lack was ultimately a good thing, and not a sign of something more ominous.

Queen Jennica was watching me closely. "And that's all there is to your story?"

"Yes." Confused, I watched as she, King Beyan, and Taryn all exchanged another three-way glance. I looked at Enlar, who face betrayed the same confusion I felt.

"Hmm." The queen folded her hands in her lap. "And your parents gave you no other information or instruction other than to come to Calia?"

"That's correct, Your Majesty."

"It's possible they didn't know," Taryn said. "It could just be coincidence."

"It's possible," the queen conceded. "But what an amazing coincidence, if that's true."

I could feel my temper starting to fray from being kept ignorant by these complete strangers. Royal or not, it was rude to discuss someone's life in front of them without any explanations. "If I may ask," I said, "what is going on?"

There was a long, weighty silence. Then, finally, from Queen Jennica:

"I wouldn't normally discuss this with anyone beyond my husband, my advisor, and a few trusted individuals who are already aware of the situation. But based on ... certain facts about you ... I feel that you have a right to know.

"For several years now, Calia has been a safe haven for people like you, Adalynn. Refugees from Rothschan who found they had magical ability, which would cause them persecution in their home country. We also have recent reports that anyone with magic in Rothschan may also be subject to military experiments, as well."

"The king's special programs!" I blurted out, finally putting the pieces together.

"Yes," the queen confirmed.

"So, Calia is housing Rothschan refugees," I said. "That's all well and good, but what does that have to do with me? Besides the fact that I am now one of those refugees."

The queen took a deep breath. "Up to this point, the refugees have been content to just stay in Calia, cultivate their talents, and live in peace. And we're happy to have them here, for as long as they want to stay. But lately we've been getting an influx of people from Rothschan. Magic seems to be creeping into the kingdom and its citizens, whether those in power like it or not. The exiles want to return home and change the country, even if they have to overthrow the government to achieve that goal.

"And their leader, Laydon Taethen, is willing to do whatever it takes to help them do it."

13

CHAPTER THIRTEEN

MY BREATH CAUGHT.

Laydon Taethen.

The name I had heard my mother whisper, wondering about his fate. And he had the same surname as me.

Searching my memory, I didn't recall a Laydon in our family. Father had never mentioned having a brother, and Mother's only sister passed away when I was young. Perhaps he was a distant cousin? That would make sense—he must be much older than me, and had probably grown up in a different household, since I didn't remember him.

Queen Jennica had a knowing look on her face, as if my reaction had confirmed her suspicions. "I could be wrong, but I don't think Taethen is a very common name."

"No, it isn't," I said, shaking my head. Then, tentatively, "Will I ... will I get to meet him?"

"I'm sure you will, soon," the queen promised. "Most of the refugees either attend the school or get private lessons, so it's likely you'll run into your countrymen at some point or another. Laydon's been in Calia for quite a while, and he's one of our best teachers." She smirked. "And a mean strategist."

"He's one of the teachers?"

"Nothing like hiding in plain sight," King Beyan commented. The queen's smirk deepened.

I looked from one to the other, not understanding what they were hinting at. Taryn, sensing my frustration, took pity on me.

"When we're done here, we'll get you settled in over at the school," she said. "Both of you."

Enlar sat back, satisfied, but I wrung my hands in worry. "I don't have any money for tuition."

"Don't fret about it for now," Queen Jennica said kindly. "Many of the people we take in from Rothschan come here with just the clothes on their back. If you'd like to give back to Calia in some way, we can figure out some form of community service for you."

Hearing this, I brightened up considerably. Although I missed my parents fiercely, and worried over their safety, knowing that I hadn't come to Calia in vain made me feel somewhat better about their sacrifice.

We chatted a little bit, about magic and lessons and life in Calia. When the conversation wound down, Taryn said, "I'll take them to the school and get them settled in, Your Majesties."

"That would be wonderful, thank you, Taryn." The queen stood up, and we all followed suit, bowing or curtseying. "And when you're done, you can just go home. Petitioners' Court is done for the day, and I think we've done everything we can, for now."

"And whatever is still undone will keep until tomorrow," Taryn commented wryly, earning answering smiles from both the king and the queen.

Taryn, Enlar, and I left the royal bedchamber. Taryn stopped a servant in the hallway, asking him to stop by the royal suite to pick up our dirty dishes. She then continued to navigate the twisty stone hallways until I was thoroughly bewildered.

Eventually we found our way back to the Great Hall and the palace doors, and then back outside to the courtyard.

"Is there anything you need to get before we head to the school?" Taryn asked us as we walked. "I assume you rode; we can pass by the stables if you want to pick up your things."

"This is all we brought," Enlar said, indicating the packs we carried.

"Oh, that's it?" Taryn raised an eyebrow. I understood her confusion. As a refugee from Rothschan, she wouldn't have expected me to be carrying much, but Enlar would most likely have prepared better for his trip and subsequent enrollment in the school.

"I travel light," was Enlar's explanation, and Taryn left it at that.

"What's the school like?" I asked Taryn.

"It's small, but steadily growing," she replied. "It's only a few years old, and started as a way to consolidate the various private magic tutors around Calia, and create a formal curriculum. We may be known for magic, but our kingdom has been very haphazard in passing down its knowledge. Usually instruction is kept within families, and outside teachers are sought if a student shows exceptional talent and the family has the means to hire a teacher. After the former king, Hendon, was deposed, Queen Jennica realized that the country needed a way to train all future magicians, regardless of family or economic status, and founded the school. If people have the means to pay then we ask them to do so, but the school doesn't rely on students' tuition to run. The Crown subsidizes most of it.

"I will admit, you're catching us at an odd time. Most of the students are gone for the summer holiday, and will be back in a few weeks. There are a few students still on campus, either getting private instruction or just staying in the dorms during the break. You'll be able to meet a few people, but there won't be any formal classes until everyone returns from holiday."

Enlar seemed fine with Taryn's explanation, but I was a little disappointed. The sooner I learned how to control my magic, the sooner I could return home and help my parents.

As we approached the school campus, I was surprised at how modest the building actually was. A three-story brick building with ivy climbing its walls and framing its ornate windows, it had the appearance of a converted mansion, with new wings recently added on. Which made sense—as we were in a primarily residential part of the capital, it would be convenient for students to live and study here. Above the door hung a simple gilded sign: Academy of Magical Arts.

Taryn seemed to sense my thoughts. "This is the school, but you will be living in one of the boardinghouses that skirt the campus. Let's get you settled in to where you'll be staying."

She led us down a side street, where I was instantly charmed by our new residence—a stately brownstone covered in ivy. Buildings in Rothschan were built for function, not for aesthetics. While I appreciated my home country's practicality, I was surprised to find there was a part of me, long dormant, that admired and longed for the adventure I was now experiencing. It was just a building enveloped by weeds, and yet to me it represented something new, foreign, and full of promise.

Taryn stepped up to the brownstone's elegant red door, knocking smartly with the shiny brass knocker affixed to it. I squinted at the knocker, momentarily taken aback at the fierce dragon head carved into the metal. Its savage smirk settled into something more neutral, and I got the odd impression of having passed some sort of unknown test.

Enlar and I joined Taryn on the doorstep, standing just behind her. I shifted my weight and hid my shaking hands behind me. A quick glance over at Enlar told me that, for all his confidence, he was now actually just as nervous as I was.

Fortunately—maybe?—we didn't have to wait long. The imposing red door swung open, and an equally formidable voice cackled, "What's this you've brought me, Taryn? Ooh, I do love fresh blood!"

14

CHAPTER FOURTEEN

PANICKED, I JERKED BACK, trying to put distance between myself and the voice. But I forgot there was a step down, and in my haste I tripped and lost my balance as I stepped backward. Arms flailing, I braced for the inevitable impact against the hard cobblestone street. To my left I heard Taryn gasp, and Enlar, whose attention had been focused on the newcomer, didn't react quickly enough to help me.

A pair of strong, pale arms shot out and grabbed my forearms, stopping my fall. Pulling me back to the relative safety of the porch, the arms released their grip on me once it was clear I had regained my balance.

I found myself staring into wide, dark brown eyes set in an openly curious heart-shaped face. My rescuer stared back at me, then a broad grin split her face as she shook her head, making her cloud of bushy brown hair billow up briefly. "Well, I'd say that's quite a welcome, wouldn't you?"

I couldn't help but grin back at the woman. Her enthusiasm was infectious. "I suppose so. Thank you for catching me, Mistress ...?"

"Fiala," the cheerful brunette said. "Just Fiala."

She stepped to the side, gesturing to the open doorway as she did so. "Please, all of you, come in and be welcome. I'm sure after your little trip you'd like to rest a bit." She laughed at her joke, emitting a sort of wheezy bark, and the rest of us joined in.

As I stepped over the threshold, something settled over me, a feeling of calm tranquility laced with an undercurrent of power. I looked at Fiala questioningly, but before I could ask our hostess what had just happened, she ushered us into the sitting room just off the foyer. She rang a little bell that sat waiting on a side table.

"Please, sit," she said, waving at the beige settee and the overstuffed chairs that were artfully arranged around the room. A servant popped her head in the doorway. "Ah, Melisande! Can you bring refreshments for our guests?"

Melisande's footsteps receded down the hallway as Fiala waved at Taryn, Enlar, and me to sit. "I always like to get to know prospective boarders."

"This is Enlar Edson of Bomora," Taryn said as we settled in. "And Adalynn Taethen of Rothschan."

Fiala gave me a sharp look, but didn't comment.

We made small talk for a bit about the weather and Fiala's lovely home until Melisande bustled into the room with a tea tray. Fiala took the tray from the servant. "That will be all. Thank you for bringing that so promptly."

As Melisande left, Fiala poured out tea for all of us, handing out the small cream-colored cups one at a time. She eyed us appraisingly, then addressed Enlar.

"Bomora, you say?" Enlar nodded at her question. "I used to live there, for a few years. Such a beautiful country, especially your forests. So majestic, so peaceful."

Enlar looked puzzled. "You lived in Bomora? In the forest? But ... the forests are uninhabitable. They're said to be haunted, no one lives there. No one sane, anyway." Enlar suddenly realized what he was implying, and coughed, embarrassed. "I mean—I didn't mean—pardon me."

Fiala smiled inscrutably, but didn't bother answering Enlar. She turned to me. "And you. You said your family name is Taethen?"

Now it was my turn to nod. Fiala's smile deepened as she tilted her head to study me. "You look just like him."

I nearly asked who she meant, then remembered my long-lost relative Laydon taught at the Academy. As Fiala was, I surmised, the House Mistress of this boardinghouse, she probably knew Laydon, the other teachers, and anyone who worked at or near the school.

As if she knew my thoughts, Fiala asked, "And are you a relation of our Professor Taethen?"

I wasn't sure how to answer that. "I … don't know?"

Fiala smirked, but didn't respond.

Like so much else about Fiala, that smirk was enigmatic. I had no idea what she was thinking. Mentally, I shrugged and filed away her mysterious response to analyze later.

Taryn leaned forward, changing the subject. "Sorry to spring this on you without warning, Fiala, but the other boardinghouses are closed for the break. Do you have any extra rooms for Enlar and Adalynn?"

Fiala nodded. "You're in luck. Several of our students left just last week, wanting to go home for the summer holiday. So I do have extra rooms available right now. If those students want their regular rooms back when they return, I'm not sure what we'll do, but for now they can stay here."

Taryn smiled, satisfied. "That will do nicely, for now. We can figure out their long-term housing later on."

"Perfect." Fiala rang the bell again. "I'll just have Melisande get some rooms ready, and then you can settle in."

Taryn looked out the parlor window, noting the fading light outside. "It's probably too late to take you two on a tour of the school today. Perhaps—"

Melisande appeared in the doorway. "Yes, Mistress Fiala?"

"Melisande, could you ready two rooms for our new guests? One each in the men's and women's wings?"

Melisande frowned thoughtfully. "I believe there are already two rooms to suit, mistress. I prepared them earlier today. On the men's side, there's the room that Tuen vacated two days ago, and on the women's side, there's the corner bedroom that faces the front of the house."

"Wonderful. Thank you, Melisande." The servant left, and Fiala turned to Enlar and me. "Shall I show you to your rooms, then?"

She stood, and we all followed suit. Taryn said, "If there's anything you need, have Fiala contact me. I'm usually up pretty early."

"I'm not," Fiala retorted with a laugh. "We're on holiday hours. I rarely stir before mid-morning."

Taryn laughed. "I wish I could be on holiday hours. But the kingdom never takes a holiday."

We exited the sitting room, walking back into the foyer. At the door, we said our goodbyes, with Taryn adding, "Enlar, Adalynn, you're in good hands with Fiala. She's one of our best House Mistresses, and she'll make sure you settle in just fine."

After Taryn left, Enlar and I followed Fiala upstairs. The House Mistress said, "Dinner won't be ready for another hour or so. I can introduce you to the other boarders. Unless you'd rather just unpack and rest?"

I opened my mouth to respond, and instead a huge yawn escaped me. I quickly covered my mouth, embarrassed, as Enlar chuckled and Fiala smiled. "I thought so. This way."

At the top of the stairs, I stopped to glance again at the front door, remembering the feeling of peace that had come over me as I entered the house. Sensing that I had stopped walking, Fiala turned around and noticed where my gaze had landed. "Ah, I'm guessing you felt it?"

I blinked away my momentary confusion. "It?"

"The spell that triggered when you entered my house," Fiala explained. "Anyone who enters this place will not cause those who are within any harm, be it physical or magical, the minute they step foot inside. That goes for both those who are invited in, and those who are uninvited but force their way in nevertheless."

My eyes grew wide even as my nerves calmed down. I was happy to know that no harm could befall me from other people while I was inside Fiala's boardinghouse, but even more shocked to realize I had felt a spell at work.

Enlar's eyes narrowed. "I didn't feel anything when we walked in."

"Most people don't," Fiala said as she started down the hallway. Enlar and I scrambled to follow. "The spell was designed to be subtle, practically undetectable. Only the original spell caster, and the client it was intended for, which would be me, would feel the spell working. The spell caster, for obvious reasons, and myself because if it was no longer active, I as the client and house owner would need to know that. Very few people know it's there, and if they do, it usually means they have an extremely strong talent for magic." She paused outside a door and eyed me appraisingly.

I shrugged, feeling a bit uncomfortable. "I just came in to my magical ability a few days ago. I barely know how to use it." *Or control it.*

Fiala smiled. "And that's why you're here. To learn how to use it, and to use it well."

She opened the door, revealing a spartan but functional room. In one corner stood a wooden bed with a matching wooden nightstand, with an open chest at the foot of the bed. The room's other corner held a worn desk and chair, with a partially used candle on the desktop. I imagined the countless hours various students had sat there, poring over magical texts or studying furiously for exams.

"This will be your room, Enlar," Fiala said. Enlar entered his new room, putting his things down on the bed as he looked around. "If you want something different in here, you can switch furniture with another room, provided it's not currently occupied. Just make sure you only check rooms on this side of the staircase, though, as this is the men's wing. During the school year, breakfast is served at first light, but since we're keeping holiday hours right now, we usually eat around mid-morning. If you need anything, please let me know."

"Thank you, Fiala," Enlar said. The House Mistress nodded, then motioned for me to follow her back down the hallway, past the staircase, and into the women's wing.

My room was similar to Enlar's, although instead of a chest to hold my things, there was a small dresser. It reminded me of my room back home in Rothschan.

"I trust this is adequate?" Fiala asked.

"It is." I didn't trust myself to say anything more. I swallowed against the sudden lump in my throat, willing myself not to cry in front of my new hostess.

Something in my voice or demeanor must have given me away, though, for Fiala gave me a hug. At first I held myself stiffly, unused to shows of affection from anyone other than my immediate family. As she continued to hold me, I slowly relaxed into the embrace.

"I know being in a new place can be scary," Fiala said. "And I'm sure you miss your family something fierce. I hope while you're here you could consider us your family as well."

I nodded, sniffling away the tears that were now definitely falling. "Thank you."

Fiala left me to settle in, and I quickly changed out of my travel-worn clothes and fell into bed for a quick nap before dinner. I was so tired that things like washing up felt like too much work.

My exhaustion, coupled with knowing that I was finally in a safe place, made sleep come quickly and easily. Blowing out the candle on my bedside table, I was asleep before my head even hit the pillow.

15

—·—

Chapter Fifteen

"I'm nervous. Why am I nervous?"

Enlar sat on the edge of the bed, watching me pace grooves into the floorboards of his bedroom. Well, it wasn't *that* bad. Yet. But the longer we stayed here, the more I was sure I would pace myself right through his floor and down into the kitchen on the first floor of the boardinghouse.

We had been in Calia's capital for three days. It was a beautiful city, full of life and color and new things to explore every day. But I was getting restless. My parents had sent me here, presumably to meet Laydon Taethen. But every time I asked Fiala when I would get to meet him, she would say, "Not this day. But soon."

Well, finally, I would get to meet him. *This day*.

"It could be because you're finally going to get to meet this Laydon Taethen that everyone but you knows so much about." Enlar grinned, knowing he was reading my mind. "Or maybe you just have first-day-of-school nerves."

"It's not like we're even going to an actual class. Fiala said most of the students are gone for the summer holiday. The only classes happening are short summer symposiums or self-studies."

"It's got to be meeting Laydon Taethen, then."

"It's so odd to think I've had family here in Calia, all these years. I hope we'll get along. I hope he likes me."

"You won't know until you actually meet him." Enlar stood up and put his hands on my shoulders, forcing me to stop pacing. "Adalynn, you have nothing to worry about. He's going to adore you. What's not to like about you?"

I blushed. "Let's see. Well, I can't control my magic. I basically ran away from home. And sometimes, if I'm in a really deep sleep, I drool a little."

"For the first thing, he—or someone else at the school—will teach you how to refine your magic, and definitely how to control it. For the second, no one can get mad at you for that; you really didn't have a choice. As for the third ..." Enlar pretended to think for a moment. "Can't help you with that one. You're right. It's hopeless."

I grabbed a pillow off his bed and smacked him lightly on the head with it. Several feathers escaped the casing and fluttered down around us.

"Hey!" he protested, laughing. "I just made my bed! And you messed up my hair!"

"You combed your hair? I couldn't even tell," I teased. I looked him over. "I think hitting you with the pillow was actually an improvement."

Enlar grabbed the other pillow, ready to engage in all-out war, when Fiala knocked on the open door. "Enlar, have you seen—oh, there you are, Adalynn. You two ready to head over to the Academy?"

We both nodded, tossing our pillows back on the bed. Fiala stepped aside to allow both of us to exit Enlar's room. As he passed her, she asked, "What happened to your hair?"

I smirked. Enlar groaned and ran a hand through his hair, coming away with a small white feather. He shot me a dirty look as I erupted into a fit of giggles.

At the Academy, Fiala took us on a brief tour of the campus, pointing out various points of interest. One school was much the same as another to me; just like my former school in Rothschan, this one had classrooms and laboratories and common areas for the students. Except instead of being decked out in the red and gray of Rothschan, this place was mostly shades of blue and white and silver. I found Calia's colors to be much more soothing.

The classrooms we passed were empty, their open doors revealing wooden tables and chairs, partial or full bookshelves, and blank chalkboards streaked with erased chalk, waiting to be cleaned.

Like its predecessors, the room Fiala brought us to also had its door open, but the slight hum of voices wafting down the hallway let us know that there was life inside. As we reached the room, we could hear a deep male voice saying, "Next week's symposium topic is on ethics in magic—when is it better to *not* use magic to get things done? You can sign up on the board outside. If you have any questions, I'll be staying in town for most of the summer, but I won't be holding regular office hours. You can leave a message at my office and I'll follow up to arrange a meeting."

Chairs scraped back and feet shuffled toward the door. Several students filed out of the room, papers in their arms or bags slung hastily over their shoulders. As they passed us, some called out, "Good morning, Mistress Fiala," or "Hello, Mistress Fiala." She nodded and raised her hand in a small wave, acknowledging their greetings. Most of the students seemed to be my age or younger, and I instantly felt self-conscious, wondering if I was too old to be here.

Some gave Enlar and me small nods or waves as they walked by, and I recognized them as Fiala's summer boarders. I smiled and waved back.

When the room had cleared, Fiala knocked on the door. The same male voice from earlier called out, "Come in."

Fiala breezed into the room, Enlar following behind. I took up the rear, shyly hanging back. I was right behind Enlar, and couldn't see around his tall form and broad shoulders, so I just gazed around the room, taking in my surroundings. This classroom was nearly identical to the others, with one exception: there was a small red-and-gray flag tucked unobtrusively into one corner of the room. I recognized it immediately.

The banner of Rothschan.

I peeked around Enlar and got my first good look at Laydon Taethen.

The man standing before us had to be a good twenty years older than me, at least. Although he was still obviously in his prime, there was a hint of gray at his temples, and the crease of laugh lines around his mouth. Of average height, he had reddish-brown hair just a few shades darker than mine. He bore a strong resemblance to my father, although Father's hair was all gray now. I studied Laydon, considering. He must be a cousin, then, from an estranged part of the family.

Enlar noticed me peeking around his shoulder and gave me an exasperated look. He feinted a move to one side and I quickly jumped to stay hidden behind him, but then he darted back the other way, leaving me exposed. I shot him a dirty look which he met with a smug smirk. *Don't you worry, Enlar, I'll pay you back for this later.*

Laydon and Fiala didn't seem to notice my awkward dance with Enlar. "It's good to see you," Laydon was saying. He paused, as if he wanted to embrace Fiala, but was conscious of the fact that they had an audience. "What brings you here today? I thought you were overseeing some repairs at the boardinghouse."

"That won't be until later today," Fiala said. "I wanted to bring two new students by, to meet you and to see the Academy."

"Ah, wonderful." Laydon finally looked over and noticed Enlar standing behind Fiala. He held out his hand. "Good to meet you. What's your name?"

"Enlar Edson, of Bomora." Enlar gave Laydon a hearty handshake. "It's a pleasure, Professor Taethen."

Laydon smiled. "There's no need to call me 'professor.' Just Laydon will do. Mr. Taethen if you feel like being formal."

"Or if you're in trouble," Fiala joked, earning a laugh from both men.

"And this must be the other new student?" Laydon looked directly at me.

Enlar smirked. Sheepishly, I extended my hand.

Laydon raised an eyebrow but took my outstretched hand. "Well met, Miss ...?"

"Taethen. Adalynn Taethen."

Laydon's gaze immediately sharpened. "Taethen? Really? You're not from Calia, are you?" It sounded more like a statement than a question.

"No, sir. I'm from Rothschan."

He didn't say anything, just continued to grip my hand and eye me like a thirsty man would eye an oasis in the desert. Full of hope—water at last! Salvation!—and full of fear at the same time. What if it's nothing but a mirage, and all you're left with is sand?

"Are you all right, Laydon?" That, from Fiala. She sounded far away, and I realized that I could barely hear her over the blood rushing in my ears.

"Do you need to sit down, Adalynn?" I was vaguely aware of Enlar grabbing a chair from somewhere nearby and placing it behind me.

Laydon came back to himself, shaking his head and releasing my hand. It was splotchy white, and numb from where he had gripped it so tightly. I hadn't even noticed. He sank down slowly on the edge of his desk, heedless of the papers scattered on top or the inkwell he nearly tipped over.

The two of us stared at each other.

Finally, Laydon spoke. "Well. This is quite ... unexpected."

"I agree." I smiled slightly. "I think you have the advantage, though. I didn't know you even existed until a few days ago. But you seem to know exactly who I am, unless I am mistaken."

"I do," Laydon concurred. "We have much to discuss."

Sitting in the chair across from him, I folded my hands in my lap and gazed at him expectantly.

Laydon glanced at Fiala, and then at Enlar. "But perhaps this isn't the best place to do it. There's not a lot of people around, since the summer holiday has begun, but still—"

Suddenly a shiver went through me, and the room felt very still and strange. The moment passed quickly, but not before I saw Fiala and Laydon exchange a loaded glance. The shiver started up again, and I felt an odd metallic taste in my mouth, but then—

"*Confuto.*" Laydon stood up, splaying his fingers toward Fiala, Enlar, and me as if he were flinging a shield or web over us. The chill feeling stopped. The air around us returned to normal.

"What did you just do?" I asked.

"Stopped a scrying spell. Seems like someone's trying to spy on us." Laydon put a finger to his lips, and indicated to Fiala that she should check the hallway. While she did so, he crossed to the window and stood to the side, trying to look out the window without being too obvious.

Fiala returned to the classroom. She shook her head at Laydon's unspoken question. "Nothing. I checked all the classrooms in this wing, and around the corner. No one's here, except us."

"It doesn't seem like anyone's outside, either." Laydon sounded frustrated. "But besides knowing who just did that, I'd like to know how they did it, too."

"How?" Enlar asked. "I don't mean to be disrespectful, but the 'how' seems rather obvious."

"Not necessarily. There are wards on the Academy and its grounds that don't allow scrying spells to work. In addition to guarding the privacy of the teachers and students here, there's a lot of magical research that takes place within these walls. Students may learn the theory of a scrying spell, but it won't work if they try to cast it in the classroom."

Enlar frowned. "Scrying often requires a focus, such as a piece of clothing the target has worn, or something sentimental to them. It's best if it's something that's been used recently, usually within the last two days."

He looked at me. I shook my head. "If it's not on my person currently, anything I've handled within the last two days is back at Fiala's." I patted my pockets. "And I'm not missing anything."

Fiala added, "And the boardinghouse wards prevent students from stealing from each other. Theft would be considered harming another person."

Enlar looked thoughtful as he continued to puzzle it out. "So if someone was able to breach the wards on the Academy, that means whoever cast that spell must have a lot of raw magical power behind it."

Laydon whistled. "That makes sense. With enough magical power, the caster may have also been nearby, but invisible. After all, we didn't see anyone, but that doesn't mean they weren't around."

Doubtfully, I asked, "So they had enough power to be invisible *and* cast a scrying spell? But I felt it. Both times."

"Both times? What do you mean, both times?"

Startled at his vehemence, I said, "We all felt it, or so I thought? When that chill went through the room? That must have been the scrying spell. But the second time, when my mouth started to taste all funny and metallic—"

"What?" Without warning, Laydon cast a quick spell at me. The metallic taste in my mouth grew stronger, and I fought the urge to spit.

Everyone was staring at me.

"What?" I said, a pale parody of Laydon's earlier question. "Why are you all looking at me like that?"

"You're …. There's two of you," Enlar said disbelievingly. "Like you have a ghostly twin."

I started, then looked around. Out of the corner of my eye, I caught a faint movement that mirrored my own flailing hand. But no matter what I did, how fast I turned, I couldn't quite see the other me. I stopped, feeling silly. I must have looked like a dog chasing its tail.

"It's a magical echo." Laydon started gathering up papers from his desk, shoving them into a satchel sitting on the floor. "Fiala, you need to get these two back to your place immediately. Be very watchful as you go, just in case of any surprise attacks."

"Surprise attacks? What are you talking about?" I asked, confused.

Laydon paused in his hasty packing long enough to address me. "Whoever our mysterious spell caster is, they must have a lot of power at their disposal. They were able to breach the wards on the school to find you, and they were able to do it without using a focus. But the fact that we felt the scrying spell means there is a limit to their power. The second spell you felt, the one that left a metallic taste in your mouth … I can only hope I was able to stop the spell in time. The magician was trying to mark you. So they can find you wherever you go."

16

— · —

CHAPTER SIXTEEN

I WAS MARKED BY magic? That didn't sound good.

Laydon escorted us out of the building, casting a quick spell of protection on Fiala, Enlar, and me right before we walked out of the Academy and into the sunshine. The cheery sky overhead seemed like such an odd contrast to the somberness that had fallen over our group, and the chill we had felt earlier in Laydon's classroom.

Laydon looked me over again, his eyes going glassy and unfocused. It unnerved me, even though I realized he was looking at me through magical eyes and not natural ones. "There's not a lot of power in the marking spell; it should disappear in a day or two. But until then ..."

He cast a second spell on me, declaring it would dim the unnatural duplicate I now had trailing me like a magical beacon. "This should shield you from whoever's marked you, but it will fade in a few hours, and then you'll be vulnerable again. But once you reach Fiala's, you'll be fine. Her wards were placed by one of the top magicians in Calia and are practically impossible to break. It's not far from here to the boardinghouse, but remain vigilant."

He promised Fiala he would try to come by the boardinghouse later, after he had looked into the scrying spell and its possible source. We parted ways with Laydon and kept a watchful eye as we headed back to Fiala's. But despite his warning, nothing occurred. I felt no more magic being performed on me, nor did we see anyone following us.

When we arrived at the boardinghouse, Fiala practically shoved Enlar and me inside before scurrying inside herself and locking the door behind her. "You're safe," she said, obvious relief coloring her voice. She relaxed against the door and turned to me. "And to remain so, I'm afraid you'll have to stay in here. I'm so sorry. But until that mark is gone, it's best for you to stay inside. If there's anything you need, I or someone on the household staff would be happy to fetch it."

"Or I can," Enlar volunteered. He could tell I wasn't happy at the prospect of basically being under house arrest.

I nodded, suddenly feeling worn out from the fading adrenaline rush. "Thank you, but I think I'll be all right. I'm going to go upstairs and rest, if that's okay with you?"

"Of course." Fiala and Enlar stepped aside to let me go upstairs.

Since I was now stuck in the boardinghouse for at least two days, I napped. And moped around. And napped some more. At one point, I plucked a book from the shelf in the parlor and tried to read. It was some novel about shapeshifters, a tribe of people who could change between their human forms and animal ones. It was a book of fiction, of course, although a note on the inside stated it was based on true occurrences. Normally, it would have held my attention, but I found I couldn't concentrate. I put the book back on the shelf with a mental note to come back to it, eventually.

My ennui carried on throughout the rest of the day. Thanks to all the napping I had done earlier, I couldn't sleep. So during the dead of night, while my housemates were all asleep, I lay in my bed wide awake, staring at the ceiling.

My sheets were a rumpled mess from my constant tossing and turning. I turned on my side, facing the wall, hoping I'd fall asleep soon. When a few minutes had gone by, and sleep still hadn't come, I sighed heavily and turned to lie on my back again.

And felt the prick of a dagger at my throat.

A hand covered my mouth. From somewhere above me, I heard a gravelly voice whisper, "Get up. Don't make a sound, or you'll regret it."

I could smell the stench of sweat and unwashed skin, grimacing inwardly at the meaty hand that prevented me from crying out. I briefly thought of biting the hand—disgusting, but I didn't have many options—but then the thought faded away. I didn't know who this person was or what they wanted, I only knew that I did *not* want to go with them. But as they had a knife at my neck, I didn't seem to have much choice.

The voice continued, "I'm going to let you get up. If you try anything, I won't be responsible for what my dagger does."

I nodded as best as I could with a knife at my throat. The pressure of the weapon eased off a bit, allowing me to slowly sit up and get a better look at the intruder.

In the darkness of my room, I couldn't make out much. In their dark clothes, speaking in a whisper, the intruder seemed to be of indeterminate height and gender. I had no weapons at hand, and the boardinghouse spell of peace dampened any feelings I may have had of wanting to fight back. *You'd think self-defense would be acceptable in this case*, I thought. *Definitely an oversight by that magician. If I survive this, I must talk to Fiala about creating loopholes in the house spell.*

Speaking of loopholes, how did this intruder get in, undetected, and be able to carry out their violent intent?

But I didn't have time to wonder about how they had breached the spell. The knife was back at my throat, and the person had my arm in a tight grip.

"Stand up, now, slowly."

I followed the stranger's instructions. I thought perhaps I could overpower them, grab the knife, call for help or incapacitate them in some way. But once I was on my feet, I still didn't have any desire to fight back. I ground my teeth and silently cursed the house spell.

While I stood there stupidly, the intruder muttered something under their breath. I stilled as I felt a spell settle around me. The intruder still held the knife in one hand, but their other hand produced a grimy strip of torn cloth.

"Put this around your mouth. Tie it tight, now."

My hands reached out for the gag and I obediently tied it—tightly—around my mouth. I tried my best to fight the magic controlling me, but the spell had me firmly in its grasp.

My kidnapper smiled in the darkness. I could feel the smugness radiating from them as they whispered, "Probably didn't even need it. You'd abduct yourself, if I asked you to. No fighting back, now. Let's go." They switched the knife to my back.

No fighting back. As if I could. The house spell and the control spell both weighed on me oppressively, confusing and clouding my mind. Prodded forward by the sharp blade, I walked out of my room and down the hallway. Moving in a still unfamiliar environment, my thoughts hazy and distracted, I stumbled and tripped, grabbing the railing for balance.

The intruder caught me before I fell. The point of the knife pricked my side as they hissed a menacing promise. "The next time you trip, it will be your last."

Still holding the railing, I glanced over at the intruder, trying to force my sluggish thoughts into some semblance of a plan. I couldn't harm them, but perhaps I could delay our departure enough to call attention to my situation or figure out another way out of this. I groaned through my gag and gestured at my ankle.

"Get up." The person brandished the knife at me, uncaring of my "injury."

I shook my head, pointing again at my ankle.

The intruder's mouth twisted in an ugly sneer. "I don't really care. Get up and let's go. If you move too slow, I will push you down the stairs myself. But I *will* get you back to Rothschan. Getting the reward will just be a bonus."

Reward? That's right, the king and queen had mentioned that. The authorities must have been really upset about that office fire....

While I was still on the ground, I had a brief moment of clarity. I wasn't fighting the house spell, or dealing with the headache its push-back was causing me. I could now sense something I hadn't earlier, due to my own fear and pain.

Magic.

Waves and waves of it, pulsing from the intruder. It was practically oozing off the person, there was so much of it.

I had never been in the presence of so much raw magic before. It was amazing, and enticing. I mentally reached toward it, wanting to touch it, for one quick moment....

The intruder smacked me and hissed. "None of that, now! Come on." Angrily, the person tugged at me, and I realized I could either go willingly or be dragged downstairs.

I stood up and slowly started walking, exaggerating the pain of my supposed twisted ankle. I could sense the intruder's agitation at moving so slowly, but our deliberate pace allowed me more time to fight the house spell. Indeed, because I was so mentally distracted, I would have moved at a snail's pace even if I wasn't pretending my ankle was hurt.

After a few more moments of trying to fight the boardinghouse's spell of peace, I gave up. It was too strong, and my magic was too untrained. But perhaps I could channel that uncontrollability into something else....

I thought about Enlar. I thought about him sleeping peacefully just down the hallway. I thought about his room, the things I remembered seeing in it. There was that half-burned candle on his desk. If it were to suddenly light up, that would wake him up, wouldn't it?

I concentrated on that candle, imagining the unlit wick blossoming into flame. I imagined the light from the candle teasing his eyelids open, the scent from the burning wick wafting on the air for him to breathe in and tickle his lungs. He'd wake up, and—

A scream erupted from down the hallway.

Enlar burst out of his room, yelling. "Fire! Fire!"

Behind him, I could see a large yellow glow and hear the fire's crackle. The little candle I had willed to alight was nowhere to be seen. Instead, the desk it had sat upon was engulfed in flames.

My eyes widened. That had definitely not been my intent.

Whoops.

Enlar glanced down the hallway, his own eyes widening as he took in my bound-and-gagged state, the knife being pressed into my side, and the shadowy figure that held the weapon against me.

"Who are you?" Enlar demanded of the intruder.

The knife glinted in the dim light. I couldn't yell to warn Enlar, only watch in horror as the knife arced through the air. Enlar dodged to one side as the knife whizzed by him, embedding itself into the wall where just a few seconds ago, Enlar's heart would have been.

The stranger dashed down the stairs, rushing out of the already opened front door. He must have left it ajar when he broke in. Enlar rushed over to me and removed the gag from my mouth. "Adalynn, are you okay?"

"I'm fine. He's getting away, though!"

Enlar darted down the stairs after the intruder just as another bedroom door opened down the hall. A pale apparition appeared, solidifying into Fiala wearing a white linen dressing gown. "What's going on?"

"Someone broke in and tried to kidnap me," I explained in a rush. "I tried to get Enlar's attention by lighting a candle. I think I accidentally set his desk on fire. The intruder fled, and Enlar ran after them."

Fiala ran to Enlar's room, weaving a spell in her hands as she went. I ran after her, thinking maybe I could help.

The fire had finished consuming the desk, and was now threatening the chair, walls, and floor. Fiala called out, waving her hands in the air, and suddenly a deluge poured from the air, thoroughly dousing the desk and effectively putting out the fire in Enlar's room.

I let out the breath I hadn't even known I had been holding.

Fiala turned, muttering, "Wait until Taryn gets the bill for the damages. The Crown won't be happy about that."

I laughed giddily at Fiala's comment, despite the seriousness of the situation. Or perhaps because of it.

Fiala eyed me warily. "Oh, dear. You might be in shock, Adalynn."

A few other doors in both the men's and women's wings cautiously opened. Various students popped their heads out. "Mistress Fiala, is everything all right?"

"Everything's fine, Diedre, go back to bed," Fiala said. "That goes for the rest of you, too."

Dull thuds peppered the hallway as the other boarders closed their bedroom doors.

"Come, let's go downstairs to wait for Enlar," Fiala said to me. "While we wait, you can tell me, in detail, what exactly happened."

We headed to the sitting room. Some of the household servants had also awakened with the commotion, and Fiala motioned at one of them. "Chara, can you bring me a lamp? And, if it's not too much trouble, perhaps some tea." She gave me a pointed look. "I think we'll need something to calm our nerves."

Chara brought the lamp and then scurried off to the kitchen. Fiala lit it—with a match, not with magic, I noted—and placed it on the table. "Now then, Adalynn, please tell me what happened, and don't leave anything out."

Just as I was about to tell Fiala my story, Enlar returned and shut the door of the boardinghouse. "They got away," Enlar said at our inquiring looks. "'They had too much of a head start, and I have no idea where they may have headed. But I did find this."

He reached into his pocket and pulled out a dirty leather necklace with a blue stone pendant. The gem had an ugly rupture in the middle of it, like a small earthquake had split the stone in two. It looked like a sapphire, perhaps? But I had never seen a sapphire look so dark and dull.

The ends of the leather looked frayed, as if the cord had caught on something and had been violently torn away, or as if the wearer had ripped the necklace from their neck in a hurry. Enlar had been fortunate to find the necklace intact; the pendant could easily have fallen off the leather cord and gotten lost in the dirt.

"Interesting," Fiala said, taking the necklace with its sorry-looking pendant from Enlar. "And you have impeccable timing. Now we can both hear Adalynn's tale."

Enlar sat down next to me on the beige settee, and both he and Fiala turned their full attention on me. I related my version of the night's events. Fiala frowned during my tale, but refrained from interrupting me.

"The house spell that stopped you from harming your would-be kidnapper should have stopped them from attempting to kidnap you in the first place," Fiala commented. "The magician who cast the peace and protection spell was very thorough, and is one of the best in Calia at charms and incantations. This shouldn't have happened. In fact, since the intruder had such obvious hostile intentions, they shouldn't have even been able to step over the threshold at all. The spell would have stopped them from gaining entry."

"I don't know how they did it, but I do know that the spell had no effect on them whatsoever," I replied, a little testily. After all, it was my person that had been threatened.

"Do you think that had anything to do with how they got past the wards on the house?" Enlar asked, pointing at the necklace he had found.

Fiala studied it. "It's quite possible. I know a little magic, but to be able to study this and know its purpose is beyond my ability. However ..."

Her eyes glazed over as she focused her thoughts inward. She touched her lips with two fingers, moving them slightly away from her face as she blew on them.

Taryn's sleepy face appeared. She yawned, shaking her head as if she could shake off her sleepiness. "Did you decide you no longer want to keep holiday hours, Fiala?"

Fiala smirked, even as her expression sharpened and sobered. "My apologies for waking you, Taryn, but we have a problem. Potentially."

As Fiala quickly relayed the night's events, Taryn's sleepy countenance rapidly disappeared. "You say the intruder left something behind?"

"Yes." Fiala held up the broken necklace.

Taryn's eyes narrowed as she studied the item through the magical connection. "I can't be entirely sure, but it looks like that gem was enchanted for a specific purpose, and once that purpose was fulfilled, the stone broke. My guess is that it was meant to help them get past your boardinghouse's wards, based on the story you told me tonight. Does it feel at all magical to you?"

Fiala held the sapphire in the palm of her hand and ran her fingers over its surface. She shook her head. "No, not right now. But if it ever held any magic, that is beyond my ability to tell."

"We'll need it analyzed, either by the queen or maybe one of the teachers at the Academy," Taryn said. "But who is even around to analyze it?"

"There's not too many teachers here right now," Fiala agreed. "But tomorrow I can ask—"

A muffled thud sounded outside the parlor window.

"What was that?" I asked, all my senses on alert.

Enlar shuttered the light and crept to the window, surreptitiously surveying the darkened lawn outside. "The tree on the lawn has been split in half."

"That tree is old, older than this house," Fiala said. "I can't think of anything that could break it in one blow other than lightning, or—"

"I don't think you can wait until tomorrow, Fiala," Taryn interrupted. "Since their charm is now useless, they'll want to try a more direct attempt to broach your house. Take Adalynn to safety. Now."

17

CHAPTER SEVENTEEN

FIALA ENDED HER CONNECTION with Taryn, with a promise to update her after I was delivered safely to—well, wherever I was supposed to be delivered to.

Enlar continued to keep watch on the grounds outside while Fiala had a hurried conference with Melisande and Chara to gather the students and inform them of the situation. "Wake the entire household. We'll need every pair of eyes available to keep watch."

"And ready to defend the house, just in case," Enlar chimed in from his position at the window.

"I'll bring her there, and come back as soon as I can," Fiala continued. "It shouldn't be more than an hour. If I'm not back in two, or if the house wards fail ..."

"Yes, madam," Melisande said. "We know what to do."

Fiala ushered me up the stairs to get my things as I pondered the exchange I had just witnessed. *The servants knew what to do? Just in case Fiala didn't return?* I shook my head, wondering what kind of place this was. It certainly was unlike any boardinghouse I had ever imagined.

I quickly changed into my pants, shirt, and jacket. There was no time to pack anything, not that I would have known what I needed to bring.

As I left my room, I saw the servants scurrying up and down the hallways, knocking on the doors and rousing the entire household. Some of the students were still awake and answered right away, heading downstairs, while others slowly and sleepily opened their doors, looking confused.

"House conference, now!" I heard Fiala call up the stairs. "Enlar, you're in charge while I'm gone."

Looking down, I saw her waving at me frantically. "Come on, Adalynn. Let's go!"

I dashed down the stairs after Fiala, who was heading toward the back of the house. She strode to the corner of the kitchen and started pushing at a metal holder full of firewood.

"Stupid thing." She grunted with the effort of trying to move the heavy object. "Why won't you move already?"

Shouldering my bag, I rushed to help her. Together we moved the unwieldy stand to the side, revealing a small hatch in the floor. Fiala flung the hatch open and motioned for me to enter the darkness within. "There's a ladder to the side, there. Hurry!"

I scrambled down the ladder as fast as I could. Fiala followed, pausing only to close the hatch. I bit back a cry as we were plunged into complete darkness.

"Keep moving, Adalynn. The ground isn't too far below us," Fiala said.

"But I ... I—" I started moving, slowly, afraid of slipping on the ladder and falling into the darkness.

"*Illumine.*"

A small, cold light appeared above Fiala's head, bobbing with her as she moved down the ladder. I breathed a small sigh of relief, and resumed a quicker pace as I descended.

True to Fiala's word, my feet soon found solid ground. Moving to the side to give her room, I looked around, unsure of which way to go. We seemed to be in some sort of underground passage, with packed dirt lining the walls and the sound of running water somewhere nearby.

Fiala stepped in front of me, heading decisively down a passageway to our left. I followed after her.

"Won't whoever's tracking me know that I'm leaving the house?" I wondered.

"Magic works differently underground," Fiala said. "Anyone aboveground would find it hard to sense magic below."

"Oh. Then why didn't I—"

Fiala smirked at me. "I thought the house wards would be enough to protect you. Besides, would you really want to stay down here for two days?"

Good point. "No."

We hadn't gone far when we heard a dull thud, and the walls around us shook a little, dirt falling off them.

I stopped. "What was that?"

Fiala stopped too. "I would guess that was some sort of physical or magical attack against the house. The 'more direct approach' that Taryn warned us about."

"You think that person is attacking the house? To get to me?"

"It seems likely," she said. "And if that's true, we should hurry."

There was another thud, and more dirt from the walls sprinkled to the ground around us. And was that a cry I heard, or was I imagining it?

Fiala looked back the way we had come from, torn. "I'm so sorry, Adalynn. But I need to go back. They'll fare better with my help. Since it's my house, I can remove the spell of peace to allow them to fight."

"I understand. I'll go back with you."

"No, you need to get to safety." She pointed down the dark passage. "Keep going until you reach an area where the path splits three ways. Pick the left hand path, and follow it until you reach the end. Can you conjure a light?"

I nodded and hastily cast a light spell. Fiala said, "Good. Good luck, Adalynn. Now, go."

She turned around and quickly disappeared into the darkness. Feeling very vulnerable, I started down the direction she had indicated. Another thud sounded somewhere above me, and I shuddered.

I'm not sure how long I followed that dark underground tunnel, or how far I traveled. I did realize after awhile the thuds had stopped. Either the attack was over, or I was too far from Fiala's boardinghouse to still hear them. Neither option made me feel better.

I came across the three paths Fiala had mentioned, and instantly made for the lefthand passage. My nose wrinkled at the slightly musty smell that slowly grew more pungent the further I walked.

The walls of the tunnel grew brighter. No, wait, that wasn't right. They were getting closer to my light, closing in the further I went.

Enclosed spaces didn't normally frighten me, but when traveling down a dark, unknown passage filled with an odd stench to who-knows-where when you've left your friends behind to fend off a magical attack, you suddenly develop an irrational fear. I clutched at the wall, trying to fight the wave of nausea building up. It was getting hard to breathe—was it the tunnel's smell, or the panic I was trying to push away?

And then my magical light went out.

I screamed. And then clamped a hand over my mouth, afraid that I might have attracted unwanted attention. While I hadn't seen anyone else in the tunnels, that didn't mean there weren't other people wandering around.

Or hiding, silently watching me.

The thought of being watched frightened me so much it took me several minutes to calm myself down, somewhat.

"*Illumine.*"

Nothing happened. I tried again, but no light appeared above my outstretched hand. Had I mispronounced the spell's trigger word? "*Illumine.*" No, that was correct. But still no light. Maybe I was too panicked to work my magic correctly.

Well, standing here in the dark wasn't going to help me any. I could go forward, or I could go back. Going back was tempting ... but I knew Fiala and Taryn would be upset with me if I disobeyed their orders. And my presence at the boardinghouse could, potentially, make things worse.

I had a brief moment of wanting to run back home to Rothschan. To be with my parents, to make sure they were all right. To go back to the way things used to be.

Except I knew that things wouldn't be the same back home, even if I returned and everything was back to normal.

No, there was only one way, and that was forward.

I just hoped that safety lay at the end of this interminable darkness.

The musty smell was practically unbearable. I stretched my arms out, my right hand catching on a jagged rock wall. Using my hand on the wall as a guide, I continued down the pitch-black passageway. I brought the sleeve of my left arm to my face, breathing shallowly. With the tunnel continuing to shrink around me, I soon had to walk hunched over, and then began crawling.

Time crawled along just as slowly as I was. My shoulders ached, and my hands hurt from where they had continuously scraped against the rock wall and dirt floor. My knees hurt as well, and I was sure my clothes were a torn and dirty mess.

I felt a blank rock wall in front of me. Feeling around, there was no other way to go.

I had reached the tunnel's end.

Behind me was the dark passage I had just traveled down. Where was I supposed to go, or do? This couldn't have been the safe place Fiala was supposed to have taken me to.

I tried again to call up a light, but still nothing happened. The panic I had felt earlier overwhelmed me.

"No! I can't have come all this way for nothing!" I screamed, not caring if anyone—or anything—could hear me. I pounded against the rock wall, tears of frustration streaming down my face.

I heard a scraping sound, and then light filled my little tunnel, temporarily blinding me. Hands reached in and grabbed both of my arms, unceremoniously plucking me out from the tunnel to dump me on the ground.

I blinked rapidly, waiting for my eyes to adjust.

When they did, I found myself staring up into five unfriendly faces.

One of them, a woman with pale blonde hair, frowned as she looked down at me. "And what do we have here?"

18

—·—

CHAPTER EIGHTEEN

I STARED AT THE woman, too dumbstruck to answer her.

I wasn't sure what to say, or how much information to give. Was this the safe haven that Fiala had intended to bring me to, or had I stumbled into another place entirely? Without Fiala here, I had no one to vouch for me.

And, remembering the incident at the boardinghouse, no weapons to defend myself. Nothing but a wayward, untrained talent for magic. Thinking of the night's events, I smirked to myself. At the very least, I was apparently good at setting things on fire, having done it twice now to get myself out of harrowing situations.

"Who are you? And where did you come from, girl?" the woman asked me. I stayed mute.

A big hearth at one end of the cavern boasted a fire that crackled and popped cheerfully. The firelight glinted off the woman's pale blonde hair. Growling, she moved a hand to her side, where I spotted a sword hanging. My breath caught as she spoke. "You should answer when spoken to. Otherwise, we may have to—shall we say, *encourage* you?—to talk."

"There's no need for that, Chandra."

The people hovering around me parted respectfully for the newcomer, whose voice was familiar. As the shadow emerged from the cavern's recesses and came closer, I recognized the man that went with that voice—my relative, Laydon Taethen.

From the way Chandra, and the rest of this interesting group, deferred to him, I surmised Laydon to be their leader. Queen Jennica's words came back to me: *And their leader, Laydon Taethen, is willing to do whatever it takes to help them do it.*

"I know you!" I blurted without thinking. "What is this place? What's going on? What—"

Laydon chuckled. "I think I'll ask the questions first, if you don't mind."

I breathed a bit easier. Although we didn't know each other very well—yet—he didn't seem to be upset at my presence here. Hopefully that would make the others accept me, too.

Laydon waved at his companions to stand down and then held out a hand to me. I took it cautiously, surprised at how easily he pulled me up. I hadn't expected a teacher of magic to be that strong. I supposed it came from all the books and papers he had to haul all over campus every day.

Releasing my hand, he led me to a small wooden table with several chairs scattered nearby. I sank down slowly into one. He pulled up a chair next to me and sat down, studying me intently.

The other members of the group wandered away to their various tasks, with Chandra muttering as she went, "People who trust too quickly shouldn't be surprised if they get a knife in their back for their trouble."

I felt better when everyone left. Having all those people watching me was unnerving.

Now that we were alone, I blurted out, "Is this the safe place Fiala was supposed to take me to?"

Laydon frowned. "We are in a safe house, yes. Of sorts. But why would Fiala take you here?" He looked back at the hole in the wall I had emerged from. "Is she here with you?"

I shook my head. "No. She had to go back, to help the rest of the students fend off the magical attack—"

"Attack?" Laydon immediately straightened. "What attack? What are you talking about?"

I quickly outlined the events of the night, starting with the intruder and their failed attempt to kidnap me, to Taryn ordering Fiala to take me away from the boardinghouse.

"But as we were leaving, we kept hearing these loud bangs above us. Fiala thought the house was being attacked by magic. She told me how to get here and went back to help. I wanted to go back with her, but ..."

"No, you were right to come here. We'll have to get back there as soon as we can to help them out. I hope her house wards are still intact." He stood, looking ready to run out of the hideaway right then and there.

"She mentioned the house wards," I said, wondering what the fuss was about them. "But why is everyone so concerned about them?"

He paused in mid-pace. "Few are foolish enough to attack a magician, especially on their home ground. And Fiala has some of the best wards money can buy. If someone is able to breach those wards, and at her home, then she and the students are definitely in a dire situation."

He called out, "Gaelen, Frist. There's trouble at Fiala's. Take the group and head over. I'll be there shortly."

Gaelan and Frist nodded, grabbing their weapons and leaving with the others. Only Chandra stayed behind.

She folded her arms across her chest and glared at me. Leaning against a wall, she said, "I'm not leaving you alone with a stranger."

Laydon shrugged, eyeing me with a smirk. "She's hardly a stranger. But fair enough. Make ready to leave immediately when we're done talking."

Chandra nodded. She began making her own preparations while keeping an eye on us.

Remembering how my own magic had failed me just a few moments before, I asked, "Why couldn't I get my light spell to work in the tunnel?"

"It's part of the wards we have on this hideaway. No magic can work within a certain distance of that entrance. It prevents us from being surprised by unwanted visitors." Laydon eyed me. "Now. To the next issue. What do I do with you?"

"What do you mean, 'what do you do with me?'" I frowned. "I go back with you, of course."

"Fiala sent you here so you'd be safe. Under orders from the Crown, or near enough. I can't just bring you back into danger."

"And I can't just stay here sitting around while my friends are in trouble!"

"And I'm not babysitting!" Chandra called from across the room.

Laydon sighed. "All right, then. Fine. Let's get going."

I stubbornly stayed where I was.

He turned back to me. "I thought you were in a hurry?"

"I am. But we also need to talk. I have so many questions."

He grimaced as he started gathering his things. Giving me a pointed once-over, he said, "You need a weapon."

"Yes, I do need something. And don't think I'm going to let you get off so easily."

He led me over to a rack filled with an assortment of weapons, most of which were in various stages of disrepair. I picked up a rusted axe that had its glory days well behind it and eyed it dubiously. I swung it experimentally. The head fell off and clattered to the floor.

"I guess not that one."

Laydon plucked a bow from the rack, along with a short sword. He handed them both to me. "Pick one. Or both, if you prefer."

Definitely not the bow. The wood was way too warped for the bow to be of any use. The sword was much better, with a good balance and a nice, sharp blade. I tossed the bow aside and hefted the sword. "This will do."

Laydon strode over to a table to grab his own sword and a pair of daggers from where they lay on top. Finding an empty, worn leather scabbard, he tossed it to me. I caught it and belted it around my waist, sheathing my sword.

"Good. Let's go. I'll try to answer your questions as we go, but some might have to wait until things are less ... hectic."

Chandra impatiently waited for us at the far end of the room. Laydon finished his own preparations and we hurried to where she was standing by a wall.

"Had a nice visit?"

"Hardly," I told her. "I have more questions than answers right now."

"That's life," she said. "Get used to it." But there was a twinkle in her eye when she spoke.

Despite her earlier hostility, I found myself beginning to like her.

Chandra turned to face the blank wall, running her hands down it on the right side.

"We're not going through the tunnel?" I indicated the way I had come, confused.

Chandra smirked. "Not if you want to get there sometime this week. I myself prefer a more direct—and less cramped—route."

On closer inspection, I realized the wall wasn't as impenetrable as I had thought. The glow of the lantern set in it faintly illustrated the hint of a door's outline.

Chandra pressed something in the rock face, and the door slid back seamlessly. A ladder stretched up into the darkness. She scrambled up the ladder.

I started to follow, but Laydon held me back. "She'll tell us when it's okay to climb."

A dull light appeared above us. I looked up. Chandra's head peeked down at me, haloed by a golden glow. "Come on up."

Her head disappeared. Laydon climbed up the ladder, leaving me to stand uncertainly inside the secret room. "How do I close the door?" I called after him.

"Don't worry about it," he called down. "It will—"

The door snapped shut behind me. I jumped out of the way, avoiding the door nearly clipping my jacket. "You could have warned me!"

Laydon paused on the ladder, grinning at me unrepentantly.

Grumbling, I climbed the ladder after him. At the top, I gasped, marveling at the scene before me.

We were in a corner at one end of what looked like a study. Deep mahogany wood shelves lined three of the four walls in the room. A dark-colored settee and two matching overstuffed chairs stood nearby. One of the chairs was partly turned away from me; with Laydon somewhat blocking my way, I couldn't see over its high back, but in the dim light I guessed it was empty. Through the bay window, I could see the sky was becoming lighter outside. Sunrise would be here soon. The whole room looked so cozy and inviting, I wished we had time to stay and relax a bit.

Laydon helped me climb up into the room and get to my feet. Once I was clear of the entrance, Chandra pushed a panel on the wall to close the secret door.

It noiselessly slid shut, looking like a regular stone fireplace in the elegant room. We had emerged from what seemed to be the fireplace that heated this room. Except the fireplace, while burning merrily, gave off no heat. Or fire.

Fascinated, I stuck my hand back in the fireplace, surprised that neither Laydon nor Chandra warned me to stop.

My hand whooshed through cold air, even though I had definitely put it in the fire. Behind me, Laydon chuckled.

"It's an illusion," he explained. "The gentleman magician who owns this home is a friend to our band of refugees."

"Really? Wow," I marveled, impressed at the rich surroundings and the idea that such a wealthy person was helping Laydon's group. "What's he like? Is he nice?"

A deep laugh emerged from one of the high-backed chairs. "I'd like to think he is, although he can get cranky when his morning meditations are interrupted."

An elderly gentleman in a rich red velvet suit stood up slowly and turned to face us. "Ah! Chandra, Laydon, it's always lovely to see you. Who's your new friend?"

19

— · —

CHAPTER NINETEEN

"I'M ADALYNN TAETHEN, SIR." I twisted my hands nervously, hoping I hadn't offended him with my earlier comment. If I could destroy things by accident with my out-of-control magic, I didn't want to think about what a full-fledged magician could do to me.

"No need to worry, my dear." The man walked over to us, surprisingly spry. "I am the magician Limande. This is my home. And any friend of Chandra and Laydon's is a friend of mine. Although—" he gave Laydon a shrewd look "—I don't know if friend is the word I would use?"

Laydon sighed. "We'll get to that. Eventually. For now, we're headed to Fiala's. The boardinghouse is under attack."

Limande frowned. "That's what the others said when they came through earlier. But that can't be right. My wards will keep any hooligans at bay."

I spoke up tentatively. "Uh, actually—"

Chandra coughed pointedly. "We need to go. Attack in progress, remember?"

Limande took the not-so-subtle hint. "Of course. You can indulge an old man's curiosity at a later time."

He whispered something and waved his hand at us. The air shimmered, and I felt a spell settle on me. I wanted to ask, *What was that?*, but held my tongue, afraid of appearing rude. Well, even ruder than I already had been.

The magician must have seen the question on my face, though, because he said, "Just a spell of protection. It will fade in about an hour."

"Thank you," Laydon said. "We'll come back to see you soon."

"Do," Limande said. "I look forward to it."

As he started walking back across the room, Chandra led the way to a small door that, before now, had gone unnoticed. She pushed it open and slipped through. Laydon followed. I hesitated, turning to give Limande one last glance. He was now standing by his chair, and gave me a small wave and a wink before settling back in, presumably to continue his meditation. I smiled to myself and slipped out the door after Chandra and Laydon.

We walked briskly, not wanting to tire ourselves out but also hoping to reach Fiala's in time. Chandra led the way. I got the impression she wanted to give us a bit of privacy to continue our conversation from earlier.

While we walked, Laydon said, "I'm not sure how old you are—"

"Twenty-one."

"Ah. Well, before you were born, the Lord High Seneschal of Rothschan visited an army camp—"

"And caught out some magical interlopers? Yes. Everyone knows that story."

Laydon coughed, uncomfortable. "Okay, then. So. The Lord High Seneschal—Renton, his name was—"

"Renton? I know who he is. But he's not the Seneschal. That position has been vacant for years, for at least as long as I've been alive."

"That would be because he lost his position when he failed to secure the 'magical interlopers,' as you call them."

"How would you know that?"

"Because." He swallowed. "I was one of the magical interlopers."

I gaped at him. I know that many stories and rumors can carry some element of truth, some small basis in fact. But to hear this man oh-so-matter-of-factly admit that one of the greatest, craziest stories to spread around Rothschan was about him! It was like ... it was like ...

Learning that magic, and the people who wield it, aren't all evil, a small, unknown, somewhat rebellious little voice inside me whispered.

Laydon was still talking. "Perhaps the story has been greatly exaggerated by now, but the basic facts are true: I was once part of the Rothschan army. My fiancée was killed because I couldn't control my magic. I deserted, out of shame and self preservation." He took a deep breath. "What the story probably doesn't tell you is how greatly my family suffered because of my actions."

Barely breathing, I asked, "Who's your family?"

"What's your mother's name?" A question for a question, apparently.

"My mother's name is Pella," I said, confused. "And my father is—"

"Mynon," he whispered. A tear slipped down his cheek.

My voice came out in a whisper as well. "How do you know them?"

"Because." Laydon stopped, swallowed, regained his composure. "They're my parents also."

20

— . —

CHAPTER TWENTY

DUMBSTRUCK, I STARED AT the man before me. The infamous Laydon Taethen. The teacher and magician everyone had kept talking about. The long-lost relative I had only recently discovered existed.

And he was my brother.

My brother!

I had a sibling.

In all my fantasies about this meeting, I had never thought I would be meeting my brother. I had assumed Laydon was an uncle, or, more likely, a cousin. To me, that neatly explained why I had never heard of him before that whispered conversation between my parents on my birthday.

"How ...?" I breathed.

Laydon smirked, his expression similar to mine. It was odd seeing my mannerisms in a masculine face. "Please don't tell me you need me to explain how basic biology works."

I blushed, even as I swatted at him in mock irritation. That had definitely been a brotherly comment to make. "No, I mean ... I'd never heard of you. Until recently, that is. I have no memories of growing up with you, or of you leaving home. I can understand our parents hiding any trace of you, especially since it sounded like you left under, uh, bad circumstances. But why don't I remember you?"

Laydon sighed. "I have to admit, I'm a bit hurt that our parents didn't talk about me at all. Although it makes sense. You're right, I didn't leave home willingly, nor under good circumstances. The reason you don't remember me is because you were barely two years old when I left Rothschan. And I understand that after I left, our parents erased any trace of my existence. Not because they didn't love me, but because ... you would be safer that way."

Ahead of us, Chandra turned around. She called out, "Pick up the pace, you two!"

I hadn't even realized Laydon and I had stopped walking. We started after Chandra. Satisfied, she shook her head and kept moving as well.

"Why didn't you ever come back? Or at least visit? When I was old enough to remember you?" My next question was barely spoken above a whisper. "Didn't you care that you had a sister?"

"Oh, Adalynn." Laydon wiped away a tear. "I did care. I wanted to come home. But I couldn't. I couldn't come home, couldn't return to Rothschan."

"Because of Renton?"

"Yes."

Remembering my meeting with the man, the conversation between Renton and Father began to make sense. "He said he wanted me for ... processing. Do you know what he meant by that?"

Laydon's mouth thinned into a straight line. "I'm not entirely sure. In the last few years, we've heard rumors…. We've sent several of our people back to Rothschan to discover what's going on, but none have been successful."

"You mean they had no information when they returned?"

"No." His face darkened. "They never returned."

Oh. I swallowed hard and looked away.

I cleared my throat and changed the subject. "Magic must run in our family, then. Strange that our parents never showed any signs of magical ability."

"It's for the best," Laydon said. "Renton has a way of ferreting out people with magic, whether it's dormant, fledgling, or full power. I think that's how our spies have all been captured. If our parents have no magic, it means they'll stay safe from him."

I was fascinated by this family history I had never known about before. And I was curious to know how the story ended. "So how did you end up in Calia?"

Laydon was about to answer when we turned a corner. His answer died in his throat. I too quieted down.

Before us was our destination: Fiala's boardinghouse.

21

Chapter Twenty-One

The sun was just peeking over the horizon as we approached the front door.

As we had made our way here, I had worried about what we'd see when we arrived. I was relieved to see her house was still standing.

Barely.

Singed bricks and the charred front stoop told us some of what had occurred. The large front window, which looked into the parlor, was shattered, the window frame mangled. The closed curtains, barely hanging onto to their overhead rod, stopped us from being able to see inside the house. The front door showed severe signs of splintering and scarring as if something had rammed it repeatedly. The door had held firm, but if it had taken a few more hits, it would have succumbed.

The house itself was eerily quiet.

Laydon strode up to the front door of the boardinghouse. Instead of knocking, he turned the handle, which surprisingly gave way to his touch. The door swung open, revealing a quiet, darkened interior.

Chandra, Laydon, and I exchanged glances. "What should we do?" Chandra whispered.

He shrugged. "Just see what there is to see, I guess." His hand moved to the weapon at his hip. "And be ready for anything."

Chandra drew her daggers, one in each hand, and cautiously moved forward. I swallowed, unhappy at taking up the rear, but followed after her.

Glass crunched underfoot as we stepped into the foyer. A slight breeze cooled the boardinghouse, twitching the closed curtains slightly open as a thin sliver of sunrise valiantly poked through them.

As my eyes adjusted to the dim interior, they idly followed the ray of light, then traced an invisible line down to the floor, where a dark, unmoving lump lay. Looking more carefully, I realized it was—

"Enlar!"

I rushed over to him as Laydon pulled back the parlor curtains, letting more light into the room. The morning sunlight revealed Enlar lying unconscious on the floor. The room looked as if a hurricane had blown through. Besides the shattered glass of the window glittering everywhere on the floor, the chairs had been pushed over, and the beige settee had been moved across the room. Books and papers were littered around the room, along with the knickknacks that had graced the mantle before.

Chandra grabbed a pillow from near the settee and tossed it to me. "You won't be of any help if you get all cut up," she said pointedly.

I plopped the pillow on the floor, hearing the muffled sound of glass breaking under my kneeling weight.

"Thank you." I eyed her quizzically. "Um. Why don't we just use magic to clean things up?"

She rolled her eyes. "Spoken like a true novice. It's never a good idea to use magic to do everyday tasks, like cleaning or cooking. It might take a little longer, but the more you use magic for mundane things, the more it becomes a crutch, and it can even hurt you in the long run.

Never anything wrong with good old-fashioned hard work. Besides, *I'm* not a magician." She started poking around the room. "There's got to be a broom around here somewhere."

"Perhaps in the kitchen," Laydon suggested. Chandra nodded and headed toward the back of the boardinghouse.

I felt Enlar's forehead, which was flush with fever. Quite the contrast to his hand, which was cold and clammy and criss-crossed with what looked like dozens of cuts. A small pool of blood spread out from under his hand. I hastily felt for a pulse, breathing easier once I detected a slow, steady heartbeat.

Hurriedly, I ripped off the bottom of my shirt, binding up Enlar's hand. I gently placed it on his chest, away from the blood and glass on the dirty floor. Meanwhile, Laydon was setting the room to rights, picking up papers and broken decorations.

I looked up at my brother worriedly. "I don't know what to do."

Laydon frowned. "There might not be much we can do, besides making him comfortable for now. We need to find the others. I know your friend is hurt, but the most important thing is to find—"

Light, tentative footsteps sounded on the stairs. A voice called out, challenging. "Who's there?"

Recognizing the voice as Fiala's, I breathed another sigh of relief. "Fiala, it's Adalynn. I came back here with—"

The footsteps were no longer hesitant as they flew down the stairs.

"Laydon!" Fiala said, breathless with joy. I looked up to see Laydon embrace Fiala tightly, only pulling back long enough to kiss her with equal passion. Suddenly feeling embarrassed, I looked away.

"I'm so sorry, Fiala," Laydon said. "We should have come sooner. We just got caught up in ... well, I'll explain it all later. I sent Gaelen and Frist ahead with most of the others. Did they get here in time to help you? What happened here? And is everyone all right?"

"One thing at a time," Fiala chided gently. "Yes, they're here, they're upstairs with the others. As to what happened—well, that's a longer tale to tell. And as far as everyone's safety, I believe nearly everyone is accounted for. Except for Enlar, who insisted on staying downstairs to guard the front. I was just coming down to see how he was …"

Fiala's voice trailed off as Laydon looked over to where I was still kneeling by Enlar's side. She gasped and joined me next to her fallen boarder.

"Oh my goodness! How long has he been like this?"

I shook my head. "I don't know, I was wondering that myself. We just got here a few minutes ago, and found him lying on the floor like this."

Fiala looked out the window, assessing the strengthening sunrise outside. "It can't have been long, then. I'd estimate the final assault was just before dawn."

More footsteps sounded on the stairs. "Mistress Fiala? Is everything okay? When you didn't come back upstairs, we thought we should check up on you."

A stocky man entered the room. I recognized him as one of the men from the cavern.

Laydon perked up upon seeing his friend. "Frist! We could use some help."

Frist saw Enlar sprawled unconscious on the floor and whistled. "Poor boy." To Fiala: "What can I do, mistress?"

"If you could bring him upstairs, I can attend to his wounds," Fiala said. "One of you at his head and one at his feet. Gently, now."

She darted ahead of them up the stairs. "Follow me, I'll show you which room to put him in."

Fiala disappeared upstairs. Laydon and Frist slowly followed, carefully balancing Enlar between them. I sat awkwardly in the parlor, still kneeling on my pillow, wondering if I should also follow, or instead look for Chandra and cleaning supplies.

My legs were beginning to cramp, so I stood up and stretched. I picked up the pillow and put it back on the settee where it had originally been. I was just about to head upstairs when I saw something that was lying where my floor pillow had been. In the originally dim lighting, and trapped underneath the pillow, I hadn't noticed the small sphere lying on the floor among the rest of the room's litter. Its soft sheen caught the light and sparkled in the sun, first an icy blue, then a pale green, and finally a vibrant purple.

Curious, I brushed aside some of the broken glass surrounding it with my foot, then carefully picked up the multicolored ball. It was warm to the touch, although it hadn't been sitting in the sunlight for long.

I rolled it between my fingers, studying all of its different facets on its unbroken, smooth surface, and marveled at the changing colors.

Laydon came down the stairs. "Adalynn, are you coming? Fiala's got your friend stabilized, and she thinks it might help his recovery if you were to sit with him for a bit, maybe even talk to him."

"Sure, I'll come." I shoved the little ball into my pocket before I followed Laydon up the stairs and into Enlar's room. He still didn't look that great to me—a touch too pale and cuts on his arms and above one eyebrow where the window glass must have struck him. But his breathing seemed to be deeper, and more even.

Fiala offered me a nearby chair. "Thank you for being here for him. Make yourself comfortable."

"Did you send for a healer?" Laydon asked her.

She shook her head. "I don't think it's necessary. My healing skills are rudimentary, but should suffice in this case. If he doesn't wake up in a few hours, then I will."

I sat down in the chair she had indicated. Laydon pulled up a chair as well. Fiala kissed him on the top of his head, then said, "I'm going to see to the staff and how the clean up is going."

As she left, Laydon and I just looked at each other. For a few moments, we sat there, listening to Enlar's breathing and watching the rise and fall of his chest.

Laydon said, "May as well finish my story from earlier."

"I'd like that," I said. "Now, where were we?"

22

CHAPTER TWENTY-TWO

"WHAT HAPPENED THAT DAY?"

That was the first thing I wanted to know. Was dying to know, actually. In all the years Laydon's story had spread around Rothschan, no one could ever say with certainty what had happened after Laydon had entered the tent, or why he had run away. But now I had the chance to find out from the very person himself what had occurred, and my curiosity demanded to be satisfied.

Laydon grimaced and looked down at his hands. "I suppose I should tell you, although I don't like talking about it. In fact, I've only told one other person—Fiala."

I stayed silent, afraid if I spoke, he'd change his mind.

Laydon's words came out haltingly. His haunted gaze showed that his thoughts were far away, caught in a horror he never wanted to relive again.

When I burst into the tent, I saw my intended—Jaynah—sitting stiffly in a chair, her head tilted at an unnatural angle. Her face was contorted in a silent scream.

Standing over her was Lord High Seneschal Renton, one of his hands outstretched toward her. He held a strange device, a silver rod with several jewels inlaid in the metal: a royal blue sapphire, a golden yellow topaz, and a blood red garnet. The first two jewels didn't sparkle in the light as you would expect. But the last gem glowed with an unnaturally bright red pulsing light. I saw a red rope of light tethering Jaynah to the silver rod Renton held in his fist.

The Seneschal ordered me to leave. With his free hand, he drew his sword and pointed it at me. I slowly began backing away. Since he thought I was following orders, Renton ignored me and turned back to Jaynah, intent on finishing whatever unholy experiment he was conducting.

I couldn't let him do it. I grabbed my dagger from my belt and lunged at him, but he blocked my blow just in time.

And somehow he still held Jaynah in thrall with that strange jeweled device.

I dodged right, feinting an attack with my knife. Renton raised his sword to strike, but I slipped under his guard and knocked the sword from his grasp. He dropped his sword. While he was distracted, I threw my dagger at his other hand—the one holding the device. I kicked Renton's sword as far as I could to one side of the tent, and rushed to Jaynah.

My aim had been true and the knife handle knocked the silver rod out of Renton's hand and onto the floor. The red light that tethered her to the wand wavered and winked out. Renton was cursing and yelling behind me, but all I cared about was Jaynah.

She slowly snapped out of her trance. She kept mumbling something, but it took a bit for me to realize what she was saying. "The wand. The wand."

I found the jeweled wand just a few feet away. But just as I grabbed it, I heard a strangled scream behind me.

In my haste I had forgotten to remove my dagger from Renton's reach. That monster had grabbed Jaynah and now held my knife against her neck. He demanded I give him the wand in exchange for Jaynah, although I didn't believe he would keep his word and return her safely to me. But I would have done anything to get her out of his grasp.

As I started to hand him the wand, the jewels began to glow, and that red line reappeared. The wand grew hot, unbearably so. The light spilling from it grew brighter, so bright it eclipsed the interior of the tent. I couldn't see anything. I was afraid I had gone blind.

Renton shouted. Jaynah cried out. Then ... silence. I still could only see whiteness, but after a moment or two my sight returned.

I wish it hadn't. Renton lay on the ground, the left half of his body and uniform charred and slightly mangled. Small smoldering patches of fire nearby hinted at what might have caused his injury. I didn't see Jaynah anywhere.

I crawled over to the Seneschal and grabbed him by the collar. "Where is she? What did you do with her?"

He groaned and tried to push me away, but he was too weak from his injuries. And I was too furious.

He said, "I didn't do anything with her. You did." And he pointedly looked at his feet.

Where a pile of ash lay.

"I don't believe you," I told him.

But then a slight breeze blew through the tent, scattering some of the ashes to one side.

A delicate gold ring glinted in the remaining pile.

I felt sick. I had placed that ring on Jaynah's finger just a few months ago. Renton had been telling the truth. I destroyed my love, and with that, my life.

So I ran. As far and as fast as I could. I still had that hateful wand with me, but no matter what I tried, I couldn't destroy it. I couldn't sell it and chance that the sale would be traced back to me. And in some strange way, I didn't want to part with it. Even if it was a painful reminder of what had happened to Jaynah, it was the only connection to her I had left.

I ended up going north, to Calia. I reasoned that the kingdom famed for its magicians would be the best place to help me understand and control my newfound magical ability. Also, perhaps someone there could give me insight on the silver wand.

In Calia, I found a private tutor who was willing to teach me despite my lack of status or funds. We had something in common—we were both expatriates from Rothschan. Under his instruction, I grew in my magical abilities, and I came to view him as a second father, a reminder of the one I unfortunately had to leave behind. When my tutor passed away, he left me his house and a modest fortune. I began teaching magic lessons in his place.

My tutor had also been able to identify the purpose of the strange device I had brought with me from Rothschan. The wand could identify if a person had magical ability, no matter how well they concealed it. If it sensed that a person had magic, the wand could use that magic against them in a temporary binding spell.

As for my true family back in Rothschan, I didn't contact them for fear that if I did send any letters, it would draw unwelcome attention to them and put them in danger.

So I was surprised when, one day, I returned to my home in Calia to find a plain linen envelope waiting for me. Just my name graced the envelope. There were no other markings to show where it had come from, or who had sent it. My heart nearly stopped when I tore open the envelope and read the letter inside.

Laydon reached into an inner pocket of his coat and retrieved a thin leather wallet, from which he withdrew a worn, yellowed piece of paper.

"I carry this with me, always," he said shyly. "To make me feel like I'm close to my family, even though it's been such a long time."

Gingerly, I took the paper from Laydon and unfolded it. I recognized my mother's elegant handwriting. In faded black ink, I read:

To our dear Laydon,

We hope this letter finds you, and hope it finds you well. Not a day goes by that we don't think of you and wonder how you are doing. We can only trust you got away safely, for though we have had no news of you these last two years, that lack gives us hope that you are still alive somewhere in the Gifted Lands. Perhaps even beyond.

We are all doing well here in Rothschan. You would be delighted to see how fast Adalynn is growing. She's now walking and getting into everything; she displays such an immense curiosity about the world around her. Just the other day she was pointing at various items around the house, asking, "What is this? What is this?" in her sweet little baby voice. I (Pella) would touch the item, and tell her, "It's a chair. This is a shoe." She would parrot back the word to me. "Chair! Shoe!"

And then she pointed to a framed picture above the mantle. Clear as day, she said, "Laydon."

My breath caught and I tried not to cry.

And then Adalynn asked, "When is Laydon coming home?"

I confess, it hurt too much to hear her ask that. After we put Adalynn to bed that night, we discussed it and, sadly, decided to remove any of your pictures and belongings that were around the house. We've already lost you, Laydon. We don't want to lose Adalynn as well, to an errant word or unwitting utterance.

I'm so sorry, Laydon. I'm sure it hurts you to read the above as much as it pains me to write it. As much as it hurt us to do it.

You may understand our caution when I tell you what is happening here. After your desertion, Lord High Seneschal Renton disappeared. Rumors abounded about the reason, but we knew that the king and queen were extremely displeased with the situation. Apparently Renton had been working on a special assignment for the Crown, and the debacle at your camp nearly gave away the secret. Then, too, he also had a long recovery time from his injuries.

When he finally emerged, there were two big surprises. The first was his appearance: half of his face and body had been badly disfigured from an extensive burn. The second, and perhaps the more shocking, is this: Renton is no longer Lord High Seneschal. His failure—and the Crown's subsequent displeasure—caused the king to strip Renton of his title, losing his lands, position, and authority in one crushing blow.

Because of his disgrace, the Crown is keeping Renton close. He is apparently not allowed to leave the capital, which limits the scope of his duties considerably. While it makes it uncomfortable on the rare occasions we run into him, we're also relieved to know that he cannot seek you out for revenge without bringing some sort of punishment down on himself.

But even those restrictions may not stop him from trying. Laydon, do be careful, wherever you are.

Speaking of which, you're probably wondering how we found you in order to send you this letter. In truth, we don't know where you are. In our desperation, and to our shame, we sought out a black market spell that supposedly could locate and deliver a message to the recipient wherever they were, as long as they were in the Gifted Lands. We'll know the spell failed if this letter returns to us within three days of sending it.

We miss you terribly and hope that wherever you are now, you are healthy and happy and safe. We sense we are being watched, and so it would probably be unwise to send us any correspondence. How it hurts us to think that we will never hear from you again! But to keep us all safe, it is probably for the best.

Know that we love you dearly and think of you every day.

Love,

Mother, Father, and Adalynn

Once I finished reading the letter, I carefully folded it up, then handed it to Laydon. He placed it back in the leather wallet and put it away.

A few moments passed in silence.

Finally, I let out a breath. "Well, this explains a lot. I wondered why Renton was so mad at Father and me. And why he hated titles. I'd never encountered him before that day, and I didn't know he had been demoted. Mother and Father certainly didn't mention it." My face fell, remembering. "Then again, it's not like we had a lot of friends in the village or the capital who would talk about it with us, anyway."

Mother's comments about Renton in the letter had certainly surprised me. The embittered man I had met was a far cry from a Lord High Seneschal. The Seneschal would have been one of the highest positions in Rothschan, appointed by the Crown. It was the most coveted title in the country. As it should be. The Seneschal was second only to the king himself, managing the entirety of the kingdom.

Losing that position would have made Renton sore indeed. And, recalling my Rothschan history, he would have been the last person to be Seneschal, as no one had held the title since. I wondered why. Was no one as good at the job as Renton had been?

Laydon's eyes were misty with unshed tears. "I'm so, so sorry. I know that what happened hurt you and our family. And there was nothing I could do to make things better. I couldn't even send money home. I tried, once. Father arranged for it to be sent back."

Thinking of our ramshackle house, threadbare furnishings, oft-mended clothes, and how much a little bit of extra money would have allowed Mother to hold her head up proudly through our village—I had to wonder. "Why?"

Laydon shrugged. "Pride? Fear? I'm not sure. Maybe he worried if he accepted it once, he'd always accept it, and the money could get traced back to me, and I would be found. He did it to keep you and Mother, and me, safe. At least, that's what I tell myself on my better days."

Seeing the tears glistening in his eyes was starting to make me emotional as well. Sniffling, I said, "All this time … they had no idea if you were all right … and I had no idea I had a brother."

Laydon leaned forward, then stopped, suddenly shy. "May I?"

I nodded. He reached out and enfolded me in his arms. As I embraced him back, my tears fell in earnest. When I pulled back from the hug, I saw tear streaks down Laydon's face as well.

Sniffling, I said, "Just curious. Whatever happened to Renton's wand?"

Laydon shrugged. "Darn thing was indestructible. I gave it to Queen Jennica for safekeeping."

On the bed, Enlar stirred slightly, but didn't open his eyes.

"Oh! He's moving!" I said, excited. Tears were still streaking down my face, although I wasn't sure if they were still for Laydon, or now for Enlar. "We should get Fiala."

Laydon strode over to the door and leaned over the railing. He called out for Fiala, but when she didn't answer, he said, "Chandra! Have you seen Fiala?"

There was the crunch of broken glass, and then Chandra called up, "She's outside. I can send her up, if you like. I could use a break from cleaning."

"Thank you, Chandra. That would be great."

More crunching of glass, and a door opened and shut somewhere in the distance. Laydon came back into Enlar's bedroom. He saw me wiping my eyes with my sleeve and began fishing in his pockets. Finding a handkerchief, he held it out to me. "Here, this is clean."

I stood up to take the handkerchief from his outstretched hand. The ball I had shoved in my pocket earlier fell out and rolled across the floor, landing at my brother's feet.

"What's this?" He bent down to retrieve it, but just before his fingers touched it, sparks shot out from the ball. Laydon hastily drew back.

"I found it lying on the floor earlier, where Enlar was," I said. "That's funny, it didn't do that when I picked it up."

"That's because it doesn't want me to touch it. Unless I want to be injured, or worse."

"What do you mean? What is it?"

"It's a message. And it's meant for you."

23

—·—

Chapter Twenty-Three

"A message? But who sent it?"

I rolled the shimmery sphere around and around in my hand as I pondered the item.

Laydon, Fiala, and I were sitting at the large wooden table in the boardinghouse's dining room, contemplating the message ball.

Chandra had finished cleaning up the broken glass from the parlor floor. Gaelen and Frist, along with some of the other refugees and students, were patrolling outside. A few students had packed up their belongings and left, presumably going back to their families. Enlar was still resting upstairs.

"I think the answer to your question is rather obvious," Fiala remarked dryly. "That certainly wasn't here when you and Enlar first arrived. It wasn't there when I sent you to Laydon. Enlar would have noticed. So it was left either by the person who tried to kidnap you, who I'm assuming is the same person who tried to set my house on fire, or by their employer."

"All right, that seems like a logical assumption," I agreed. "So what do I do with it?"

My brother chuckled. "That's pretty obvious, too. You open it."

I frowned, holding the message ball up to the light and turning it this way and that. The sphere was seamless, with no way of breaking it open as far as I could tell. Experimentally, I tapped the ball on the wooden table, trying to crack it open like an egg. There was a clanging noise that echoed lightly throughout the dining room, but the ball remained intact.

"Well, that didn't work." My frown deepened. "Maybe I should try throwing it in the fire, to see if it will melt open?"

Laydon grinned. "That's not how those work. Magic created it; you need to use magic to undo it."

I gave my brother a pained look. "You forget, I'm new to this whole magic thing."

"Think of it as a test then, to see if you have the ability to control it and make it conform to your will." His grin grew wider. "If you pass, we'll count it as extra credit."

I stuck my tongue out at him, even while his comment elicited an involuntary chuckle. "How can I have extra credit when I haven't even started classes?"

He shrugged and waggled his eyebrows at me. I rolled my eyes. Fiala looked between us, shaking her head as a smile teased her lips. "Hard to believe that you two only just met. You certainly squabble like siblings who've grown up together."

"Hush, you," Laydon told her, but his smile took the edge off his words. He reached over and captured Fiala's hand in his own. She smiled back at him before he turned his attention back to me.

"All right then, how do I open this?" I tapped my fingernail against the sphere.

He stood up, grabbing his chair and bringing it around the table to sit next to me. "Hold it up a bit higher, if you don't mind?"

I obligingly raised my hand. The ball wasn't heavy, although it was quite solid. Laydon craned his neck forward, putting his face as close as he could to the glittering sphere without touching it. I held my hand as still as possible, afraid of accidentally dropping it. If those earlier sparks were any indication, prolonged contact would be quite bad for my brother.

After a few minutes' careful study, Laydon straightened up in his chair and looked at me. "I never asked you, what can you do magically?"

I quickly outlined the things I had done, most of them by accident, since my powers had awakened about a week earlier. Laydon listened carefully, looking thoughtful as he studied me, then the message ball. When I finished my recitation, he didn't say anything for several long moments. Finally, I said, "Well?"

Laydon blinked, coming out of his ruminations. "Hmm?"

Exasperated, I said, "So ... what are you thinking?"

He grinned at me. "I'm thinking you're a natural talent. It obviously runs in the family—" both Fiala and I groaned simultaneously "—so this should be no problem for you at all. Now, then. Are you ready for some magic practice?"

24

CHAPTER TWENTY-FOUR

I WASN'T IN THE mood for practicing my magic, not really, but there was no help for it. I'd have to keep working at it so I could learn how to channel and control my magic properly.

I guess I had been hoping it wouldn't be under such a pressured situation. *Nothing else seems to be going the way I had hoped it would. Why should this be any different?*

"Is there anything I can do to assist?" Fiala asked Laydon. "Do you need any ingredients, or anything special for spell casting?"

Laydon shook his head. "No, this will rely more on Adalynn's intuitive use of magic more than anything else. But if I were you, I'd leave the room. Just in case she loses control ..."

Fiala nodded in understanding. "I'll go check on the students that are still here. And see about the house wards." To me, she said warmly, "You'll do fine, Adalynn. I'm not worried." With that, she left the room.

Fiala might not be worried, but I certainly was.

"Now, then," Laydon said, pulling my attention back to him. "When you've done magic so far, you usually want for something to be true, and then it happens, is that correct?"

At my nod, he continued. His voice had taken on a lecturing qual-
ity, and I hid a smile. *Now I know how his students feel.*

"That's the most basic form of doing magic. Most babies or young
children start showing their abilities that way; they lack the understanding or knowledge to take their powers and shape it into anything
more complex than a simple wish. Because they are so young, their
magical ability is still growing. It's like if you add water to a glass. A
child would start with a glass about a quarter full. As they grow older,
more water would be added to the glass. As an adult, their glass would
be full. In your case, because you came into your magic as an adult, you
not only have a full well of power, it's also more concentrated, because
it's been lying dormant inside you for so long.

"When you cast a spell, there's two parts to it. The first is control,
the second is creation. Going back to my glass analogy, when you dip
into your power, imagine pouring out only some of the water, just
enough to use for your spell. Simple spells just need a sip of power.
Complex or more powerful spells might require a long drink, or even
the entire glass. More water, so to speak, will also put more power
behind your spell. So you need to get adept at drinking only what you
need. Draining the entire glass could be dangerous, both for your spell
and for you as a magician. You don't want to entirely deplete your
magical reserves unless there's no other option.

"You've already experienced the creation element of magic, by accidentally willing things into existence. Now, you have to learn how to
be deliberate in choosing the things or actions you want your magic to
create. When you put careful thought and specificity into your spells,
you will not only get the results you want, but those results will be
better. Does that make sense?"

I nodded slowly, thinking over the magic I had unwittingly performed over the last week. "But I *did* get good results. It's not like I

ended up with dirty water in the pitcher back at home. My bath at the inn was pleasantly warm, not scalding. So doesn't that mean I already have some measure of control?"

"No, not in the way you assume," my brother said. "Your magic is just awakening. So even though it feels like a sudden rush of power to you, since you've never experienced it before, it's actually just beginning to trickle out of you. Remember that glass? Without you consciously pushing back against it, it's going to keep tipping, pouring out water, until it's been upended completely and comes out in a flood. Give it a few more weeks, without any training, and you'd be at that point."

I frowned. "Then why was your coming-into-magical-ability story so much more ... extreme ... than mine?"

Laydon laughed. "Strong emotion can open the magical floodgates more than one wants. And, if you remember, you had a similar experience yourself. With the same person, even."

My lips twisted wryly as I recalled the scene in Renton's office. "We really don't like that man, do we?"

"Yet another thing that runs in the family," Laydon agreed.

I smiled at him, then turned my attention back to the colorful ball in my hand. It shimmered blue, then purple, then green, as I turned it continuously. "All right, I think I understand the theory. But how do I actually apply it?"

"Concentrate, but stay relaxed."

I did as my brother said, closing my eyes so I could better focus. After a brief moment, I heard him pointedly say, "I said, relax. If you keep holding that thing any tighter, you won't ever be able to open your hand again."

I opened my eyes and looked down where my hands rested in my lap. I hadn't realized I had tightened my grip around the message ball.

My hand was turning white from the pressure. Sheepishly, I loosened my grip.

"That's better. Now, you mentioned that you can create a basic light. Why don't you do that for me now?"

I nodded, remembering my on-the-road magic lessons with Enlar. His instruction, about letting out just enough magical power, had been much the same as Laydon's. It was easy enough to conjure up a small light in the palm of my free hand. I beamed at my light, then grinned triumphantly at my brother.

He smiled back. "Good. Can you explain to me exactly how you did that?"

I frowned, thinking through the steps. "I ... unlocked my power, grabbing just enough to use for the spell. I closed off my magical reservoir so there wouldn't be an accidental overflow, then used the magic that was available to create the light."

"Good," he said again. "And if you're not in a hurry, or just need to do one small, easy spell, that would be an acceptable way of approaching spell casting. But let's say you have to do more complex work. Or you are in a situation, such as a possible fight or self-defense, and you need to access your ability quickly. You can't just stop and take a few moments to parcel out the power you need for whatever spells you want to cast. So you'll need to learn how to subconsciously keep the lines of power open, without letting it overwhelm you. This will also help you when you do bigger spells because then you can continuously access your magic. Does this make sense?"

"I—I think so," I stammered, unsure I would be able to do that.

He laughed. "I know it sounds impossible, but don't worry. With enough time and practice, it will become as second nature to you as breathing."

"If you say so," I muttered. I took a deep breath. "Okay, then. What do I need to do?"

"Close your eyes again, focus on what I'm saying, but keep your mind and body as relaxed as you can."

I closed my eyes once more and nodded to let Laydon know I was ready.

From somewhere to my right, I heard him say, "All right. Imagine your magical reservoir. A box, a glass, whatever feels right to you. Got it?"

I nodded again.

"Good. Now, remember what I said about how you don't want all your power to seep out of its container, because it would take hours, maybe even days, for your magic to replenish. But you still need to access your magic at all times. So, instead of thinking of your magic as a linear ability, channel it into a loop, so it's constantly replenishing itself."

I paused, pondering Laydon's words. I felt fairly confident I could do what he and Enlar had taught me, about taking sips from my magical reservoir as needed. Now, I had to think about actually controlling it, bending it to my will. Instead of being controlled by it, which had been the case up to this point.

Combining the imagery that both Enlar and Laydon had used, I envisioned my magical ability contained in a single vessel, a clear jar with a partially open lid. My magical essence filled the jar to the brim, shimmering with an inner glow as it shifted in a rainbow of colors. The rainbow trickled down one side of the jar, and if I opened the lid wider, more of the multicolored essence would flow out.

Right now the magic poured out into a vast nothingness. But how to get it to flow back into the jar?

In my mind, I imagined the jar sitting in the middle of a small table, just big enough to hold the jar and nothing else. The tabletop allowed my magic to pool on the surface, but not slosh over the sides and fall away.

That took care of losing any more of my magic. So, now ... I thinned the walls of the jar, making one part of it porous enough to soak up the magic that was lying on the table. Everything on the table's surface slammed back into the jar.

And I instantly doubled over in my chair, overwhelmed by the magnitude of the magic that had suddenly flowed back into my vessel.

Through the blood rushing in my ears, I heard Laydon say, "I can tell you've figured it out, just control the flow to a manageable level."

Panting and light-headed, I nodded slightly to show I had heard and understood him. I closed down part of my jar that was re-absorbing magic so it wasn't soaking up quite so much magic, quite so fast.

Slowly, I felt a pressure in my chest ease, and I found I could breathe easier. The feeling of nausea passed. I sat back up and looked at my brother.

"I think I understand what you were talking about," I said.

"Good." His look of satisfaction warmed my heart more than any words of praise. "That was the hardest part. Now, to unlock your message."

25

·—·

CHAPTER TWENTY-FIVE

"THE MESSAGE IS KEYED to you, which is why your magic needs to settle around it for a bit," Laydon explained. "Once the spell recognizes you, then it will be more receptive to opening. You'll need to use your magic to encase the message ball, and more magic to open it, but you don't want to overwhelm it, or you'll destroy the item and the message along with it."

"All right. I'm ready."

"Good. Send your magic out."

I frowned, a bit distracted, as I mentally pulled some of my magic forward, sending it to enclose the little round object in my hand. Perhaps it was my imagination—I had certainly never seen my magic take physical form before—but it seemed to me that a thin multicolored ribbon, the same as I had imagined my magical essence, bloomed in my chest and arced down my arm, coating the ball until I couldn't distinguish the ever-changing blue-green-purple of the ball from my own brightly colored magic.

When my magic shifted from blue, to green, to purple, I felt the ball shift slightly. Closer study of it showed that there was now a slight crack in the middle, where there hadn't been any gaps previously.

I gasped in understanding. Laydon had been correct; the spell on this had been keyed to me. My magic had unlocked a secret sequence that let the spell know that the message had reached the right recipient.

"Good job. Now, open it."

Brows furrowed, I reached out and tentatively jabbed at the crack with my finger. Instead of catching in the crack so I could wedge it open further, my finger slipped off the surface, which felt as smooth and unbroken as before.

My brother smiled wryly. "I didn't think I had to specify, *with your magic*."

I laughed. "It was worth a try."

Turning my attention back to my spell casting, I took stock. The ball was tethered to me, both by my physical hold on it and the magic threading down my arms anchoring it. I imagined my jar, opening the lid wider, and willed more magic to course down my arm. The rainbow-colored light around the ball grew thicker, nearly so opaque that I couldn't see the ball in my hand anymore.

Laydon whistled. "Not so much."

"Oops." I hastily closed the lid so less magic was spilling out, and tipped my hand so some of the magic pooling in my palm could escape. The power tumbled down in a multicolored waterfall and onto the floor, becoming a puddle of light before disappearing and leaving a hand-sized hole in the ground.

"Oh, dear," I said when I saw what I had done. I felt the magic in my arm shift a bit uncontrollably, and quickly sat up straight, afraid of inflicting more damage to the poor boardinghouse. It had already endured enough.

"It's all right," Laydon said, a laugh lacing his voice. "I'll fix it later. Trust me, I did way worse when I was first learning how to use my magic. Now, concentrate."

I nodded, following his instructions. With the extra magic I had pulled forth, I sent it through the crack in the message ball and whispered to it as it went, "Open."

My magic went through the same light sequence as before, overpowering the shimmering colors inside the ball. The light grew brighter, so much that I closed my eyes and turned my face away. When I felt brave enough to open my eyes and look, two halves of the once smooth sphere were lying in my hand. One half held a small, folded piece of cream-colored paper.

For a few long seconds, neither Laydon nor I spoke. Then, finally, my brother broke the silence.

"Congratulations. That, Adalynn, was your first complex spell."

Completing my first complex spell was easy in comparison to figuring out what to do about the note it uncovered.

Laydon and I sat in the same places as we had during my spell casting, our heads bowed over the piece of paper. Chandra joined us in the dining room, pulling up a chair so she was sitting opposite us. "The parlor's all cleaned up, if you two want to sit in there. It's probably more comfortable. More light, too."

Laydon looked at me, but I shrugged and shook my head. Chandra was right, but I still didn't feel comfortable being in that room, after discovering Enlar unconscious in there.

Fiala appeared and sat down between Laydon and Chandra. "Everyone's doing fine, if a little shaken up," she announced. She looked at me. "And your friend Enlar is awake, although the poor boy has a nasty headache. He was asking for you."

"Really?" I perked up.

She nodded. "I told him I'd send you up when you had a free moment. But honestly, he should just rest as much as possible right now."

I pushed my chair back. "I should go to him."

Laydon put a hand on my arm. "Maybe after we figure this out?" he said pointedly.

"Oh, of course." I settled back in my seat.

"What are we figuring out?" Fiala asked. Laydon put the note in her hand. The two halves of the ball that used to contain the note lay in the center of the wooden table. Now that the spell was broken, its shimmery blue-green-purple tint had dulled to a static dark gray.

Fiala looked over the little paper, then looked up, her eyes troubled.

"What do you think?" Laydon asked her.

"What's going on?" Chandra asked.

"Are you going to do this?" Fiala asked me, worry lacing her tone.

"What? What are you going to do?" Chandra tried again.

"I—I'm not sure," I said. "It doesn't seem wise, but at the same time ..."

"What are you all talking about?" Chandra exploded.

She snatched the paper out of Fiala's hand. Scowling at it, she turned it this way and that, squinting as she tried to make sense of what she was seeing. Frustrated, she thrust the paper back at me and said, "Tell me what's going on."

Confused, I waved the paper in the air. "You just saw what the note says."

"No, I didn't." Her deepening scowl dared me to comment.

Mildly, Laydon commented, "The offer still stands, Chandra."

Chandra huffed, "I don't see a need for it. If I'm in the thick of a fight, all I need to know is how to stop my opponent. We're not going to sit down and discuss what we read in that day's paper."

Gently, Fiala said, "Regardless, you know either Laydon or I would be happy to teach you how to read."

Chandra frowned, first at Fiala, and then at Laydon. Her frown grew when she caught sight of their clasped hands. Pursing her lips, she looked away and stared at the far wall. Fiala and Laydon pointedly ignored her behavior, giving her a chance to recover.

And in that moment, I wondered: *Is Chandra in love with my brother?*

Trying to cover the awkward moment, I blurted out, "Sorry about your floor, Fiala."

"My floor?" She glanced down to where I was pointing. "Oh, my. How did that happen?"

I explained what had occurred, finishing with, "I'd be happy to pay for the repairs." Although with what money, I didn't know.

Fiala waved away my offer. "Don't worry about it."

During my story, Chandra had time to regain her composure, and my revelation of the hole in the floor had piqued her curiosity. I smiled at her, hoping to convey some encouragement, and was rewarded with a small tug of a smirk at the corner of her lips. She nodded at me, ever so slightly. It seemed we had reached some sort of mutual understanding.

"Back to the matter at hand," Laydon said. "What are you going to do, Adalynn?"

I looked back down at the cream-colored paper, now slightly wrinkled from being passed around to multiple hands. The strong, blocky handwriting stared back up at me as I read it aloud, partly for Chandra's benefit but also because I still couldn't quite believe what it said.

Adalynn Taethen: Return to Rothschan immediately, or your parents' lives are forfeit. If you value their safety, then come to the Iron Bridge two weeks hence, at midnight. Alone.

The note wasn't signed.

"Well, of course you can't give in to their demand," Fiala said.

"Where's the Iron Bridge?" Chandra said at the same time.

"The Iron Bridge is in Rothschan, just outside the capital city," I said. "It used to be the only way you could reach the royal residence, before more of the city was built up, and the royal family outgrew the original palace and moved to the current one."

"Is the old palace used for anything?"

I paused for a moment, thinking. "I think it's just storage, now, if it's used at all. When the new palace was built, the capital was built around it, so the original palace is kind of out of the way of anything. There was talk of converting it into a museum, since it is a part of Rothschan's history, but it's fallen into disrepair, and the Crown always has something more important to spend our taxes on than fixing it up."

Chandra fell silent, allowing Fiala to finish her earlier thought. "You're not going to go to this meeting, are you? Who's to say they—whoever *they* are—will keep their word? This is just an easy way for them to get their hands on you."

"I think I know who may have written it, or at least who had it sent," I said slowly. "And if my guess is correct, then he obviously already knows where I am. It wouldn't matter if I returned to Rothschan or fled Calia. I wouldn't be safe anywhere I go."

I sighed, running my fingers over the paper. "Besides, he has my parents." I looked at Laydon. "Our parents."

"That alone would be reason to go back," Laydon agreed. "But don't worry. Renton may think you're walking into his trap, but he'll be walking right into ours."

26

—·—

Chapter Twenty-Six

"How are you feeling?"

I carefully placed the tray I was carrying on the nightstand by Enlar's bed. After our meeting in the dining room, Fiala had sent me upstairs with a glass of water and a plate piled high with sandwiches for Enlar.

He sat up in bed, his movements careful. "I'm sore all over, and my head hurts something fierce. But Fiala told me that in a day or two, I should be mostly healed." He flexed his arm reflectively, twisting his wrist and wiggling his fingers. "Whatever Fiala did to heal me, it was pretty amazing. A blow like the one I took should have laid me out for several days, not just a few hours."

I stood awkwardly by Enlar's bedside. Enlar waved for me to sit, which I did, being careful to avoid jostling him.

"What happened, exactly?" I asked.

Enlar grimaced. "After you and Fiala left, the magical attack on the house grew more intense. Whoever was attacking us conjured several elementals. One was an elemental of fire—apparently the choice form of destruction—to burn us out, or trap us inside and kill us. One was an earth elemental, repeatedly pounding on the door, trying to gain entry. And when those failed, a wind elemental was summoned, to lift the house off of its very foundations."

I gaped at Enlar. "I can't believe this old boardinghouse was able to withstand all of that."

He smiled grimly. "The wards on this place are unbelievable. Fiala got her money's worth on them, that's for sure. But after repeated assault the house wards started to fail. Fiala dissolved the peace spell, and the students staying here did their best to fight back, but they're at all different levels of talent and experience. I tried too, but I'm still a novice myself. We were barely holding our own until some random people came to our aid."

"They weren't random," I said, remembering how Laydon had sent some of his comrades ahead of us to assist at Fiala's house.

Enlar snorted. "Well, when you're in the middle of a battle, unknown people showing up claiming to want to help you seems a bit suspicious. But I'm glad they were on our side; they really helped make the difference.

"Anyway, we were able to push back the magical onslaught with their help, and it seemed like we would be victorious, when the wind elemental suddenly appeared with a blast of power. It blew out the windows." He shook his head ruefully. "That wind tossed me aside like an unwanted toy. When I finally came to ..." He smiled at me. "You'll have to fill me in on the rest."

I told Enlar what had happened after I left the house with Fiala, including discovering that Laydon was my long-lost brother, returning back to the house and the battle's aftermath, and ending with the mysterious message that was sent to me.

"Of course I'm going to go with you," Enlar said, sitting up straighter. He winced at the sudden pain, holding his side.

"Of course you're not," Fiala said, entering the room with Laydon on her heels. "You're not in any condition to travel right now."

"You said that I should be back to normal in a day or two," Enlar argued.

"*If* you rest, and don't do anything unnecessary," Fiala shot back. "Traveling with Adalynn is unnecessary."

"I don't think it is," Laydon spoke up. There was a thoughtful gleam in his eye.

"Laydon," Fiala began, sounding exasperated.

"No, I'm serious." He looked at me, then Enlar. "Adalynn shouldn't travel by herself; it would make her too easy a target. It takes about a week to travel from Calia to Rothschan, and that's at a normal pace. Adalynn doesn't have to leave right away for Rothschan, which should give Enlar the day or two you recommended for him to recover completely."

Fiala looked like she wanted to argue, so Laydon rushed on, "And I'll send Chandra with them."

"You sure she's not needed here?"

Laydon frowned as he thought it over. "Chandra's an irreplaceable second, but Frist should be able to fill in for her fairly well."

I wondered how Chandra would feel when she heard the plan. She'd follow Laydon's orders, of course, but that didn't mean she'd be happy about it.

Now it was Fiala's turn to frown. "I don't agree, Laydon, but if you think it's necessary—"

"It is."

"—Then I'll go along with it." She turned her frown on Enlar. "Young man, your only job for the next two days is to stay in bed. I'll assign two of the students to take shifts helping you out. Any travel preparations you need to make, I can take care of. If I see you pushing yourself for any reason ..." She left the unspoken threat hanging in the air.

"Yes, Mistress Fiala," Enlar said meekly.

Fiala sniffed at his use of "Mistress" but didn't comment. Instead, she swept out of the room, no doubt to find two hapless souls who would serve as Enlar's unwitting nursemaids over the next two days.

"I need to check in with Gaelan and Frist, and let Chandra know what's happening," Laydon said. "You should get some rest yourself, Adalynn. Come by the hideout tomorrow, and we can make our own preparations."

Laydon turned to leave. I stood up abruptly. "Wait."

Laydon turned back, a question in his eyes. I threw my arms around him. "Thank you."

He stood stiffly in my arms, then slowly relaxed and returned my embrace. "You're welcome, Adalynn. You're welcome."

27

—·—

CHAPTER TWENTY-SEVEN

THE NEXT MORNING, OVER breakfast, Fiala announced that we would be paying a house call.

"I'm supposed to see Laydon in the hideaway," I said.

Fiala smiled. "And how do you think you're going to get there?"

I hadn't been sure, actually. "Through the tunnels?"

She laughed. "There's an easier way."

I gave her a skeptical look as I finished the rest of my bread. "I can't just stroll into Limande's house. I don't even know how to work the secret passage in his study."

Not to mention, in the wake of an attempted kidnapping, discovering I had a long-lost older brother, and rushing back to help my friends in the midst of a magical battle, I hadn't really been paying attention to little details like how to get to Limande's house from Fiala's.

"Of course you can't." She daintily wiped at her mouth, then put her napkin down on the table. "Which is why Limande himself will tell you how."

She started toward the kitchen doorway, leaving me sitting stunned at the table. At the entry, she turned around. "Well? Are you coming?"

I hastily scraped my chair back from the table. "Of course! Yes. Yes, I am."

"Mistress Fiala, welcome. The master has been expecting you. Right this way." A butler ushered Fiala and me through the doorway of Limande's townhouse and into the parlor, where the elderly magician stately sat in a royal blue high-backed chair. The butler hurried away to see to refreshments for us.

Not only does magic make things easier, it apparently pays very well, I thought as we entered the room. If the rich velvet furnishings and exotic art on display were any indication, the magician Limande was extremely well off.

"Ah, Mistress Fiala, it's good to see you again," Limande said warmly as he stood to greet us.

"Likewise, Master Limande," Fiala said, crossing to the man and clasping his outstretched hand. He turned her hand and placed a kiss on the back of it.

"Always the charmer." She smiled, turning to me. "And I believe you know my companion?"

"Miss Adalynn." Limande smiled at me. "I'm so glad you were able to come today."

"It's nice to see you again, sir," I said.

"And now to business," Limande said. "Mistress Fiala, I believe your note said something about your house wards?"

"Yes, but before we get to that—Laydon asked Adalynn to come see him in the hideout this morning. Could you help her find her way?"

"Oh, of course. It's quite easy, Miss Adalynn. Just look for a small latch, partially concealed, on the same wall as the fireplace. It should be at the same height as the mantle."

"Thank you." I hesitated, unsure if I should get up and leave to go find Laydon, or stay here and visit with the elderly magician for a while.

The butler returned to the room bearing a tea tray.

"Ah, Prein." Limande waved at a side table. "Please put that tray over here. Then, could you escort Miss Adalynn to my library? There are a few books she'll be borrowing for her magic studies."

"Of course, sir." Prein put the tray down and then motioned to me. "If you would follow me, miss."

I stood up and walked to the doorway. Just before leaving, I turned to Limande. "Thank you for your help, sir."

"I'm happy to be of assistance," he said, a twinkle in his eyes. "You're welcome to borrow books from my library at any time."

The butler had already started down the hallway, and so he missed the wink Limande gave me. I grinned and winked back. As I walked away, I heard the magician say to Fiala, "Now, then. About these wards?"

The butler led me straight to Limande's study, and after opening the door for me, left without another word. I breathed a sigh of relief, glad I didn't have to hunt for the hideout's secret door with the butler standing nearby watching me.

The study appeared much the same as it had yesterday. Looking around, I got the impression that the magician's household servants rarely came in here. Running a finger on the windowsill, I changed my initial thought: the servants *never* came in here. My finger was now stained black. I sneezed from the dust I had inadvertently stirred up.

I crossed to the false fireplace and felt along the wall, near the mantle like Limande had said. It wasn't long until I found the concealed latch and flipped it, marveling at how quietly and seamlessly the secret door opened.

Peering into the darkness below, I hastily called forth a light and sent it down about halfway. Carefully, I climbed down the ladder, pausing in the middle to move the light further down, ahead of me.

Now on the ground, I stared at the blank black wall. I had forgotten to ask Limande how to open the door to the hideout from this side. But I also refused to give up right away. I'd pound on the secret door as a last resort.

Recalling how Chandra had opened the door yesterday, I felt along the wall to my left. Which would have been, on the other side of the wall, the door's right side. If I remembered correctly, she had pressed something about a third of the way down, somewhere at the level of my stomach....

The door slid open.

On the other side, Laydon, Chandra, and some others in the hideout blinked at me, surprised at my sudden appearance. Above me, the fireplace entrance closed, leaving me with only my magical light and the sporadic lanterns and wall-set torches in the cavern for my eyes to adjust to.

"Hello, everyone," I said brightly. "Here I am."

"Perfect. Come here." My brother waved me over to the table, and the others shifted to make room for me. I ended my light spell and walked over.

A large piece of paper lay on top of a table. On it, I saw a drawing of some sort. A diagram? No, it was a floor plan of a building.

My eyes widened.

It was the layout of the former Rothschan palace.

"How did you get this?" I breathed. "Laydon said none of the spies returned."

Chandra chuckled. "Your country is famed for its might, not its minds. Rothschan's sorry excuse for a library is terribly understaffed. It was painfully easy to, ah, indefinitely borrow this document."

At my scandalized look, she shrugged. "I'm planning on returning it. Eventually."

"Your late fees are going to be outrageous," I muttered. And then it dawned on me. "And, you're not a magician. So, unlike the other spies, you'd have no magic that could be traced."

Chandra smiled. "Hard for magic-soaked Calians to believe, but sometimes a lack of magical talent can actually be useful."

"Now, then," Laydon said, calling our attention back. "Let's discuss what we're going to do."

"What *are* we going to do?" I wondered. "And more importantly, *why*?"

Laydon paused. "I never did explain, did I?"

"Not that I recall. Or if you did, not to my satisfaction."

"Have you ever heard what happened here in Calia a few years back, with the king? Not the current one, King Beyan. But Hendon, the one before him?"

I nodded.

"Ah, good. Then you probably know that relations between Calia and Rothschan are strained, at best."

"So? Rothschan doesn't have the best relationship with many of the countries in the Gifted Lands."

"Yes, but it also doesn't have a very personal score to settle with any of the other kingdoms. Hendon was one of the best knights Rothschan had to offer, and many from that kingdom considered it a waste of his talent when he left Rothschan and moved to Calia. Even if he did become a king. And then he was shamed so publicly at the hands of his queen and supposed daughter, and Rothschan's Prince Anders was also shamed .... Well, it's a wonder Rothschan hasn't tried to annihilate Calia."

"That's what Queen Jennica said." I shrugged. "But it hasn't happened."

"Yet." My brother leaned forward and gripped the table. "You mentioned Renton wanted you for processing. It was something Rothschan was dabbling in many years ago—trying to find people with magic, and experiment on them. But the rumors from the refugees since then have confirmed that the experiments have become more frequent and, worse, organized. It seems there are specific things Rothschan is looking for, with specific, but unknown, goals. And all the stories point to here." He pointed at the map of the old palace.

His hands swept the cavern, indicating everyone around us. "And with the full support and blessing of Queen Jennica, we mean to stop these experiments. Permanently."

28

CHAPTER TWENTY-EIGHT

SO, WE WERE GOING home. To save my parents. And to stop the vengeful, displaced former Seneschal, who somehow wielded both great magical power and the famed mighty military of Rothschan, known throughout the Gifted Lands.

Easier said than done, I thought sourly, as I watched Laydon secure the tack on my horse. *I think I liked life better when magic was just creating baths that stayed warm and conjuring pretty lights.*

Something of my thoughts must have shown on my face, because my brother turned to me, his eyes soft. "Hey. I'm worried, too. But it will be okay. Really."

"And if it's not?" I searched his face, but couldn't find the answers I was looking for. Truthfully, I didn't even know the questions.

"Let's not think about that." My brother smiled wryly. "You're in good hands. Enlar and Chandra will be with you in case anything goes wrong. The three of you will get to Rothschan faster than if you traveled with my group."

I grimaced, knowing he was right.

Enlar, who had mostly recovered from the magical attack on Fiala's house, had insisted on accompanying me personally, instead of staying behind in Calia or traveling with Laydon's team. When I had asked him about his reasons for wanting to come, he had grinned at me.

"Why not? We're still on summer break. Think of the stories we'll be able to tell our classmates! And besides, King told me he'd kick me hard if I let my only friend in Calia ride off into danger alone."

I had laughed. "You talk to horses?"

His grin had just gotten wider. "Unlike some people I know, I'm unable to charm animals with my sheer presence alone."

I had blushed, even as I had laughed again, walking away to make my own preparations to leave. Secretly I had been pleased. It was nice to know Enlar wanted to make sure I stayed safe.

Chandra, Laydon's second-in-command, had been less than pleased with my brother's decision that she should go to Rothschan with me instead of Laydon's group.

"Enlar and Adalynn will be fine. Besides, I'm the best spy we've got." She had crossed her arms across her chest and glared at him. "It's your parents that our mysterious madman is holding captive. Perhaps you and your sister should go together."

"My group will be just a few days behind yours," Laydon had pointed out. "You and Enlar and Adalynn can prepare for the meeting. My group will scout out the old palace and then join you."

"I still say I should be in your group. Send someone else with your sister and her friend."

"Chandra." Something in Laydon's tone had made her close her mouth on her next argument. "You are our best spy, that's true. You're our best *everything*. That's why I'm entrusting my sister's safety, and recovering our parents, to you. Because I know you're the best person we've got to make sure it happens."

Chandra hadn't said anything. When she finally did speak, it had been to reluctantly agree.

Now, as we were about to depart, she grumbled once more, "I still say I'd be more useful if I stayed with your group."

"I know you would be," Laydon said, surprisingly gentle. "But I'm counting on you to get Adalynn and Enlar to Rothschan safely."

"Playing nursemaid to a pair of baby magicians," Chandra muttered as she mounted her horse and spurred it forward.

Enlar and I exchanged skeptical looks. Catching our glances, Laydon said, "She'll grouse about it, but she'll be there when you need her."

"If you say so," Enlar said under his breath. He gave me one last loaded look, then mounted his own horse and followed after Chandra.

First Fiala, then Laydon, embraced me. Holding me at arm's length, my brother said, "Be safe."

"That's easy for you to say." I sounded as grumpy as Chanrda. "You're not the one who's returning to certain death."

"I wouldn't say it's *certain*. Just because Renton's tried to kidnap you and attacked your new home, doesn't mean he wants you dead."

"That doesn't make me feel any better." I sighed. "I can think of a million things that could go wrong, but I understand. This is probably the best plan we've got."

Laydon sighed as well. "If I could think of some way to keep you out of harm's way, you know I would do that in a heartbeat. But we have to save Mother and Father, if we can. And then—hopefully we can find a way to stop whatever Renton—and Rothschan—are planning."

I laughed weakly, trying to stop the tears that threatened to fall. "Since when did you become a rebel leader? I thought you were just a magic teacher."

My brother's face remained somber. "Why can't I be both? We become what we need to be when the situation calls for it."

He gave me one more big hug, then helped me mount my horse. I spurred my horse forward, turning at the gate to wave to Laydon and Fiala. They waved back, with Fiala blowing me a kiss goodbye.

Enlar and Chandra were waiting for me just down the main road that led south from Calia's gates. Enlar noticed me surreptitiously wiping tears from my eyes. "Are you okay?"

"Yes," I said, a slight sniffle in my voice. "I just hope I'll see them again. Soon."

"You will," Chandra said sardonically. "In what condition remains to be seen." She clicked at her horse to set it in motion, leaving Enlar and me staring at her retreating back.

"This is going to be a long week," Enlar commented.

"I agree." I spurred my mount, catching up to Chandra.

"Chandra." She didn't look at me, but I knew she was listening. "Thank you. For coming with us, when you'd rather have stayed with Laydon's group."

"You're welcome. I guess," Chandra said ungraciously. She pursed her lips. "I just don't like being away from ... everybody. A lot can happen in even just a day. If something does, I won't be around to help."

I glanced behind us. Enlar was following at a careful distance, close enough to keep us in sight, but far enough away to allow Chandra and me to have a private conversation.

I lowered my voice. "I understand that you want to be there to help my brother. Because you're in love with him."

Chandra's eyes widened. This time she did look at me, horrified that I knew her secret.

"No one said anything," I quickly reassured her. "I figured it out on my own."

"Please don't say anything to anyone."

"I won't," I promised. "But, if it helps, would you want to talk about it?"

She took a deep breath. "They're engaged, did you know that? Fiala and ... your brother."

She faced forward again, her back rigid as she rode. Now that she wasn't looking at me, the words came out in a rush, as if she had held them back for a long time. "Fiala and I used to run the boardinghouse together, even before Queen Jennica opened the magic school. We didn't get as much business as Fiala does now, but it was enough to keep the boardinghouse running.

"I overheard Laydon telling you how he came to Calia. Well, his former tutor was our parents' next door neighbor." At my gasp, Chandra nodded, still carefully not looking at me. "Yes, Fiala is my sister. And Laydon moved in next door to our parents' home while he was learning magic. I met Laydon when I moved home; our father had an accident, and I returned home to help around the house while he recovered. Our mother had passed away a few years earlier. I couldn't leave him alone to fend for himself."

"Very commendable of you," I said.

"Is it? It's hard enough to put your own life on hold to help another, no matter how much you love them. It's harder still to watch the man of your dreams fall in love with your sister." She blinked, and a single tear spilled down her cheek. "It was inevitable, I suppose. If they hadn't met when Fiala came to visit, they would have met some other way around Calia. I was just lucky enough to witness them falling in love." Bitterness tinged her voice, but underneath I could hear her hurt and sadness as well.

"Then why stick around?" I wondered. "I understand your father was hurt, but surely once he was well you were free to leave. You didn't have to stay in Calia, much less its capital. And you certainly didn't have to join Laydon's group and become his second-in-command."

Chandra snorted softly. "I made a promise."

"To your father?"

"No. He eventually recovered, but his injuries left him weak and he passed away about a year after I returned home. When he died, Fiala was inconsolable. I was grieving, too, but I think I was better prepared to come to terms with it. Anyway, she can't handle any more loss—first our mother, then our father. If she lost Laydon, it would break her. So I promised her I'd keep an eye on him, and make sure he stayed alive."

I eyed Chandra curiously. "Is it really that dangerous, teaching at the Academy?"

Chandra turned to face me. "Teaching at Queen Jennica's school was never Laydon's ultimate goal. You know that."

I swallowed. "I do know that, now." It was part of the reason we were going back to Rothschan at this very moment. I met her gaze. "And I hope you know that I am your friend, no matter what. I would be honored if you would allow me to consider you my friend as well."

Chandra didn't respond, just sniffed and wiped at her eyes with the back of her hand.

I turned slightly in my saddle and caught Enlar's eye. He raised his eyebrow, a question on his face. I nodded, letting him know my private conversation with Chandra was done.

As Enlar approached, I asked, "Do you think we need to worry about being followed?"

"It's possible they're tracking us somehow," Chandra said. Her voice was steadier now that we were talking about strategies and not emotions. "After all, they were able to find you in Calia." She eyed me suspiciously. "You're not still marked, are you?"

I shook my head. She relaxed.

Enlar offered, "Laydon showed me how to create wards, and I can teach Adaylnn. Between the two of us, we should be able to handle any trouble, at least magically."

Chandra shook her head. "I'll be honest, I don't think we're being followed. Still practice your magic, of course. And we should definitely keep a watch at night, as well as be vigilant while on the road. But I don't think the person who delivered Adalynn's message is still here."

"Why not?" Enlar and I spoke at the same time.

She shrugged as she glanced at me. "There's really no point. Either you show up at the Iron Bridge at the appointed time, or you don't. You stand more to lose than they do. If you show up, then they get you and can set whatever nefarious plan they have in motion. If you don't, you lose your parents, and they don't have to worry about their hostages anymore."

Enlar whistled. "Crass, but true."

Chandra shrugged again, not seeming to care about Enlar's assessment of her. "I learned long ago there's no sense in prettying up reality. It's much better if you face it head on, and accept it as it is."

"Ah, well ... I suppose that's one way of looking at it."

"It's the only way of looking at it." She clicked her tongue at her horse, spurring it into a trot as she left Enlar and me behind.

Enlar made a move like he was going to follow, but I stopped him. "Let her be for a bit."

He stared at her retreating back, now a good ways down the road. "What did I say to make her so upset?"

"Nothing. Nothing at all."

29

— · —

Chapter Twenty-Nine

We made good time as we traveled back to Rothschan. When Fiala had informed Taryn that we would be leaving Calia and heading back to my home country, Taryn had in turn informed Queen Jennica, who gifted us with a generous purse to aid us in our travels. So the return journey was much easier—and more comfortable, thanks to spending the majority of our nights at various roadside inns—than the original trek to Calia had been.

Not having to camp at night had an additional advantage. While Enlar and I still set wards at night, it was mostly for practice. The inns we stayed at were well populated, making Chandra even more confident that no one was following us. "And even if they were, they'd be stupid to try anything with so many people about."

Even though I remained wary, Chandra was right. Nobody tried to attack us, and our wards remained untouched each night.

Near the end of the week, we reached the outskirts of Rothschan's capital city. I urged my horse to move faster, impatient to reach the end of our journey. Dread settled in my stomach as we approached the small village where my family lived.

Used to live.

Don't think that way, I chided myself. *We'll get them back.*

Somehow.

I swallowed the lump that had lodged itself in my throat as we approached. My childhood home appeared untouched and serene, if a bit quiet. A random passerby would think that maybe the inhabitants were still sleeping, even though it was late morning. Or perhaps the inhabitants were on a trip. If Renton or his lackeys had forced their way in to capture my parents, the peaceful façade of the house didn't betray that.

The curtains of my neighbor's house twitched back, and a pale face peered out at us, partially obscured by the blue fabric. I dismounted and started toward her house, calling, "Brynn? It's me, Adalynn."

But the curtains abruptly shut, slightly twitching, then stilled. Despondent, I turned away, knowing that if Brynn was unwilling to welcome me, none of my other neighbors would help me either.

I moved toward the door of my house. Behind me, Enlar hastily dismounted and said, "Adalynn, wait!"

But I had already turned the handle and walked inside.

I was so stunned by the scene before me it didn't even register right away that the front door had been unlocked.

Although by the look of things inside, it wouldn't have mattered if the door had been locked. Not anymore.

While the front door showed no signs of damage, the interior of my childhood home hadn't been so fortunate. The curtains could barely keep out the daylight, now that they had been slashed to ribbons. By the fireplace, my mother's and father's twin plush chairs had been cut open, with the feathers that had stuffed them scattered on the floor or bursting through the split seams. The wooden side tables, a gift my father had carved for my mother, had been knocked over, the legs dangling haphazardly or broken off altogether. It looked like someone had taken an axe to them. Shards of jade green glass lay near one of the tables, along with a bouquet of trampled, withered daisies. I recognized the dried flowers from my mother's garden, and knew the green glass was the remnants of the vase passed down from my grandmother.

My heart hurt at the destruction.

Numbly, I walked through the rest of the house. As I entered the kitchen, I heard footsteps at the front door, but didn't bother to turn around. "Adalynn." Enlar's voice trailed off as he, too, took in the state of the house.

The kitchen hadn't fared much better, showing the same signs of willful damage that the front room had. Except in the kitchen it was much worse, as the cupboards, pantry, and icebox had all been raided. If whoever-had-done-this couldn't take the food, then they had made sure no one could. Dried egg yolk painted the counters, and a sticky substance was ground into the cupboard doors. Closer inspection made me think someone had smashed some apples into the wood. A thin trail of ants were making their way up the cupboard, while a sour smell permeated the air. If the cluster of flies hadn't alerted me, the yellow-white liquid and broken glass let me know that the gooey puddle on the floor used to be fresh milk.

I walked down the hallway, desperate to know how badly my childhood bedroom had been damaged. Nothing else in this house had been sacred, but how much of my former life had they violated?

When I reached my bedroom, I held my breath, afraid of what I might see. Heart racing, my sweaty palm slid off the cool door handle. I wiped my hand on my pants and grasped it again. *One ... two ...*

I turned the handle and pushed the door open, gasping in surprise.

My room was untouched.

Sure this was a trick, I looked around my bedroom wildly, looking for any sign of damage. But, at least to my fevered overview, it looked just as it had before.

I dashed across the hall and opened the door to my parents' bedroom. Their room, too, was unscathed.

Footsteps sounded in the hallway behind me. Enlar peered over my shoulder. "Well, that's interesting. I wonder why they didn't destroy these rooms?"

Chandra spoke up behind Enlar, causing us both to jump. "It's possible they ran out of time." We both turned to look at her. "And the horses are tied up out front, by the way. You're welcome."

Enlar surveyed the room, then looked down the hallway. "You didn't touch anything, did you, Adalynn? Chandra, how about you?"

"Besides the door handles to these rooms, no," I replied, confused.

Chandra snorted. "You two left the doors wide open, so I didn't have to touch anything. Not that I'd want to. What a mess."

"Good." He frowned. "I'd like to check for any residual magic, and it will be easier if you both leave everything alone. Once I'm done, we can clean up the place."

Chandra groaned. "Do we have to?"

"We have a few days before that meeting," Enlar pointed out. "And this is probably our best place to camp out in the meantime."

"You sure about that? What if the place is being watched?"

Enlar stilled, mumbling a spell under his breath as he stretched his hands out, palms up, toward the door. After a moment, he withdrew his hands and shook his head. "I don't sense anything. We're safe, at least from magical means. I'll set some stronger wards later tonight, after I've had a chance to rest."

"Well then, what about good old-fashioned spying? People skulking about in the forest, and all that?"

I looked around at the sorry mess that was my childhood home. "Maybe, but I doubt it. After all, they got what they wanted. My parents. Why keep watching the place?"

Chandra muttered something under her breath. I couldn't quite make out the words, but it sounded something like, "Can't help people who insist on making stupid decisions."

I ignored the comment. My throat tight, I said, "We can't leave my home in such a state. Enlar, if you're satisfied with your magical investigations?" He nodded. "All right, then. Let's get to cleaning."

Chandra groaned again, shaking her head. She grumbled as she stalked down the hallway. "Nursemaid and house cleaner, that's all I'm apparently good for. When I see Laydon next ..."

30

---·---

Chapter Thirty

We didn't get to cleaning right away, though. Enlar insisted on doing one more magical sweep before we did anything, and a thorough investigation left him satisfied that there were no magical traps waiting for us. However, he did find evidence that a spell had been in use recently.

"But I can't tell if the spell was cast here, or if an object infused with magic was brought in and used," he said, as he looked around the damaged drawing room.

"Does it matter?" Chandra asked from the kitchen doorway. She grasped a handful of rags in one hand and an old broom in another.

"It could, when you consider the proficiency required to do each. Casting a spell requires control and ability, while using an object containing magic requires less. Depending on the spell contained within, you might not need any magical ability at all."

His eyes met mine, and I caught his meaning. "Magic is forbidden in this kingdom. Are you saying that someone, connected to Rothschan's government, is using magic?"

"It seems possible," Enlar said. "My guess is that it was used on your parents in some way, perhaps to subdue them. The damage here and in the kitchen was purely out of spite, but no magic was used to destroy things."

"So whoever did this is either a proficient magician, or has the assistance of one," I said slowly. "Both of those are punishable offenses, although the first one would get a more severe penalty. But why risk the Crown's wrath like that? Who would do that, and what do they hope to gain from it?"

"We still have time to figure out all those answers," Chandra said. "In the meantime—" she shook the rags and broom she was holding "—I'd like to get this over with, if either of you don't mind?"

Even though I was distraught by the damage to my family home, I was also strangely glad to have something to fill my days. I couldn't leave the house, since I'd be recognized. I was worried that my neighbors might report my return, but as the days wore on and nothing happened, I relaxed a bit. Perhaps they didn't want to call any trouble on their own heads by drawing attention back to the area.

When I offhandedly mentioned this to Enlar, he said, "I doubt it. If anything, your neighbors would have a lot to gain by letting the authorities know you're back. But don't worry, I've taken care of it."

"Taken care of it?" I echoed, confused. Enlar didn't seem like a naturally violent sort.

He grinned. "Part of the wards I put up on this place. In addition to protecting us from attacks and intruders, it also keeps curious eyes, both magical and mundane, from noticing us."

"Really? How?" A spell like that would take a lot of power to set up and maintain.

"I modified an invisibility spell," Enlar said. "Instead of the house, and its inhabitants, being completely invisible to outsiders, there's just a suggestion that we're not there. If anyone tries to look at this house, or its surrounding area, they just ... get distracted. The power of suggestion over actually changing the physical environment. The spell makes them think nothing's there. It takes less magic to create, which is why I was able to extend the spell from the house all the way to the road leading into Rothschan."

"Wow," I said, impressed. "That sounds like a major magical accomplishment."

He shrugged modestly, but I could tell he was pleased at my praise. "I'd be happy to show you how to do it, if you like."

I smiled back. "I'd love that."

While I stayed home, practicing the limited magic I knew, tending the overgrown garden or fixing things, Chandra and Enlar went into the capital city to get supplies and to try to glean some gossip from the merchants.

To blend in, Chandra, who was around my height, borrowed some items from my closet, giving her grudging approval to the practicality of my outfits. Enlar's attempt to adopt Rothschan attire wasn't as successful—he was several inches taller than my father, and his borrowed clothes made him look like a teenager who had gone through an unexpected growth spurt. I giggled when he emerged from my parents' bedroom fully dressed in one of Father's outfits. Enlar's expression forbade comment.

His unluckiness extended to talking to the locals, but Chandra proved to be surprisingly adept at gathering information. People found her charming, Enlar told me one day when Chandra had gone into town by herself. His wondering tone reflected my own awe when he relayed that to me.

"When did you leave here, again?" Chandra asked me over dinner.

I counted out the days on my fingers as I thought it over. "About three weeks ago, give or take a few days. Why do you ask?"

"Just three weeks? Interesting."

"Interesting? What's so interesting about it?" Enlar asked.

Chandra popped a stewed carrot in her mouth. She chewed slowly, deliberately savoring every bite. Enlar and I both watched her in suspense, waiting for her to share her news.

She finished her bite, swallowed, and reached for another one. I made a small noise of protest. Enlar cleared his throat, brows raised.

Chandra put her fork down and grinned. "I just wanted to see how long you two could hold out. Apparently not long. No patience, either of you."

Enlar sighed. I could sympathize. Chandra in a good mood was more unsettling than her usual sour one, but it was so rare that I felt it should be indulged. Even if it was maddening.

"Well, then?" Enlar drummed his fingers on the table impatiently.

Chandra sobered instantly. "It's interesting news, but it's not necessarily good. Apparently right after you left, Adalynn, the raids started happening."

I frowned. "Raids? Why?"

"No one really knows why. And no one really wants to talk about it, at least not openly. I was lucky to get Neera, one of the merchants, to tell me anything. I think she was afraid I would draw attention with my ignorance.

"But from what Neera said, the raids have been happening fairly frequently. Every few days or so, and a handful of people get taken every time. Men and women, mostly adults, but some in their late teens, and even some elderly, too. No one very young, though. There's no reasoning behind it either, as the ones hauled off haven't caused any trouble—some were even staunch loyalists to Rothschan. But they're taken away, and they haven't returned."

My mind racing, I gazed out the window toward where my neighbor's house was. That explained why Brynn hadn't wanted to open the door to me. And it also explained why Brynn, or any of my other neighbors, hadn't reported my return to the authorities, although by now Enlar's spell would have made any of them forget I was here. To make a report would have brought attention to them. And it didn't sound like anyone in Rothschan wanted to attract any attention at all right now.

"Is this normal?" Enlar asked me, interrupting my thoughts.

"Raids? No," I said. "At least, I've never known of it happening as long as I've been alive. My parents might know if it's happened in the past, but ..." I shrugged, uncomfortable with finishing my statement.

"Adalynn's right," Chandra put in. "Neera and the other merchants said raids are unusual. From what I understand, they're unusual because they're unnecessary. If you choose to live in Rothschan, then you choose to abide by all of the country's rules. Spoken or unspoken."

I nodded. Rothschan had a reputation in the Gifted Lands for being a harsh place to live, but what outsiders didn't always understand was that many of us *liked* the black-and-white, "this is the law and the law is absolute" culture of our country. It made things easier for us, knowing exactly what was acceptable and what was not, with no gray areas or deviations.

So, then. The Rothschan authorities weren't gathering people up because they were rebels or lawbreakers, necessarily. But if the people they were arresting weren't troublemakers, then why would they be in trouble?

"What should we do?" I wondered aloud.

"Do?" Chandra snorted. "Nothing. For right now, anyway. Best just to keep our heads down and try to lay low. Get through your meeting, and then ... we'll see."

Slowly, I nodded again, trying to ignore the queasiness growing in my stomach and the dread filling my chest. Chandra was right about the best course of action. But that didn't make me feel any better.

31

CHAPTER THIRTY-ONE

SIGHING, I LET THE curtain fall back into place, and turned away from the window overlooking the front of the house. Twilight had darkened into true night, and there was still no sign of Laydon or his group. Not that I had necessarily expected them to be in Rothschan by now, or to just show up on my doorstep. But still. I hoped they were all right, wherever they were.

I also hoped *I* would be all right. In a few short hours, I would head to the Iron Bridge to meet with the mysterious messenger, and hopefully get my parents back. I knew I should try to sleep, at least a little, but anticipation and worry had me too wound up to rest.

Since I was alone in the house, every shadow made me jumpy. I had to calm down, or I would be too riled up to think straight during my clandestine midnight meeting. I desperately wanted to get it over with so I could return home.

If I returned home.

Don't think that way. Everything will be fine.

I hope.

Chandra and Enlar had just left the house. Chandra had gone to take up position near the Iron Bridge, where she could keep an eye on me from a hidden location. Enlar had accompanied her, even though she had insisted she could take care of herself and didn't need his chivalry. I think he wanted to get familiar with the route at night, though, since he would be returning to the house so he could follow me discreetly as I made my own way to the Iron Bridge later on. Partly for my protection, and partly to observe if anyone else was following me.

I reached for a lamp on a nearby table, with the intent of lighting it, when I heard a fumbling at the back door, the one leading into the kitchen. I froze, heart pounding. It couldn't be Chandra; she wouldn't abandon her post. And I doubted it was Enlar, either—it was too soon for him to return from escorting Chandra.

Should I call out to whoever it was? As I was debating, I heard the lock click open, and the door handle turned slowly. No, definitely not my friends. They would have no need to sneak around. I grabbed the unlit lamp from the table and crept toward the back of the house. The person entering quietly closed the door, then started walking through the kitchen. They moved deliberately, as if they had a vague idea of the room's layout but weren't entirely confident of where they were going.

At the kitchen's entrance, I stopped and stepped to the side of the doorway, doing my best to blend into the room's shadows.

I tensed, raising the lamp above my head.

"*Illumine.*" The intruder's whisper caused a cold ball of light to flare into existence, temporarily blinding me. I swung the lamp, aiming for the spot where I remembered the person had been standing. I heard a hasty curse, and felt the impact up my arms as my swing—and makeshift weapon—were deflected.

Blinking furiously as my eyes adjusted, I wildly swung again, only to have the lamp knocked out of my hands. It clattered to the floor somewhere to my left. I reached out to hit the intruder, and the person easily clamped a hand over my wrist, effectively stopping me.

"Adalynn, stop! It's me, Laydon!"

I struggled to break the intruder's grasp, and then the words registered in my brain and I stopped fighting him. My eyes had now adjusted enough to see my brother's wide-eyed face just inches from my own. When he was sure that I wasn't going to fight him anymore, he released my wrist and stepped back.

"Laydon?" I squeaked, trying to calm down from the adrenaline still surging through me.

"Yes." He squinted at me through the pool of magical light hovering between us. "Is this how you normally greet your visitors?"

"Visitors usually use the front door. In broad daylight." I peered over his shoulder to assess the back door, which didn't show any signs that Laydon had forced his way in. "Why didn't you call out? How did you get in here, anyway?"

My brother shrugged. "Lucky guess. When you see our parents next, tell them they really should get more creative about their hiding spots."

I grimaced. There was a spare key hidden in the lantern to the left of the back door, and had been there for as long as I could remember. Which meant it had probably been there when Laydon had lived here, too.

"I'm impressed you remembered that," I commented.

He laughed, a rich echo in the darkness. "You wouldn't be if you knew how many times I had snuck in that way."

I knelt down and felt around for my dropped lamp. Laydon pushed his magical light towards the floor, and a metal glint near one of the chairs caught my attention. I picked it up and lit the lamp, then moved around the room to light the wall sconces. With the room softly illuminated from the various firelight, Laydon extinguished his magical light and sat down.

"Well, I made it here," he announced unnecessarily.

"Apparently so, and then you decided to scare your sister silly before her big meeting," I grumbled. "You know, the one where she's going into certain danger. That's fine, though. It's not like I can calm down enough to rest before it, anyway."

"That's why I'm here. The rest of the group is about a day or so behind me. When I realized the group was traveling too slow to get here in time, I left Gaelen in charge, then took one of the horses and traveled day and night to get here. I've barely slept. But I'm here, and that's what matters."

"Thank you, I really do appreciate it. Now that I know you're you and not a burglar or an assassin."

"I've been called upon to be both on occasion, but not tonight," Laydon said cheerfully. At my sharp look, he added, "Relax. I've never been an assassin."

"Yet."

He chuckled. "Remind me to tell you some stories later. For now, what's the plan?"

I outlined what Enlar, Chandra, and I had decided to do in preparation for tonight's meeting, and where they currently were.

"Since Chandra's got the bridge covered, why don't I go with you and Enlar?" Laydon said. "I know it's been a while, but I probably know this area better than Enlar does. And it will be better to have two sets of eyes looking out for you."

"That sounds like a good idea to me," I said. "When Enlar gets back, you two can decide who will do what."

"Great." Laydon stretched out in his chair, slouching down as his long legs sprawled out in front of him. "Wake me up when he's here."

He closed his eyes, and within moments his breathing had evened out into the rhythmic pattern of sleep.

"He makes it look so easy," I grumbled as I settled into another chair. I closed my eyes as well, but my racing thoughts made it impossible for me to drift off into slumber.

The sound of a key turning in the lock in the front door startled me out of the semi-doze I was in. The lights in the wall sconces had burned low, putting the room in near-darkness.

I looked over to see Enlar stepping through the front door. "Did everything go all right?" I asked, yawning. "I take it Chandra is in place?"

Enlar nodded as he shut the door. "She is, and I didn't see anything suspicious on my return trip." Noticing the other chair was occupied, he frowned. "Who's that?"

"It's Laydon. You remember Laydon, right?" I reached out and nudged my brother. "Hey, wake up."

Laydon groaned as I poked him awake. "Yeah, yeah, I'm awake. What do you want?"

"You told me to wake you when Enlar got here," I said unrepentantly. "Well, he's here."

"Thanks," Laydon said dryly. He cracked a yawn, then sat up slowly. "Give me a moment to wake up, and then we can make our plans."

I offered my seat to Enlar, who took it gratefully. While he was resting and my brother was still shaking off his sleepiness, I went to the kitchen and quickly put together a tray of refreshments for everyone, grabbing some leftover rolls, apples, three cups and a pitcher of water.

By the time I returned, Laydon was more awake and discussing the night's plans and route with Enlar. I put the tray down on an end table and sat down, listening in on their conversation.

"I'll stay to the southwest side, near where Chandra is," Laydon was saying. He grabbed an apple off the tray and bit into it. "It'll be good to have more coverage on that side anyway, since if someone tries to escape in the other direction, they'd run into the city wall fairly quickly."

"That sounds good," Enlar agreed. "Shall we go together, or would you prefer one of us goes a bit ahead while the other stays behind with Adalynn?"

Laydon frowned. "That's a good question. Two of us blundering about in the dark would attract more attention than just one person. It's been many years, but I grew up here, so it's likely I know this area better than you do."

"But, as you just said, it *has* been a while, and some things have probably changed around here," I pointed out.

"A fair point."

"If you think it's best we go separately, I can go ahead, and alert you to anything I see on your route," Enlar said. "I just came back from the bridge, so I know my way from here to there, at least."

"All right," Laydon said. "If you see something, come back and warn us. Otherwise, we'll meet you at the bridge."

"Oh, that reminds me." Enlar reached into his pocket and withdrew a closed fist full of something. "Hold out your hands, Adalynn."

I did, and he poured a bunch of little rocks into them. "What's this for?"

"When Chandra and I checked out the bridge, I saw all these pebbles and thought they might be useful. Toss them on the bridge if you're in trouble. We'll hear the echo against the bridge's metal slats and come to your aid."

"Huh." I stuffed the pebbles into my pocket. "Thanks."

With our plans settled, Laydon finished his apple while Enlar started in on a bread roll. The hours passed by in a quiet camaraderie. I still didn't get any sleep in, but the time flew by anyway, and soon it was time for Enlar, and then Laydon, to slip into the night.

I moved around the room, extinguishing the various lights while counting to one hundred to allow both men time to get into their places. As I neared the end of my count, I shuttered the last lamp and quietly left the house as well.

32

— • —

Chapter Thirty-Two

Even though the night air was mild, I couldn't shake off the chill of apprehension that crept down my spine. Knowing Laydon was nearby helped, but I still felt very much alone as I set out on the half hour walk to Rothschan's capital city. I also felt very vulnerable. It had been decided that I should go unarmed to the midnight meeting—or at least, have the appearance of being unarmed. All I had on my person was a single dagger hidden in my boot. I just hoped that if things went poorly, I'd be able to grab my weapon in time.

Or get out of there in one piece.

Breathe. Don't think that way. Just focus, one foot at a time.

The full moon overhead bathed the area in a hazy glow, allowing me enough light to follow the road that led to the city. The walk there was both interminably long and surprisingly short. Each footstep sounded loud in my ears, and every shadow seemed to hide some unknown threat. And yet I soon found myself just outside the capital.

Before reaching the main gate, I turned off the road, following a smaller path around the city walls that would take me to the old palace. Along the way, I passed a smaller, rusty-looking gate set into the wall. Most people used the main gate to gain entry or leave the city, but it made sense that there might be other exits, especially if people needed to access the old palace quickly and didn't want to go around half of the city. I had never noticed the rusted gate before, but then again, I had never thought to explore this part of the capital.

It was nearing midnight, and I was near my destination. The Iron Bridge loomed before me, and behind it, the old palace. The shadows didn't betray its true condition, but if I had been here in the daytime, I would have seen the ivy taking over the walls and windows of the building, and noticed the dilapidated roof.

But what I did notice was the tall person standing at the far end of the bridge.

My steps faltered, and I swallowed hard, trying to fight my rising feelings of panic. I willed myself to keep putting one foot in front of the other, instead of turning and running all the way back to my childhood home, locking the door, and lighting every single lamp until the house was in danger of catching fire.

As I approached, the shadow turned, presumably to face me. They were wearing a dark cloak, and their face was hooded. At this distance, I couldn't make out any details about my mysterious contact.

The hooded person called out to me, softly, but their voice carried clearly through the still night air. It was deep, definitely male, and vaguely familiar. "Are you alone?"

"Yes." My voice was unsteady, and I hoped he would take it as nerves and not as me being a poor liar.

The shadowy figure didn't say anything, just stood tall and still, waiting for my approach. A quick glance around told me that he, too, was alone. "Where are my parents?"

"They're ... close by."

I stopped before setting foot on the bridge, facing down its length at the mysterious person on the other side. My eyes narrowed. "Are they well? Unharmed?"

"Yes. For now."

I lifted my chin defiantly. "Let me see them."

The man laughed unpleasantly. "Don't worry, you'll see them soon enough."

I ground my teeth, fighting to keep my fear and anger in check. Losing control of my emotions and my abilities wouldn't help me right now, and it definitely wouldn't help my parents. My next question came out slowly, each word precise and deliberate as I tamped down my feelings. "What is it that you want?"

The figure started walking toward me, his footsteps echoing off the metal slats of the bridge. "Why, my dear girl, what do you think? You."

His familiar voice teased at the edges of my memory. My mind raced, remembering all the times I had heard it before. Just recently, that grating whisper of my would-be kidnapper. And, before that, in an office lit up by the flames of my fear....

His hood fell back, revealing Renton's disfigured face.

The man who had sent the message spell. Who had tried to destroy Fiala's house in an effort to lure me out after his kidnapping attempt had failed. Who had denied me my proper place in Rothschan society, because of a decades-long grudge against my brother.

And who now held my parents captive.

I started to turn, intending to run. Or at least, I tried. As I moved, Renton pointed at me and snapped his fingers, muttering something unintelligible under his breath. My body instantly seized up, and I realized with growing horror that I couldn't move at all.

My heart raced in fear as I stared at Renton leisurely approaching me. *He's such a powerful magician! How can I ever hope to stand against him?*

And then my mind caught up to the rest of me, and another thought surfaced: *How does Renton know magic?*

The moonlight cast strange alternating pockets of illumination and shadow on his face, occasionally highlighting the manic gleam in his eyes. He stopped just inches from my frozen form.

"How—" I stopped, surprised my voice still worked. For some reason, I thought I had been rendered mute, since the rest of my body wouldn't obey. My voice sounded unnaturally loud in the quiet of darkness. "How did you do that?"

He smirked. "You'd like to know, wouldn't you?"

I caught a whiff of his sour breath, and wished I could plug my nose or turn my face away. The cheap whiskey he had imbibed before our meeting wafted off him, and despite the danger I knew I was in, one small part of me snidely wondered if he had needed the liquid courage in order to face me.

I also wondered how I could alert my companions to my trouble. The pebbles Enlar had given me lay in my pocket, ready to be used to signal my friends to come to my aid. But with my body frozen, I wouldn't be able to grab them, let alone throw anything. I could still yell for help, but that would be a last resort, especially with Renton so close to me. He could easily plunge a knife into my heart the moment the scream left my mouth.

No, I would have to wait for a more opportune moment.

Renton waggled his fingers at me. "As you can see, I know a few tricks."

How? I thought in disbelief. I didn't realize I had actually spoken the words aloud until Renton answered me.

"I've been studying magic for quite some time. It's the first rule of battle—know your enemy. I spent close to two decades trying to figure out a way to destroy magic. But in the last few years, I realized: why destroy it when I can harness its power, instead?"

"Y-You've learned magic?" I spoke as loud as I dared without outright yelling, hoping that my raised tone would catch my friends' attention. "Why would you do that?"

Renton snorted. "Asks the stupid girl who blew up my office with her own, out-of-control magical powers. You of all people should know how exhilarating it is to have that kind of power."

"It's not always exhilarating," I muttered. I raised my voice again. "So you have no qualms about breaking the ironclad laws of Rothschan. What does that have to do with me, or my parents? And where are they? I did as you asked and came here tonight. I expect you to release them as you said you would."

"I don't think you're in much of a position to bargain." Renton circled me slowly, relishing his control over me. Sarcasm dripped from his voice. "But since you were so kind as to come here tonight, I'll give you a little bit of information. Your parents are alive and ... well, perhaps not *well*, but they're alive. As my ... guests."

"What do you mean? *Where are they*?"

"Don't worry, my dear, you'll see them soon enough. I'm sure they'll be delighted to see you."

Renton clamped a hand around my arm. I stumbled forward as his spell on me broke, allowing me to move again. Instantly I twisted in his grasp, but I wasn't strong enough to break his hold on me.

"Let go of me!" I cried out. I braced myself as best I could, trying to slow us down.

Renton's grip on my arm grew tighter. "I'd prefer not to waste any more magic on you, but if you won't shut up and come quietly, I will. And I promise you, you won't like it."

Were those footsteps coming up behind us? I fervently hoped so.

As Renton dragged me along, I reached into my pocket. My hand closed around a handful of pebbles. As the footsteps became louder,

I threw the pebbles at Renton's face. He swore as he stepped back, trying to avoid the gravel showering his face. Unfortunately, though, he didn't loosen his hold on my arm, and my shoulder was practically wrenched out of its socket as he yanked me with him.

"Hurry up!" I yelled over my shoulder.

Chandra was the first one to reach us. She pulled a dagger from inside her sleeve as she ran and threw it. I flinched, but I needn't have worried: her aim was true. The knife sliced through the air, and was about to embed itself deep in Renton's shoulder—

—When it stopped just inches from his arm and clattered harmlessly to the ground.

I gasped.

Chandra pulled another knife and threw. This time, Renton flicked the fingers of his free hand, and the knife abruptly turned around mid-air and arced back toward her.

"Chandra!" I screamed in warning.

She twisted, dodging just in time. The knife just grazed her, and I saw several inches of light blonde hair fall to the ground to her left. Chandra didn't break stride, though, and came running at us full speed. She jumped up and kicked at Renton's arm, trying to get him to break his hold. With her momentum, I definitely felt the force behind that kick. I yelped at the sudden jolt running up my arm. Chandra yelped as well, since her boot ricocheted off Renton's arm and didn't even touch him. The blow intended for him instead doubled back on her. She flinched back violently, as if an invisible force had pushed her away from Renton. She fell to the ground.

Renton didn't even break stride, just growled at Chandra as he continued to drag me behind him.

Then Laydon and Enlar were there. Enlar hastily helped Chandra to her feet as Laydon ran after Renton and me.

"Don't try attacking him, he's got some kind of magical shield!" I yelled at my brother.

Laydon stopped short, his hand on the hilt of his sword, ready to pull it free. Instead, he muttered something under his breath, culminating in a shout as he pointed at Renton. A bolt of cerulean light shot toward Renton, but didn't make contact. Instead, it fell harmlessly to the side and fizzled out.

Laydon turned stricken eyes on me. "Adalynn, I'm sorry!"

Enlar and Chandra reached Laydon's side, their expressions equally troubled. Knowing their efforts would be futile, none of them raised a weapon or cast a spell.

Renton cackled, and a flash of anger replaced my fear. As he was under quite an impressive protection spell, none of my friends could harm him. But since he was holding me, perhaps that protection spell extended to me too. And if that was true, perhaps that meant I was also unwittingly under his guard....

I focused my attention inward, pulling all my magical power forward as fast as I could. Heat bloomed in my chest and spread across my shoulder, concentrating in my upper arm where Renton still held me in an iron grip.

For a second, I didn't think it was going to work. Renton's hold didn't break, and we were across the bridge and nearly at the old palace.

But then he suddenly screamed in pain and dropped my arm, shaking his hand as if he could make the burning sensation go away by doing so. "Not again, you—"

He broke off, howling again as a knife planted itself in his thigh. Chandra had pulled two more daggers from somewhere about her person. One of them had made its way into Renton's leg. She held the other in her hand, poised to throw.

Laydon and Enlar also had their weapons in hand. Now that his protection spell was broken, Chandra, Enlar, and Laydon advanced.

Renton snarled as he grabbed me once more. The magical heat still infused my body, and he hissed as he spun me around, twisting my arm behind my back before he shoved me at my friends.

They hastily dropped their weapons as I was flung toward them, not willing to risk accidentally injuring me. Enlar caught me as Renton yelled again, disappearing in a flash of red smoke. Chandra and Laydon ran toward the haze, but the smoke quickly cleared, revealing nothing but an empty space where Renton had just stood.

"He's gone." Laydon looked around, as if he couldn't believe what he was seeing. Or rather, what he wasn't seeing. "How could he have just disappeared like that?"

"Apparently he's been studying magic in secret for years, and now has the ability to back it up," I explained. I looked at the entrance to the old palace. "Do you think he just ran inside?"

"I doubt it." Enlar had retrieved Chandra's dropped weapons and now handed them back to their owner. "That would just be too easy."

"I agree." I eyed the dark doorway with apprehension. "But then why would he want to meet me here?"

Chandra moved to the entrance, her hand hovering just above the handle. "Shall we find out?"

33

CHAPTER THIRTY-THREE

"WAIT!" LAYDON SAID BEFORE Chandra could touch the handle. He gently pushed her aside, his own hand hovering just above the door handle as he murmured a spell to check it. The handle glowed briefly, and Laydon stepped back.

"There's a spell on the lock. I'm not sure what it would do to intruders, but it wouldn't be wise to test it to find out." He surveyed the front of the former palace, noting the shuttered windows and the overall unwelcoming feel of the place. "It's probably safe to say that the windows would be warded as well."

"Can we break the wards?" Enlar asked.

"I think so, but it will take time," Laydon said. "How much, I'm not sure." He continued to study the lock, brow furrowed in concentration.

Chandra, who had been examining the door, turned to Laydon. "You magicians are all the same. Taking forever thinking about theory and subtlety. Sometimes the most direct route is the best one." It was her turn to push Laydon aside as she squarely faced the door. To Laydon, Enlar, and me, she said, "Ward the group, and do something to muffle the sound."

We barely had enough time to cast our spells as Chandra stepped back a few paces, then spun and solidly kicked the door just to the right of the magically locked handle. Her boot slammed against the door, and the handle exploded in a shower of gold sparks. Whatever magical attack had been set off by the breached ward jolted our shield. It slid off to the side where it harmlessly went off. The explosion made a dull thump, no louder than a single soft footstep, and then was gone.

Before us, the door to the old palace hung haphazardly open on its now-broken hinges.

Laydon turned to Chandra. "Next time, some advance warning would be nice."

"I did give you advance warning," Chandra said unrepentantly. "Anyway, all of you should get used to quicker spell casting. Keeps you sharp."

She sauntered into the darkness, as if we were visiting someone for afternoon tea instead of looking for a madman. The rest of us exchanged glances, shrugged, and followed her in.

I muttered a quick spell. A cold ball of light flared above my open palm, and after a moment of brief concentration, it floated just above my head.

"Good job," Laydon said behind me.

"Thank you." I beamed with pride, even though I knew in the darkness he couldn't see the expression on my face.

Laydon and Enlar also called forth some lights, giving us enough illumination to see our surroundings.

We were standing in the large foyer of the former royal residence. The building was little more than a glorified mansion: palatial by the country's standards decades ago, but now just another oversized house. One that was falling apart, to boot. Parts of the wooden floor were warped or had rotted away. There were holes in the faded and peeling paisley wallpaper where vermin had chewed away at it over the years.

Enlar swatted away a cobweb that hung from the ceiling. Darkened entryways yawned to the right and left; if the layout was typical of standard Rothschan houses, I guessed they led to the parlor and dining room, with the kitchen in the back. The servants' quarters would either be in the back of the house as well, or upstairs in the attic, with a separate staircase for them so they wouldn't disturb the royal family as they went about their duties. The private rooms for the royal family would be upstairs. I eyed the rickety-looking staircase ahead of us. Parts of the railing were damaged or completely missing, and the wooden steps didn't look much better.

"What a dump," Chandra snorted.

"I understand the current palace is kept in much better condition," I said.

"This doesn't make sense." Enlar was inspecting the staircase, running his hand down the warped wood of the railing.

"What doesn't make sense?" Laydon asked.

Enlar looked up. "How long has this place been vacant?"

"At least as long as I've been alive." I shrugged, looking at Laydon. "Do you know? Was the royal family living here when you still lived here?"

Laydon frowned, thinking. "I vaguely remember the new palace being built when I was little.... I think by the time I was ten or so the new palace was finished and the royal family had moved in."

"So that's been at least, what? Twenty or thirty years since anyone's lived here?" I guessed.

Enlar frowned as well. "If that's true, then this place should be covered in more dust and dirt." He held up his hand, displaying completely clean fingers. "But there's hardly any dust on this railing." He knelt down and ran a hand over one of the stairs. "And not on this, either." He looked at the broken front door thoughtfully. "I'm not familiar with the ways of your country. Would you normally ward an abandoned building?"

I shook my head. "Normally? No, because we don't use magic in Rothschan. And there's not really a problem with theft, or vandalism, or any other crime, really. The punishments for crime are extremely severe. Most people wouldn't chance it, unless they were foolish or desperate. And by now, there would be nothing in a building this old that anyone would want. It would either be in bad shape, or have been taken already."

"What about squatters?"

Again, I shook my head. "If you're that poor that you can't afford housing, the Crown puts you to work. You have to pay off your debt to them over a number of years, but at least you get three meals a day and a roof over your head."

"So then there's no reason for this building to have any protections, either magical or mundane," Enlar mused. He stood up and moved toward one of the darkened rooms. I trailed behind.

Our combined magical lights revealed a dining room. The wooden floor and papered walls were in the same shape as the foyer's had been, but what really drew our attention was the massive wooden table in the center of the room. Polished and gleaming, its sleek lines and lack of decoration meant that it was new, too modern for this house. The furniture styles favored years ago when this residence was in use had tended to be very ornate, with a myriad of carvings to show off the maker's artistry.

Dozens of clear glass bottles in various shapes and sizes littered the top of the table. Most looked like they had once contained something, but were now empty. A few still held small amounts of colored liquids.

In the glow of our magical lights, the liquids sparkled, changing colors constantly. First blue, then green. From another angle, red. Then gold. Some of the bottles had labels on them. Curious, I picked one up and read it aloud.

"T. Quentin." I looked at Enlar. "T. Quentin? What does that mean?"

He shrugged, just as confused as I was. He picked up another bottle. "I don't know. But this one says E. Wexlar. Maybe they're ingredients?"

"Maybe," I said doubtfully. "But I've never heard of any ingredients with these names."

Laydon and Chandra had entered the room after us and now fanned out, examining the various bottles with the same confusion and curiosity. Chandra picked up two bottles. One was empty, with a label. The other was half full of the color-changing liquid, but had no label on it.

"I don't get it. Why is this one labeled, but this one isn't?" She waved her bottles in the air.

At the far end of the table, Laydon held an empty bottle in his hands and was staring at the label as if he couldn't tear his eyes away.

"What do you have there?" I asked my brother.

Slowly, hands shaking, he held the bottle up so the rest of us could see.

There, written in simple black letters against a plain white label, were the words: *A. Taethen*.

34

— · —

Chapter Thirty-Four

I took the bottle from Laydon, my hands unsteady as well. "What does this mean? Why ... why is my name on this?"

"Is there one for you?" Chandra asked Laydon.

Laydon scanned the bottles in front of him. "I see nothing over here. I'd assume if there was, they'd be grouped together. Unless any of you see something at your ends?"

A quick scan by the rest of us in our respective areas did not turn up any bottles labeled *L. Taethen*.

Chandra said, "Maybe he thought you were dead, Laydon."

"What's going on?" I burst out, the bottle—*my* bottle—clenched tightly in my fist.

"They're meant to hold people's magical essences." Laydon spoke quietly. It took me a minute to realize that his low volume meant he was trying to hold in his anger.

"This has to be Renton's doing," I said, my voice tight. "He admitted as much on the bridge. He wants magical power, and this is how he's getting it. All these names ... they must be people with magical power. That's why the raids started, to find them."

"It's him, for sure," Enlar said. "But how?"

"That's the question, isn't it?" Laydon surveyed the bottles on the table. "We'll find him, soon. And make him talk."

We searched the rest of the room, but didn't turn up any other clues. Laydon grabbed a few of the filled bottles, selecting some with labels and some without. "For study later. And I'm sure Queen Jennica will want to know about this."

"I'll search the kitchen," Chandra offered.

"You just want to see if there's anything to eat," Laydon teased.

Chandra snorted. "Not that I'd trust anything in *this* place." She motioned at Enlar. "Come with me? I could use a light."

The two of them disappeared through a doorway in the back of the room. As if by unspoken agreement, Laydon and I both headed back the way we had entered, crossing the foyer and entering the other shuttered room.

At first glance, this room was severely disappointing, compared to the room we had just explored. We were standing in what had once been a parlor or reception room for the royal family, if the gilt edging the walls and fireplace and the heavy velvet curtains were any indication. But the red fabric was faded, hanging in tatters to the floor. The room was devoid of any furniture, and there was a discolored indent in the wall above the mantle where, I guessed, a portrait of the royal family must have once hung.

"There's nothing here." I couldn't keep the disappointment from creeping into my voice.

"Wait." Laydon sniffed the air. "Do you smell that?"

I gave an experimental sniff. Aside from the mustiness of the room and the layers of ancient dust, I caught a faint scent of stale smoke floating in the air.

"Someone's been in here recently," I commented. I looked around the room doubtfully, noting the lack of furniture. "Smoking a pipe?"

"Unlikely." My brother knelt down before the unlit fireplace. He brought his magical light forward and sent it into the recess.

I joined him on the ground and sent my ball of light to join his. "What are we looking for?"

Laydon pushed a partially burnt log to the side. The burnt part crumbled at his touch. The rest of the log rolled away, revealing something thin and pale under our lights.

He fished it out and scrutinized it. "Hmm. Interesting."

I poked around in the fireplace, uncovering more half-burnt sheets of paper. Gingerly, I plucked them out and handed them to Laydon.

He flipped through the various pieces of paper. I peered at the pages in his hands, unable to make anything of the random words and strange symbols on them. "What are they?"

"They look like notes for a spell." Laydon held up two pages side by side, comparing them. The first page was still fairly legible despite the burn marks on the edges, but the second page was darkened from fire and harder to read. "From what I can tell, the same spell. With variations and changes. But I can't tell what the original spell was, or what the final spell ended up being. There's too much missing."

Chandra and Enlar walked into the parlor. Looking down at us, Chandra said, "What's so fascinating about the floor, you two?"

Laydon told her what we had found, finishing with, "I'll need to get in touch with Taryn as soon as I can. Or Fiala, if I can't reach Taryn."

I couldn't help the small laugh that escaped me as I watched Chandra casually toss a small bread roll between her hands. "I thought you said you wouldn't eat anything you found here. Changed your mind?"

In response, Chandra threw the roll at me. I just barely caught it. "No," she said. "But I thought this might be of interest."

The bread definitely wasn't straight from the oven, but it was still surprisingly fresh. It was completely intact; no mice or other vermin had discovered it yet. There was no hint of mold on it, only a slight staleness that suggested it was just a few days old.

"Was there more food?" I asked.

"No," Enlar said. "The larder and cupboards were empty. If there had been any food stored, it's either been long gone, or someone packed everything up and took it away."

"And in a hurry," Chandra added. "The larder and cupboard doors were wide open. We found this on the floor in one corner of the kitchen."

"Packed and in a hurry," Laydon mused as he stood. He offered his hand to help me up. "With every storage area used. That's a lot of food. This place used to house the Rothschan royal family, their servants, and it would also have had to have food on reserve for any unexpected visitors."

We brushed the dust from our clothes as our entire group moved back into the foyer.

"Do you think—"

A groaning noise made the words die in my throat. We instantly stilled, straining to figure out where the sound came from.

We didn't have to wait long. The noise came again, followed by a weak, "Hello? Is ... is someone there?"

I was up the stairs before I thought, calling out, "Hello? Who's there? Hello?"

The decrepit hallways of the former royal residence were eerie in the dark, but fortunately I had a good amount of light to see. Not just from my own magical light, which was still bobbing just above my head. But from the moonlight spilling into the hallways from all the open doors on the second floor. Just like Chandra and Enlar had found the kitchen, the upper level looked to be in a state of disrepair, yet the rooms had been recently occupied and vacated in a hurry.

As I walked down the hall, I peered into the open rooms, but each one was empty, at least of people. I noticed that many of the rooms had chains on the walls. I highly doubted the royal family would have had their private rooms outfitted in such a way, although who knew about the habits of royalty. I ground my teeth, anger bubbling inside me at the atrocities that must have been committed here.

At the end of the hall was a door, left slightly open, but not wide enough for me to see what was inside that room.

The voice called out again, weakly. "Please ... we need help." The last word broke on a cough.

I followed the sound to the last room. I hadn't even been aware that my friends had joined me until I realized the light around the door had grown much brighter.

"Do you think it's a trap?" Enlar asked softly.

"It's always a trap." Chandra nodded at the door, where my hand was hovering just by it, ready to push it open. "But at least we'll know it's coming."

I drew my weapon. My friends did the same. Taking a deep breath, I thrust open the door and moved to the side to allow the others to enter.

Two pitiful, huddled figures were chained to the wall. One lay unmoving, while the wheezing one finally got their coughing under control. The cougher turned a bruised and battered face toward me, scared and wary.

My sword clanged to the ground. "Mother? Father?"

"Adalynn?" My father's voice was weak, but he smiled at me as I rushed to their side. He looked up at the rest of our group, and then his jaw dropped in shock.

"*Laydon?*"

35

—·—

CHAPTER THIRTY-FIVE

LAYDON COUGHED, ALTHOUGH WHETHER it was from the dust we had kicked up or in discomfort, I couldn't tell. "Father. It's been a long time. It's ... good to see you."

"You're alive." Father's voice was full of wonder. "All these years, we had hoped ... I wish your mother could see you right now."

Frantic, I reached out toward Mother. "Are you saying ... is she—?"

"No." Father's body convulsed into a coughing spasm again. Now that I was up close to him, I could see in detail the dark bruises on his eyes and cheeks, his swollen nose, and the dried blood on his face and shoulders. The chains holding his hands to the wall were just short enough that he hadn't been able to wipe his face with his hands. Next to him, Mother was also chained to the wall, but she was curled in a ball, unmoving. The noise of my group's arrival hadn't stirred her out of the deep sleep she seemed to be in.

"What's happened, then? We need to get you out of here." I tried to remain calm as I examined his chains. Laydon knelt down by Mother to do the same.

"The experiments ... took too much ... out of her," Father rasped. At my horrified look, he continued, "Explain ... later. But just know ... you won't be able to ... wake her. Right now."

Indeed, Laydon had been shaking Mother gently, trying to elicit any sort of reaction from her. He shook his head, concerned. "She's breathing, but just barely. I can't tell what, exactly, her injuries are. But there's no help for it, we'll have to move her. And hope we don't hurt her more in the process."

"These are incredibly solid," I said, tugging on the chain. "I don't think I can break them. Does anyone see a key?"

Chandra nudged me gently to the side. "If I may?"

Confused, I stood up and let her take my place on the floor. Chandra looked at Laydon. "Any magic?"

Laydon put his hand on Mother's chains and briefly concentrated. "No."

"Perfect." She eyed the ball of light hovering over Laydon's head. "Some light, please?"

He obligingly sent his light toward her, where it floated right by Father's chains. Chandra pulled a small bit of wire from her pocket and started working on the lock. Impressed, I admired her skill even while wishing she would hurry up. And then I realized ...

"Chandra, are you *humming*?"

Our apparent thief was also cheerfully humming under her breath while she picked the lock on Father's chains. I recognized the tune as a popular drinking song about a fairy sprite and a dragon.

"Do you have to hum? It's a bit ... maddening, don't you think?"

Enlar elbowed me, clearly enjoying my dismay. "Who's around to hear her? Besides, this is a great song!" He joined in, singing lustily when Chandra reached the chorus.

"You don't prefer to use an actual lock pick?" I asked, trying to distract them from their singing.

She shrugged. "I keep losing them. Not worth the hassle of constantly buying them. And now, if you could *please* be quiet. I need to concentrate."

She returned to her lock picking. And her humming.

I glared at Laydon, mostly because both Chandra and Enlar were impervious to my dirty looks. He shrugged apologetically. "She's told me it helps her focus."

Father's chains fell away, now unlocked. Chandra moved to Mother's side to free her.

I sighed in annoyance. "Remind me not to do any more clandestine missions with you two."

The last lock clicked, and Mother's chains fell away.

"She's all set," Chandra said, putting away her wire. She turned to Father to help him to his feet.

I sprang to my father's side to help. I didn't have a waterskin on me—none of my companions had carried extra supplies either—but in the corner of the room was a battered metal bucket with an equally beat up looking ladle. I hastily scooped up some water and brought it to my Father's parched lips. Gratefully, he drank the entire ladleful. He slowly got to his feet, but swayed alarmingly when he was fully upright. Hastily, I put my arm around his waist to steady him. He stood a good head above me, and I was grateful that Chandra was there to help carry some of his weight.

Laydon scooped up Mother, holding her carefully in his arms. I blinked away the sudden tears that sprang to my eyes. She looked incredibly frail. As her head lolled to the side, I saw that the bones of her cheeks had sunken in, most likely from lack of food. I didn't know how long she'd been unconscious, but I guessed she hadn't eaten in several days.

Enlar offered to take my place at Father's side, but I shook my head, even though it would probably have been smarter to let him help. I just didn't want to be away from my family, now that we'd been reunited. "I'm good for now, thanks." Enlar nodded in understanding.

He led the way back downstairs, with Laydon holding Mother right behind him. Chandra and I moved slower, supporting my weakened father between us.

The moon lit our way as we left the old palace, moving as quickly and quietly as we could even with two injured people among us. Although we were watchful, Renton didn't reappear, and we made our careful way around the city and down the road toward home. The trip back took much longer, since we had to make frequent stops for both my father and Laydon to rest. Enlar insisted on helping, either by supporting my father, or with carrying my mother, and eventually both Laydon and I gave in to his offers of assistance.

We finally made it back home under a decidedly lighter nighttime sky. We were all exhausted and desperately needed rest, but with the coming dawn Laydon was also impatient to get in touch with Taryn and through her, Queen Jennica.

After my parents were settled in their bedroom, Laydon pulled the rest of us aside. "I want to know what happened, but they need to sleep, too," he said. "But daylight will be here soon, and Renton may start looking for us. If he isn't already."

"I hate to say it, but we probably shouldn't stay here," I said. "It's too obvious a place to start searching."

"I agree." He frowned. "I wonder why Renton wasn't here already, when we got back?"

Remembering Enlar's forgetful spell, I explained what wards Enlar had placed on the house. "It's late, and it's dark, and perhaps that did the trick."

"Clever idea, but Renton won't be fooled for long. He'll know where the house is, and if he checks for magic, he'll see through it." He frowned. "My group should get here sometime tomorrow. With their help ..."

He looked over to where our parents were sleeping. "I don't want to move Mother and Father again, but it's too risky to stay put. We'll go at first light, right after I contact Taryn."

"Do you think she will know how to help Mother?"

"I hope so, but regardless, we need to call Taryn. It's imperative that Queen Jennica knows what we found. If Taryn can't help with Mother, then I'll contact Fiala."

"What if Mother doesn't wake up?" I whispered. Laydon put his hand on my shoulder and squeezed in sympathy.

Thankfully, the night passed uneventfully. We tried to keep a watch, but by the time the sunlight peeked through a slit in the curtains, Laydon, Enlar, Chandra, and I were all fast asleep.

I had given Chandra my bedroom to use, while Enlar slept on the floor in the sitting room. He had claimed it was more comfortable than trying to sleep in a chair or on the settee.

Father was fully awake by the time Laydon and I stirred. Neither of us had wanted to leave our parents alone overnight, and had just slept on the floor by their bed. I tried to work out the stiffness in my back and neck as I sat up and stretched, knowing it was futile and I'd be paying for my night sleeping on the floor. But the smile on my father's face was worth the pain.

He reached out, taking my hand in one of his and Laydon's hand in the other one. "I thought maybe my mind had finally broke, and I had dreamed seeing the two of you. But here you are."

I pressed my face, damp with tears, to his hand. Laydon embraced him, reluctantly letting go after a long time. My brother's eyes were suspiciously shiny as well.

On the other side of the bed, Mother was still unconscious.

Laydon looked at her still form, swallowing hard. "I'm so sorry, Father, but we're going to have to move you and Mother again. Before Renton finds us here."

Father took a deep breath, which turned into a cough. Wheezing slightly, he said, "No need. Renton was running out of time. He'll have left Rothschan by now."

"How do you know that?"

Father took another deep breath, smiling slightly when he realized it wouldn't turn into another coughing fit. "While I've got the strength, let me tell you what happened."

"Hold on." Laydon quickly cast the calling spell as Enlar and Chandra entered the bedroom, stretching and rubbing their eyes. Chandra took up a watchful position by the door, while Enlar leaned against a wall.

Taryn's face shimmered above Laydon's open palm. She looked fairly put together for such an early morning summons, although closer inspection showed wisps of her hair escaping from her hasty attempt at a bun, and the collar of her dress was slightly crooked. She clapped a hand to her mouth as an impromptu yawn escaped it.

"Good morning, Laydon. Being that it's so early, you must have important news."

"I'm not entirely sure," Laydon admitted. He quickly outlined the events of last night. "But my father has some additional insights, and I thought you would prefer to hear his thoughts and experiences firsthand."

Taryn's face had grown grim during Laydon's tale, and now her frown grew deeper. "Yes, of course."

I sprang to help my father, who was struggling to sit up a bit straighter. He gratefully leaned against me for support, regarding me quizzically.

"It's all right, Father," I said. "You can trust her."

When he still didn't say anything, I said, "Don't worry about her. Don't worry about anyone else in this room. Why don't you just tell *me* what happened?"

My father nodded slowly. "As you say. Well. After you left Rothschan, your mother and I were taken to the former palace. For safe-keeping, we were told, from an unknown enemy. But the enemy was actually our own people.

"We were questioned, tortured, and experimented upon. Pella bore the brunt of it." He turned to look at Mother. Tears shimmered in his eyes. "Adalynn, remember how your magic showed up around your birthday? Did you know your brother also had magic?"

"Still does," I said. "And he's an extremely talented magician."

Father smiled sadly. "We failed you both. Couldn't keep either of you safe. But we honestly had no idea ..." He broke off coughing.

"You didn't fail us," I said softly.

Father squeezed my hand. "Your mother and I know little about magic, but during the experiments, we learned much, rather quickly. Did you know magical ability is passed down through the mother? That's why they put Pella through more trials than me. I tried to fight them, but ..." He swallowed hard.

"They drained her of her dormant magical essence, although they couldn't get all of it. They took what little I possessed—I didn't even know I had magic. They had forced the other prisoners to take some strange concoction, and they tried to get me to take it too. But then they just ... abandoned their plans."

"Why? Why would they do that?" I asked.

Father took a deep breath, his gaze going glassy. He was reliving some horror I couldn't see, couldn't fathom. "Renton was talking one night about it. Bragging, really. He said something about the former king of Calia, Rothschan's Sir Hendon, conducting similar experiments. But whereas Hendon wanted magical power for himself, Renton did something else with that magic. With the blessing of the Rothschan monarchy, and the aid of our country's best researchers, he's found a way to use magic to enhance the Rothschan army while keeping the ability to use magic of their own free will from them. It makes our knights stronger, faster, able to exert themselves further than normal, with little rest or need for food. Wounds seal almost immediately. They're practically invincible."

There was a collective gasp of horror from the rest of us in the room. Taryn's disembodied voice floated in the air. "But Rothschan is already the most feared country in the Gifted Lands when it comes to military might. No one would dare raise a hand against them. So, why would they do this now?"

Father started to answer, but whatever he was going to say was lost in a fit of coughing. Chandra disappeared into the kitchen, returning with a full glass of water. Father took a long drink. When he recovered, Chandra took the glass from his hand. "Thank you, young lady." A rare smile bloomed across her face.

Even though Taryn had asked the question, when Father spoke, it was directly to me. His haunted eyes pierced my soul, and my heart hurt at seeing my strong, proud father now so afraid and defeated.

Father took a deep breath. "Renton said Hendon was a dear friend of his. Hendon stayed in touch with him even though most people shunned Renton after the disgrace of being stripped of the Lord High Seneschal position. Renton plans to use these magical experiments to get back in the Crown's good favor. Rothschan hasn't forgotten the kingdom of Calia's many slights against it—the fall of our beloved knight Hendon, the failed engagement between Prince Anders and Queen Jennica. Rothschan wants revenge. They're marching to Calia as we speak."

36

—·—

Chapter Thirty-Six

For a few moments, no one spoke, or even dared to breathe.

"Oh dear," Taryn said, breaking the silence. "Calia would be hard pressed to withstand such an assault. We don't have a standing army, and we've never trained our people in any sort of skills for war."

"Not even battle magic?" Laydon interjected.

Taryn shook her head. "We've had battle mages in the past, but it's a magical skill we've let lapse. Plus, with Queen Jennica and Royal Consort Joichan present, an army didn't really seem necessary. Although, right now Royal Consort Joichan is traveling the continent with his wife Melandria, the former queen, so Calia only has Queen Jennica to defend it."

Laydon nodded in understanding, but I was confused. How could an entire kingdom rely on only two people to keep them safe? Across the room, I saw my confusion mirrored on Enlar's face, but then his puzzled expression changed to thoughtfulness. Chandra seemed to know what Taryn was talking about, but her expression forbade any questions. Father simply closed his eyes and leaned back, trying to steady his breathing.

"I need to tell the queen right away," Taryn said. "Laydon, contact me if—"

"Wait," Father interrupted her. "There's one more thing."

Taryn paused, turning an expectant face to my father.

Father opened his eyes slowly. We could see the effort it was costing him to talk even for just this small amount of time. "Renton still hasn't perfected his magical concoction. He was yelling at one of the researchers about it. While it's been used on the entire army, it doesn't work on everyone. I think about half, maybe more, of our people remain unaffected. That was the second part of Renton's experiments, trying to figure out why it worked on some but not others, but the tests remained unfinished because the attack on Calia was moved forward."

With that, Father closed his eyes again and sat back. "I need to rest."

I fluttered around my father, adjusting his pillows and helping him resettle under the bedcovers.

Laydon outlined our plans to Taryn. "We'll get these bottles back to Queen Jennica as soon as we can so she can examine them." He frowned at our parents, both lying in the bed looking frail. "But we might be moving a bit slowly."

"I understand," Taryn said. "But do your best to hurry back to Calia. If what your father says is correct ... the Rothschan army should be on Calia's doorstep within a matter of days."

We all agreed we needed to return to Calia, and soon, but the practicalities of doing so—and quickly—eluded us. Mother was still unconscious, and Father wasn't really in a state to be moved again, although it would have to be done. Whatever was afflicting Mother was magical in nature. The journey would be rough, but perhaps in Calia we could find magical healers who knew how to release her from her coma.

After talking to Taryn, Laydon left to try to intercept his group. Although we could have sought help in Rothschan, we didn't want to risk the attention—or the time it would take to find someone trustworthy.

Chandra and I did our best to make Mother and Father comfortable while Enlar gathered supplies for the upcoming trip. Although I was impatient to get on the road and get back to Calia, the rest definitely helped Father, as did the little bit of food he was able to swallow. By the time Laydon returned, Father actually had some color back in his face and his breathing sounded more even.

I flung open the door as Laydon dismounted. He hugged me like he hadn't seen me in days, even though it had only been an hour or so since he'd left. "Any change?"

I shook my head. "None, at least for Mother. Father looks a bit better, though."

"Well enough to move?"

I grimaced. "If we go slowly and carefully."

Laydon turned to the group accompanying him, including one fragile-looking elderly woman. He helped the woman dismount. Her graceful landing, rather robust for her frail appearance, surprised me. She caught me staring and grinned at me, eyes twinkling. "You'll have to forgive me, my dear. I'm the reason everyone traveled so slowly. My old bones can't handle horseback the way they used to. I keep telling these youngsters to leave an old biddy like me behind, but they don't listen to their elders."

"Oh, Ulla," said one of her companions, a man still seated on his horse. "You're never any trouble at all. Besides, we'd be lost without you."

Ulla chuckled. "That's right, Gaelen, flatter your healer. Maybe it'll give you higher priority when you're wounded." She winked at me.

Laydon led Ulla into the house. "If anyone can help Mother, it will be you, Ulla."

The other two people who had accompanied Laydon, the man Ulla had named Gaelen and a woman, both looked to be middle-aged. They busied themselves with the horses—their own mounts, plus Laydon's and Ulla's.

When I invited them inside, they declined. Gaelen said, "We came to help Laydon search the old palace, and get him out of trouble if necessary, but when he met us on the road, he told us you and your friends already did that. Seems we missed all the action."

"I'm sorry?" I said, not sure how to respond.

"I'm not," the woman replied, laughing. "Missing the action makes my life much easier."

I left them to their work, hoping Enlar's attention-elsewhere spell was still working. I smirked as I thought of what the neighbors would say at the goings-on at my house—if they could see them.

Back inside, Ulla stood by Father's bedside, assessing his condition. "A few more days of complete rest, coupled with some good, hearty meals, and you'll be well on your way to full recovery." Father smiled weakly at her words as she patted his arm. She looked up at Laydon. "He can be moved, but we must be very careful we don't go too fast and reopen any injuries. Other than that, he'll be just fine."

She moved on to look at Mother. The easy manner she had displayed with Father fell away as she studied Mother's condition more closely. Her smile slipped, her brow furrowed, and her eyes sharpened as she poked and prodded and listened, all the while keeping up a constant flow of muttering. At one point, she ceased her inaudible chatter and placed her hands on my mother's inert form, one hand on her head and one on her chest. Ulla closed her eyes and grew very still, and it seemed that everyone in the room froze and held their breaths as well, not wanting to break her concentration.

And then Ulla began to shake. Small vibrations at first, and then suddenly her small frame was racked with such severe tremors that I feared she would shatter before us. Her eyes shot open, wide and focused on something only she could see. Her mouth fell open in a wordless scream as her hands tightened on Mother.

Mother's body bucked under her hands, but from what I could see, Mother was still unconscious. Whatever Ulla was doing wasn't healing Mother; I feared it was quite the opposite. And I also was afraid Ulla would succumb to whatever was trying to control her.

I started toward Ulla, reaching out to pull her away from Mother. The movement caught Laydon's attention, and he frowned and shook his head at me, warning me away. I opened my mouth to protest. Laydon's head shake grew fiercer as he put a finger to his lips. *Don't speak, don't do anything to interrupt her concentration!* I understood Laydon's unspoken warning as clearly as if he had shouted it aloud at me.

I backed away, but not too far. If it looked like Ulla was going to completely lose control, I was going to force her away from Mother, regardless of the consequences.

And then Ulla took in a heaving breath, held it, and then exhaled soundlessly. Her gaping mouth expelled a stream of colored haze, a sickly mix of green and gray and black. I quickly stepped out of the way, unsure of what that multi-colored mist was but knowing instinctively I didn't want it to touch me.

Laydon hastily moved to the window, flinging the curtains back and opening the window wide. A fresh breeze carried the ugly haze from the room, where the greenish-gray mist dissipated in the outside air.

Finally, Ulla stopped breathing out that odd colored air, and the stiffness left her body. Her hands relaxed, although I wondered if her grip on my mother would leave bruises. Ulla grew extremely still.

And then my mother's chest heaved as she coughed slightly, and her eyes fluttered open.

"Mother?" I breathed.

Her eyes flicked to me, a slight smile playing on her lips. She opened her mouth to speak, but started coughing again.

Above her, Ulla slowly opened her eyes. The person staring out from them was completely in control of herself once more. She looked at her patient, then looked at the rest of us. "That was some nasty bit of magic."

She swayed on her feet, and Laydon jumped to her side, helping her sit down at the foot of the bed. She leaned heavily on him, her head lolling back. Meanwhile, I helped Mother sit up in bed.

"Don't try to talk just yet," I told her. She nodded and squeezed my hand.

"What just happened? What *was* that?" Laydon wondered.

Ulla wiped her mouth with the back of her hand, as if she could physically scrub away the remnants of the tainted magic. She was panting heavily, trying to recover from whatever ordeal she had just gone through. "I'm not entirely sure. When I examined the patient, I saw that she was fine, physically. So I suspected that whatever ailed her was entirely magical in nature."

Laydon and I regarded Ulla, unsurprised. Father had said as much, but I suppose it was comforting to know that Mother hadn't been hurt beyond whatever magical experiments Renton had conducted on her. Those were bad enough.

"When I examined your mother internally, I saw that her magical essence was fighting off some sort of ... black, slimy substance. I don't know quite what it was, but it seemed like every time her power slipped free of it, that ... *thing* ... would find a way to reattach itself to her magic and eat away at it. A magical leech, if you will. I got here just in time. Any longer, and her magical essence would have been completely devoured. And as one's magic is tied to one's soul ... well, thank goodness I got here in time."

"She's been fighting it off for nearly a week," I said.

Ulla shook her head in wonder as she regarded Mother, who was holding hands with Father and looking much more alert. "I'm impressed. She must be a very strong woman."

I leaned over and enveloped Mother in a big hug. Her free hand reached up to embrace me. "She is. She really is."

37

CHAPTER THIRTY-SEVEN

"CAN'T SLEEP, HUH?"

The fire's embers had burned low, but there was just enough of a glow for me to see Enlar's face looking down at me. I shrugged as he sat down next to me, being careful not to wake the others in our camp.

"I'm just worried," I admitted quietly. "I don't think we're moving fast enough. What if we don't get back to Calia in time? But what if Mother and Father don't recover fast enough? What if—"

Enlar put a finger over my lips to shush me. "I completely understand. But fretting yourself to pieces won't help anything."

"I'm also wondering why we haven't seen any trace of the Rothschan army while we've been out here. They had a head start, didn't they? They should definitely have reached Calia by now. But why haven't we heard anything?"

Now it was Enlar's turn to shrug. "If there was anything to report, Taryn would have told us. I don't like this prolonged silence any more than you do, but there's not much we can do."

I threw a twig into the fire, entranced by the sparks that briefly shot up. "I know, and I *hate* that feeling. I hate just waiting. Did you ever realize that *wait* and *weight* sound the same? I don't think that's a coincidence. Right now, I just feel anxious and worried and *heavy*."

Enlar put his arm around me and gave me a brief hug. "Your parents will be fine. I promise." He sighed heavily. He wisely didn't say what we were both thinking: *I hope.*

Even though Mother had regained consciousness, she was still worryingly weak from her ordeal. Father, too, needed time to rest and recover. But we couldn't leave them behind, nor did we have the time to stay in Rothschan and wait for them to recover. So we had brought them with us on the journey to Calia. But, unfortunately, their frail condition was greatly slowing us down.

"Can't sleep either, huh?"

We looked up at my brother's worn face. He sat down heavily on my other side, sighing.

"I know what's keeping *me* up," I said.

"Our parents?"

I nodded. "You, too?"

"Partly." He looked over to where our parents lay nearby, curled in a bedroll by the fire. "They really should be in a comfortable bed, not out here in the wilderness, exposed to the elements and other things."

He withdrew the bottles he had taken from the former palace and shook them in the firelight. "This is the other thing that's keeping me awake. It's been hard to test these while we travel, but there's no help for it. I'm worried that if we wait until we get back to Calia to work on these, it will be too late. But I just wish I had more time to study them, instead of the moments here and there I can grab while we're resting or camping."

"What do you know so far?" Enlar asked.

Laydon sighed again. "I know how to steal someone's magical essence, for one thing. Queen Jennica hadn't destroyed Hendon's notes, but instead has them locked away in a magically sealed vault that only she can access. I think she worried that, if anyone ever tried to harness stolen magic like Hendon had, she didn't want to be unprepared. Destroying his notes would have left her and her kingdom vulnerable if they lost that knowledge, evil as it may be."

"Smart lady," Enlar commented. "Although I'm sure she didn't expect to have to use that knowledge so soon."

"I'm surprised that it took this long for Renton to avenge Hendon, so to speak," I said. "Although I guess revenge takes time."

"I suppose so, if you're going to do it right," Enlar agreed, a slight smirk on his lips. "Although from the things you two have said about this Renton person, I'm surprised he's that patient."

"I don't think he had a choice." I thought about everything we had learned so far, about Hendon's failed experiments, Renton's involvement with Hendon, and Renton's relationship to Rothschan's rulers. "Thanks to the incident with my brother, he fell from grace years ago, and it's not easy to climb your way back to the top. In fact ..." I paused, remembering my first encounter with Renton. "There was something about a special, secret program happening, that Renton was heading. Carrying on Hendon's magical project was probably what it was. But they couldn't announce it, not after generations of Rothschan leaders denouncing magic."

"Well, creating an unbeatable army and destroying Calia would certainly put Renton back in your Crown's good graces," Enlar said. "And if Rothschan subdues Calia, they would have a near endless supply of power."

Laydon and I exchanged horrified glances. As one, we turned to Enlar.

"The citizens of Calia," Laydon said slowly.

"All those people ... and Calia is a peaceful nation. It would be so easy to overrun." I shuddered, thinking of Calia's fate. And all the lovely people I had met—Taryn, Fiala, Queen Jennica, King Beyan. They didn't deserve that.

"Why stop at Calia?" Enlar looked grim. "With all that untapped magical potential, Rothschan could easily take over the rest of the kingdoms in the Gifted Lands."

"Which is what Hendon had been trying to do." Laydon's expression matched Enlar's. "Which is why we need to stop Renton." He shook the bottles again, frustrated. Their variable colors danced in the firelight. "I wish I knew how he was able to modify it."

I reached for a bottle, giving Laydon a confused look. "But you said you had Hendon's notes. And you have Renton's notes as well. Didn't you figure out the modifications?"

"In theory, yes." Laydon raked his hands through his hair. Since it was already messy from tossing and turning in his bedroll, his impromptu styling just made his hair look even crazier, sticking out at all sorts of odd angles. I made a mental note to remind him to comb his hair. "But there's not enough in these bottles to test my theory. And without being able to run a proper test, I can't figure out a way to counteract Renton's magical enhancements."

He lapsed into a frustrated silence. Then:

"Use my magic."

Laydon slowly turned to look at me. "What?"

"Use my magic," I repeated. I spread my hands wide. "What do you need me to do? Do you need my blood? Do you need to say a spell over me? Whatever you need, I'll do it."

Laydon shook his head, horrified. "No, Adalynn. To steal your essence, it's unconscionable. It's monstrous. It's ... no."

"If I'm volunteering, then it's not really stealing, now is it?" I studied the bottle in my hand. I had grabbed the empty one that had my name on it. "Besides, Renton wanted to get his hands on me. We might as well find out why, right?"

Laydon didn't say anything for a minute. I lightly punched his shoulder. "Come on, you know it's a good idea."

"I hate to agree with you, but you're right." I smirked and started to speak, but Laydon cut me off before I could say anything. "But even if I wanted to do this—which I don't, really—your magical essence alone isn't enough. From what I read in Renton's notes, part of the modifications he made include mixing together several people's power. He tried different concoctions, such as blending the power from a fire mage and an earth mage. Or, mixing magic from people of varying levels of power. What would happen if he mixed power from untried magicians with dormant ability with trained magicians? Things like that. So taking your magic alone wouldn't work. I would need more."

"Could you use your own?"

He pursed his lips, thinking. "I could try, but I don't know if it's a good idea to pull my own power right now. The more magic you use, the longer it takes for your magical reserves to replenish. Although you have a lot of natural talent, I've still got more training and experience than you, so it might be unwise to deliberately weaken myself, when we don't know what we're facing back in Calia."

Enlar spoke up. "Then take my magic."

I turned a triumphant grin on Laydon. "Now you have no excuse not to test your theories."

Laydon sighed, exasperated. "Fine! I know when I'm outnumbered. One would think you two planned this."

"One better stop complaining and get started on experimenting," I said pointedly.

Laydon rolled his eyes and stood up. "I'll be right back. Wait here."

"Where does he think we'd go?" Enlar muttered as Laydon walked into the relative darkness at one end of the camp.

"Hush." I eyed him closely. "You're worried, aren't you?"

"Well, yes. Aren't you? Someone's going to take your magic from you. I don't know what you're taught in Rothschan, but in Bomora, we're told that having magic is not just a skill or talent. It's a part of your soul. So, yes, I'm a little nervous that someone's going to rip part of my soul out. Even if I did volunteer."

I pursed my lips thoughtfully. "We're not taught anything about magic in Rothschan, except that it's superstition and dangerous and only the weak-willed rely on it. So I guess giving my magic away wouldn't be such a big deal to me, as it is to you or probably anyone else in the Gifted Lands."

It was Enlar's turn to look thoughtful. "If that's what you're taught to believe, then I would think it would be frightfully easy to take the magic from your kingdom's citizens. After all, if it means so little to your people, you'd hardly miss it. And it would be contributing to the cause, so it would appeal to your country's rabid and unquestioning loyalty."

"It's nice knowing your place in the world," I protested, but my well-worn argument now sounded weak to my ears. Enlar's skeptical glance told me he wasn't convinced either.

Laydon returned, his pack with him. He sat and rummaged through it, bringing out a small ceramic bowl and a few packets containing what I recognized as dried herbs. The empty bottles he had taken from Renton's workshop also appeared, as well as a very sharp-looking knife. He pulled out Renton's burned spell notes, which now boasted some of Laydon's own scribblings where he had added his own notes. Finally, he took out his waterskin and poured some of the water into the ceramic bowl.

"I had no idea your bag could hold so much," I commented.

"You never know when you'll have to set up complex spells while traveling," Laydon said, picking up the papers and studying them in the firelight. Enlar and I watched in silence, fascinated, as Laydon worked. He added various herbs from each packet, in varying amounts. At one point he frowned at his notes, muttering, "Is it two parts rosemary to one part rue? Or the other way around? No, I think Queen Jennica said ..." His voice trailed off as he continued his spell preparation.

When he had finished, he held the bowl in both of his hands and spoke a quick spell. The water in the bowl instantly heated and bubbled, and the scent of mixed herbs floated in the air. Setting the bowl aside, Laydon picked up the knife and repeated his spell. The blade briefly flashed blue, then settled back to its original shiny silver. Laydon held out his empty hand to me. "Give me your hand."

I recoiled. "No. I mean, at least wait until the knife has cooled."

He placed the flat of the knife against his empty palm. I flinched, but the metal didn't burn his skin. I cautiously held out my hand.

"This will sting for a second," Laydon warned. Then, before I knew what was happening, the metal flashed in the firelight and there was a bright red slash across my palm. I hissed at the pain.

Laydon held my bleeding hand over the still-hot bowl of herbal water, squeezing slightly and counting silently as he watched my blood drip, drip, drip into the bowl. Twenty drops later, he released my hand and then felt around in his pack again. Finding a clean piece of cloth, he handed it to me. I started to thank him, but he shook his head at me, indicating that he was still in the middle of a spell and shouldn't be interrupted.

He picked up the bowl again and slowly tipped it this way and that, mixing my blood thoroughly into the herbal water. He then picked up

Renton's notes and slowly repeated the modified spell written on the pages. Meanwhile, Enlar helped me bind my wound, after which we both turned our attention back to Laydon, not wanting to miss any part of his magical working.

The throbbing in my hand faded away as I watched the bright crimson liquid swirl around and around in the bowl of its own accord. Laydon had carefully placed the bowl on the ground before picking up the notes, and I was fascinated by the small red whirlpool that was even now picking up speed as it swirled. As Laydon spoke, the concoction cycled through several colors—first blood red, then gold, then black, until it finally slowed and faded into a purple-blue tinged with a green sheen. Curious, I leaned over to examine the bowl's contents more closely. The liquid had also thickened, and there were no longer any herbs floating in it. I sniffed the air. The herbal scent had also disappeared, replaced by something more bitter and metallic.

Laydon picked up the bowl and carefully poured its contents into a waiting empty bottle. The one that happened to have my name on it. *How funny that my brother could accomplish what Renton could not*, I thought wryly, recalling my midnight meeting with the hateful man a few nights previous.

Laydon held up the now full and corked bottle to the light, admiring his handiwork. "Truth be told, I wasn't completely sure that would work. Queen Jennica helped me fill in some of the gaps in Renton's notes. But without actively testing the new incantation ... well, there's a lot of things that can go wrong with an untried spell."

"Glad I could be your test subject," I said sarcastically, but my grin let Laydon know I wasn't truly upset. Now that the spell was completed, my attention refocused on my slashed palm. "You didn't tell me that magic could, quite literally, hurt."

"Blood—or other facets of the body—is sometimes a necessary component in spell casting. Fortunately, we didn't need too much of yours to make this."

"It makes me wonder how much Renton took from others to make enough to create his magical army," Enlar said. "And how much blood—and magic—one can lose before they go mad."

"That's the question, isn't it?" Laydon said somberly. "When we find him, be assured he will pay for that, and much more. And we *will* find him."

We all fell silent for a minute, lost in our separate thoughts. Then Laydon cleared his throat. "All right, Enlar. It's your turn."

Laydon repeated the process with Enlar, and soon there was another full bottle of magical essence to join mine. Instead of the same purple-blue color as my essence, Enlar's magical essence was a warm golden yellow that reminded me of morning sunlight gilding a field of daffodils.

I grabbed a clean bandage from Laydon's pack and bound Enlar's hand while Laydon cleaned up. By the time Laydon was finished, Enlar was staring at his bandaged hand thoughtfully. "Will this leave a scar?"

"It shouldn't," Laydon said. "I know it looked bad, but I didn't cut too deep. Just make sure to keep it clean, and it should heal nicely." He rummaged around in his bag once more, frowning. "I know I have ... oh, here it is!" He pulled out a small jar and handed it to me. "Ulla gave me this balm before we left Rothschan, just in case. It will help those cuts heal faster."

He stood up, slinging his bag over his shoulder, the bottles containing Enlar's and my magical essences in his hands.

"Where are you going?" I smeared some salve on my cut and then, with Enlar's help, rebandaged it.

"To study these," Laydon said.

"Now? It's getting late. Or rather, it's so late, it's practically early." Enlar finished putting the salve on his own hand, and I reached over to help him redo his bandage.

Laydon looked up, noting that the night sky was beginning to lighten. "Good point," he said sheepishly. "I just get so excited about research. But I don't know when I'll have another chance to work on these bottles."

"Well, you won't be much use to anyone if you're falling out of the saddle sleeping," I said. "I know we need to get back to Calia quickly, but you *are* the leader. Just make sure we stop a little more often, or take longer when we do."

Laydon eyed me wonderingly. "I don't know why I never thought of that."

I rolled my eyes as I headed back to my bedroll near the fire. Enlar had already made himself comfortable and would soon be asleep, I was sure. "How did you ever survive so long without me around to give you these great ideas?"

"Is that what you call them? I would have called it nagging." Laydon chuckled quietly, then jumped when I pitched a small rock at his shoe. He turned to go to his spot in the camp. "Good night, Adalynn."

38

CHAPTER THIRTY-EIGHT

THE NEXT MORNING, LAYDON pulled me aside as everyone was packing up camp.

"I'm leaving," he announced abruptly.

"What? Why?"

"I need to get those bottles to Calia—and the queen—as soon as I can," Laydon said. "I'll go faster if I don't travel with the group. I can travel overnight, swap horses when necessary, and hopefully reach Calia in three days or less." He glanced over his shoulder, surveying our little party who already looked spent, even though we hadn't even begun the day's travel. "We're moving much slower than I would like. Gaelen has agreed to handle things here. You can all rest for a day or two."

He lowered his voice further. "I've asked Gaelen to bring everyone back to Rothschan and wait there while our parents recover. Ulla's already furious at me for having moved them in the first place."

"You're right, our parents should go back. Although I don't like the idea of you going alone," I said. "Too many things could go wrong, and there'd be no one to help you. I'll go with you."

"You're safer if you stay with the group."

"Maybe. Or maybe not. Besides, if you need more magical essence, how will you get any between here and Calia?"

Laydon frowned. "I wasn't planning on breaking the bottles."

"You never know what might happen. Anyway, I don't want to worry about you while you're on the road. I'm going."

"Where are you going?" Enlar said, overhearing the last part of our conversation as he approached us.

"Laydon's headed back to Calia by himself, and I'm going with him," I said.

"Oh, good. I'll go too. I'll go get my things, we'll gather up our horses, and then we'll be ready to go." Enlar hurried off, nearly knocking Chandra over in his haste.

She walked over to us. "What's he in such a hurry about?"

"Nothing," Laydon growled.

"Laydon's going on a solo mission, and Enlar and I are accompanying him," I said at the same time.

"Perfect, I've been wanting some action. It's been so boring lately," Chandra said. "Let me grab my bag, and I'll meet you back here." Briskly, she walked away.

"Thanks a lot." Laydon's mouth was turned down in a scowl.

"Don't be so grumpy," I said as Enlar returned, leading our horses and with both of our bags slung over his shoulders. I thanked him as he gave me my bag, then turned back to Laydon. "You obviously didn't get enough sleep last night."

Chandra came back just then, also ready to go. "Laydon? Where's your horse? I thought you were in a hurry."

He ground his teeth, rolled his eyes, and stalked off to get his horse. Chandra, Enlar, and I shared a laugh as we watched him go.

As we continued our journey to Calia, we didn't catch any trace of Renton or the Rothschan army. We didn't stop often, but when we did, inquiries at roadside inns or of other travelers yielded nothing—no news, and not even any rumors. The countryside seemed untouched by the passage of a large group of people, let alone an army. It should have made us feel confident, knowing that, despite our fears, we were perhaps, miraculously, moving ahead of Renton and might reach Calia before him.

But instinctively, we knew that wasn't correct. It didn't make sense. We *knew* that Renton and a partial group of knights—the ones Father had said were successfully "changed"—had a several days' lead over us, not to mention their magically enhanced march. They should have passed our way. They should have been seen.

And the prolonged peace as we traveled made us uneasy.

Thinking back to my time in Calia, I remembered how much magic Renton had thrown around in his efforts to try to kidnap me and destroy Fiala's boardinghouse. Not to mention breaching the wards at both the Academy and at Fiala's. And he must have been at the Academy when he cast that scrying spell, but invisible....

"Do you think Renton made the army invisible?" I asked.

Enlar and Laydon both turned to me as we rode, identical looks of horror dawning on their faces. "It's possible," Laydon said slowly. "But it would take an awful amount of power."

"How much power? The magical ability of a dozen people? Fifty? More?"

My companions instantly understood my meaning. Enlar remarked soberly, "As many as you would need to accomplish your goals, I suppose."

Like conquering another kingdom.

We didn't say anything after that, just spurred our horses to move faster.

Within two days of hard riding, we saw the gates of Calia on the horizon. We passed through a small town on the outskirts of the kingdom, which Laydon informed us was Taryn's hometown. "I believe she still has family here, a brother? But she moved away years ago, when she first started working at the palace as then-Princess Jennica's lady-in-waiting."

The town was abustle with its normal day-to-day doings. Some people would occasionally smile or wave at us, but for the most part we passed through, unregarded.

"We must have made it here before Rosthschan," Enlar commented. "If the army had gotten here before us, they would have tried to take over the town. It's a perfect staging point before an assault on Calia's capital city. Right? But everything seems completely fine."

Chandra shook her head. "Magic is involved. I don't know how, but I never trust anything when magic is involved."

"Spoken like a true citizen of Rothschan," I said.

She shrugged. "It's not that, necessarily. I've lived in Calia long enough to see what powerful magicians can do. Alter reality, confuse the mind. Even raise the dead, if they want to pursue dark magic. Since magic is mixed up in this whole thing ... it doesn't sit well with me. I just don't trust it."

We passed through the gates of the capital, heading straight for the palace. Dismounting, we left our horses with two pages at the front of the palace. A guard at the palace doors barred our way when we approached. "State your business."

Before any of us could answer, the heavy wooden doors pushed open from the inside, nearly knocking the guard over. He hastily stepped back, about to reprimand the person on the other side, but swallowed his words when he saw who it was.

Taryn was holding the door open for Queen Jennica, who stood at the threshold, blinking into the sunlight at us. Laydon and Enlar sketched quick bows while Chandra and I both fell into hasty curtsies.

The queen waved away our formalities. "Don't worry about that now. We've been keeping an eye out for all of you since Taryn told us you were coming. Please, come in. We have much to discuss."

The guard collected our weapons, promising they would be returned to us upon leaving the castle. The queen turned and walked back into the castle, her voluminous satin skirt swirling around her. The four of us followed her and Taryn down one of the cool stone side hallways, passing a seemingly endless row of paintings. We were moving at too quick a pace for me to inspect them thoroughly, but I noticed a resemblance between some of the people depicted and Queen Jennica. The clothing worn in the paintings also seemed to get older the further we moved down the hallway. These must be historical family portraits, then.

The queen stopped before a nondescript wooden door near the end of the hallway. I was so engrossed in the paintings lining the hallway that I nearly didn't stop in time, catching myself just before I plowed into Enlar. Who would have probably bumped into Taryn, who would have definitely bumped into Queen Jennica. The queen pulled a key from her pocket and unlocked the door, gesturing that we should all enter. As we dutifully filed in, Enlar gave me a pointed look, raising his eyebrows at me. I gave him a sheepish grin and stepped through the doorway.

The room on the other side seemed to be a small workroom of sorts. A large window overlooked the palace courtyard, covered with sheer white curtains to give the occupants of the room privacy but still allow the light in. Bookshelves lined the walls, but not all of them were full. Some titles caught my eye: *The History of Magic in the Gifted Lands; Calian Folk Spells; Advanced Magical Adaptation.* I realized this must be a private workshop for the queen and her select companions, and when I spotted the jars of herbs and other spell components on a small side table, I knew my hunch was correct.

"Do you still have those bottles, Laydon?" Queen Jennica asked. When he nodded, she pointed to an empty table at one end of the room. "Good. You can put them over there, please, along with Renton's notes. Taryn, you remember the ingredients we'll need? Can you gather them up and bring them here? Thank you."

While Laydon and Taryn fluttered around the room following the queen's orders, the rest of us stood in the center awkwardly, unsure of what to do. The queen noticed our discomfort, and said in a friendly tone, "You must be exhausted from your travels. Let me summon a page to escort you."

"If it's all right with you, Your Majesty, I'd prefer to stay and watch," I said. "I'd like to learn about magic as much as I can. I'll do my best to either help or stay out of the way." Enlar nodded his agreement.

"Not me," said Chandra. "I'd prefer to eat, then sleep. But it doesn't have to be in that order. As long as they both happen sometime, and soon."

Queen Jennica smiled as she moved toward a cord hanging on one of the walls. "I completely understand. Let me just call for—"

Before she could pull the cord, a page appeared in the doorway. Wow. The palace staff in Calia was extremely efficient. Rothschan could learn a thing or two.

The young man bowed, then said, "Pardon the intrusion, Your Majesty, but the King requests your presence in the Great Hall."

Queen Jennica sighed. "I was hoping I didn't have to go back to listening to citizen petitions for the rest of the day. Beyan is more than capable of deciding things fairly for the people."

"That is true, Your Majesty," the page answered. He coughed slightly and looked a little uncomfortable. "I, ah, believe he wants you there more for, uh, as he phrased it, moral support."

The queen chuckled. "What you mean, but are too well-trained to say, is that it's extremely boring and he needs me there to nudge him awake when necessary. Yes, please let him know I'll be in the Great Hall shortly." She gestured to Chandra. "And after you deliver your message, could you show this young lady either to a guest room or to the kitchen? Whichever she prefers."

The page bowed again and left, Chandra in his wake. "Perhaps someone could just bring food to my room directly? That way I don't have to worry about falling asleep in my soup...." Her hopeful voice trailed off as they continued down the hallway, out of earshot.

"I wish I could be here to help research, but unfortunately, duty calls." The queen surveyed the items Taryn and Laydon had gathered, and opened a slim brown leather-bound journal. She flipped through the pages until she found the entry she was looking for, and held it out to Laydon. "This was Hendon's grimoire, where we found the original magic stealing spell. From what you told Taryn, Renton has modified it somewhat, creating more powerful magic by combining different people's essences together. But consuming someone's magic doesn't mean you can instantly use it; magic has its own special imprint, inherent to each individual. There are additional steps one must take in order to tap into the stolen magic. I doubt that each person in the Rothschan army would have performed the spell that would have allowed them to do that, as it requires training and precision to make it work correctly. Any mistakes would harm the spell caster, either incapacitating them or killing them outright. Which makes me think that Renton has figured out a way to trigger the magic in each person who's taken one of his stolen magic concoctions, which also means he is magically connected to each person in the Rosthchan army."

Laydon gasped in sudden understanding. "Of course. The principle of reciprocity."

"What does that mean, exactly?" Enlar wondered.

Queen Jennica looked grim. "It means that if Renton can tap into the magic that each person in his army now possesses to awaken it in all of them, then he can also gather all that magic from them and concentrate it solely in his person. And use it."

39

CHAPTER THIRTY-NINE

QUEEN JENNICA LEFT US to start our research, obviously reluctant to leave. I think she might have "forgotten" to go to the Great Hall, but once she had settled us properly, Taryn gently but pointedly said, "And now, shouldn't you be on your way before the petitions conclude?"

The queen let out a huge, exaggerated sigh, and said with a touch of sarcasm, "What would I do without you, Taryn?"

"A good question, Your Majesty," Taryn said cheerfully as she took the queen's arm and steered her toward the door. "Let's hope we'll never have to find out."

"Wait," I said. Taryn and Queen Jennica both turned to look at me. To Taryn, I said, "Aren't you going to stay and help us?"

Taryn laughed and shook her head. "I get by in Calia, but I have no head for magic. You'll be fine in Laydon's capable hands. Besides, someone has to make sure this one—" she playfully pointed at the queen "—gets to where she needs to be."

Queen Jennica groaned, sounding very un-queenly. Taryn laughed again, and the two women left the room, presumably headed to the Great Hall.

"It still surprises me that Taryn acts so informally with her sovereign," I remarked after I was sure they were out of earshot. "That kind of behavior would never happen in Rothschan."

"They grew up together, so they're more friends than queen and servant, despite their stations." Laydon sounded somewhat distracted as he studied Hendon's grimoire. "In some respects, Calia is a lot more relaxed than Rothschan about those things."

I picked up Renton's spell notes, flipping through them without really understanding what I was reading. Enlar peeked over my shoulder, curious. I held the notes out to him. "Does this make any sense to you?"

He took the notes from me, comparing the pages against each other. "Not entirely, but that's why we have Laydon, here."

Laydon chuckled. "Of all the things to teach you as one of your foundational magic lessons. How to steal someone else's magical ability. But, I could use the help. Let me show you some things, so you understand what I did, and what we're trying to do." He put Hendon's spell book down on the table, keeping it open to two specific pages. He pointed to the text. "This was the original spell for siphoning magical power from an individual."

He took Renton's notes from Enlar, and spread them out on the table next to Hendon's book. "This is the same spell, along with my personal notes, to fill in what was missing. That's the basic spell, again. These, here, are Renton's modifications to the basic spell. From Hendon's notes, he had tried combining people's magic after removing it from them, but since magic is unique to each individual, it resisted Hendon's efforts. It was like trying to mix oil and water. But somehow, Renton figured out how to create certain effects in his test subjects by merging magical essences." My brother's voice held a grudging respect. "If it wasn't such an immoral, horrendous thing to do, it would be almost admirable. What a feat to accomplish in the name of magic study."

"How was Hendon able to tap into multiple people's magic, if they resist combination?" Enlar, ever the scholar, asked.

"I believe he would consume one person's essence at a time," Laydon said. "When his magical reserves were fairly low, that's when he would use another person's magic to bolster him."

"I wonder how he came to those conclusions?"

"It's in his journal." Laydon wore a fierce grin. "I believe he tried to consume more than one person's magic, early on, and became violently ill. More in a mental sense than anything, including nearly going insane, and his magic just spontaneously making random things occur. There were some physical side effects, as well. Magical indigestion, if you will."

I giggled at the thought of the former great knight Hendon, Rothschan's favorite son, having a magical upset stomach. "I wonder if we can make Renton feel those same effects?"

"He seems to have a failsafe against it, but I'm certainly not opposed to trying." He turned to the two bottles containing Enlar's and my magic. "But first we need to successfully recreate what Renton was doing, and then we can move beyond that to see how we can alter it to our advantage."

Enlar and I nodded in agreement. "So, what should we do first?" I asked.

Laydon was intently studying one of Renton's notes. "I don't think you're going to like this," he said slowly.

"What? What won't we like?"

He picked up the paper and read it over carefully, frowned, then re-read the page like perhaps the words scrawled there would have changed. His expression didn't lighten, so I guessed the words remained the same. He looked up. "I didn't understand this when I first read it, but now that I have Hendon's original notes to compare this to ... It explains why these mashed-up magics are working on Renton and the people of Rothschan, for the most part."

"What? What is it?"

"According to Renton's notes, here, these new magical essences, the combined ones, work best on people with innate magical ability, but who have yet to harness that power. Meaning, the more experienced you are as a magician, the less likely you are able to meld with Renton's concoctions."

"It sort of makes sense," Enlar commented. "If magic is a part of your soul, then it would become entrenched in who you are the more you use it. Someone who's just starting out in their magical journey wouldn't be as entwined with their magic, unlike someone who has consistently used their abilities."

Laydon paused, regarding Enlar with renewed respect. "Yes. That's it, exactly."

"Well, what do we have to do?" I said. My voice sounded uncomfortably loud, but then again, *I* was feeling a bit uncomfortable. While I had accepted the idea of magic—and that it was a part of me—I was still unsure how I felt about all this talk of souls and magic and philosophy. Esoteric concepts were for people who had that kind of patience. To me, a sword was way more logical—clean, sharp, and to the point.

"I'm going to recreate the spell we did before, but this time take some of my magic for it," Laydon said. Taking a deep breath, he slowly turned to look at me. I instantly felt a prickle down my spine.

"And then?" I asked apprehensively, instinctively knowing I wouldn't like the answer.

"And then," Laydon said, drawing each word out slowly. "Then, we will add our combined magic to you, Adalynn."

"What? Why me?" I tried for strong and defiant, but it came out sounding more petulant and annoyed.

"Several reasons," Laydon said, waving both Hendon's journal and Renton's notes in the air. "One, because unlike me, you're still a fairly new magician."

"So is Enlar!"

"Hey!" Enlar interjected. "Who says I want to become a magical experiment?"

"And two," Laydon continued, ignoring both of our outbursts. "Because like calls to like."

"What does that mean?" I said, exasperated.

"It was in Renton's notes, but I didn't quite understand it until just now, comparing Hendon's pages to Renton's," Laydon explained. "Hendon gained strength from his stolen magic, but he wasn't originally from Calia. He could only use their magic to a certain point. But Renton is from Rothschan—as is the army he's enhanced through his magical experiments. Their shared culture strengthens their magical bond and allows them to tap into each other's powers. That's why Enlar can't be a conduit to the Rothschan army. But you can, Adalynn."

40

— · —

Chapter Forty

A STUNNED SILENCE FILLED the room. Then, from me: "Is that why Renton was so keen to get his hands on me?"

"It makes sense," Laydon said. "Not that he couldn't have used someone already in the army. Although it's likely anyone currently enlisted has already ingested the experimental magic. But you're a known commodity, Adalynn. You already proved you had untried magic, when you accidentally attacked him and set his office on fire."

"Which is why showing off our talents unnecessarily is never a good idea," Enlar murmured. Cheeky. I stuck my tongue out at him and he grinned back.

"Besides," Laydon added, "I'm sure when he realized who you were, the idea of subduing my sister and her magic greatly appealed to him."

I snorted. "Spare me from Renton's revenge fantasies." Sighing heavily, I continued, "If there are no other options ..."

"Very few, and even if there were, they'd be practically impossible to find at this late hour," Laydon interjected.

"Then, okay. I'll do it."

Enlar blinked, surprised. Laydon abruptly closed his mouth on the argument he had no doubt been preparing to use to persuade me. "Ah, um, great. That was a quick decision."

"What else could I say?" I said practically. "Shall we get on with it?"

Laydon didn't answer, just ducked his head and busied himself with the papers and ingredients and bottles in front of him, but I caught the slight smirk on his face as he started his preparations. In short order he had recreated the spell from last night, and had gathered some of his own magic in a bottle. His magic was a shimmery silvery-gray.

Carefully following Renton's instructions, he soon combined his magic with mine and Enlar's. I had thought that the mix of colored magical essences might turn the contents into some odd, muddy color, but the trio of magic settled on each other like some sort of glittery parfait: Laydon's silver on the bottom, my purple in the middle, and Enlar's yellow on top.

"It's kind of pretty," I commented.

"Let's hope it's as pretty going down as it is in the bottle," Laydon said, admiring his handiwork.

I gave him a funny look. "Excuse me?"

"You heard me." He grinned and held the bottle out to me. "Bottoms up."

Gingerly, I took the bottle from him, but didn't drink from it. "Are you sure this is a good idea? What's it going to do to me?"

"Besides give you enhanced magical abilities and increased power? Not sure of any other side effects. You might not feel a thing. Then again, all that mixed-up magic might give you a bad stomachache."

"Let's hope that's the only side effect," I muttered. I gave the bottle an experimental sniff. Nothing. Apparently, magical essences were odorless. I pursed my lips. "I'm probably going to seriously regret this." I upended the bottle and gulped down its contents in one long swig.

The essences may have been odorless, but they stung as I drank them. A tingly sensation, like I had swallowed copious amounts of peppermint. I couldn't help it; I sneezed as the last drop slid down my throat and plunked the empty bottle down on the table.

Both Laydon and Enlar stared at me curiously. "Well?" Enlar said anxiously. "How do you feel?"

I blinked, taking stock of myself. "So far, so good." I sneezed again. And again. And, again. "Phew! Of all the things I've thought about magic, I never guessed it would be ticklish."

Laydon laughed. "We probably shouldn't let that one get out. The idea of a wise, powerful magician is a bit at odds with ticklish magic."

I started to laugh too, but then suddenly felt faint, like the breath had been knocked out of me. The room grew overly bright, and my breath started coming in short gasps.

"Adalynn? Adalynn!" Enlar's voice sounded far away. Or maybe it was just hard to hear him over the blood rushing in my ears.

"I ... don't feel ... well," I said, and then my world went black.

I opened my eyes to see Enlar peering at me anxiously, his face hovering way too close to mine. I was lying on something soft—they must have moved me to the low velvet sofa. I squinted into the sunlight that was streaming through the window, right into my eyes. "Mmm ... Enlar, could you move a little to the right? That light is bothering me."

"You're awake," he said. He called to Laydon across the room, "She's awake!"

I groaned, feeling a headache blooming in my skull. "And could you yell a little quieter, please?"

"Sorry," Enlar whispered sheepishly. He helped me sit up slightly, although I was still reclining on the sofa, propped up against the pillows. "How are you feeling?"

"Like I overate at breakfast and then got a surprise ride from one of your mythical dragons. And then it decided to drop me mid-air, with no warning." I burrowed into my pillows, curling up in a ball. "If the future of Calia depends on me, then we're in trouble."

Laydon came over to us, grimoire and burnt notes in hand. His finger was holding a place in Hendon's book; he must have been searching for answers on how to help my condition when I fainted.

"I'm sorry, I should have anticipated this," he said. "I thought perhaps since your magic was included in the concoction, it wouldn't have any adverse effects on you."

"Was this common?" I asked, indicating his marked page.

"Surprisingly, no. It seems that neither Hendon nor Renton suffered any ill effects when they ingested someone else's magic. They didn't keep detailed notes beyond that, but my guess is it's because they didn't have any magic to begin with, so there was nothing for new magic to interact and, er, 'compete' with."

"Lucky me," I said dryly.

"You weren't out for long, if it's any consolation."

"It's not." I sat up fully, putting my feet on the floor. "Good news, I don't feel like throwing up anymore. But I still have this stupid headache."

"Are you okay to continue?"

I brushed away Laydon's concern. "I'll be fine. So, I've got all this mixed-up magic in me. Now what?"

"Well, in theory, you are now connected to Enlar and me," Laydon said. "You should be able to feel our magic, and thus influence it. We can do the same, I think, but to a lesser extent."

"In *theory*," I grumbled. "I'd prefer to deal in concrete, well-tested, established *knowledge*."

He shrugged helplessly. "That's it. That's all I've got. After the how-to of successfully stealing someone's magic and incorporating it into one's person, all of these notes are remarkably vague on what happens next."

"Typical," I muttered. "After you figure out how to achieve world domination, the practicals of maintaining it aren't considered necessary."

"There's one more thing," Laydon began, but he was interrupted by a low boom outside the palace that shook the workshop's windows.

"What in the Gifted Lands—?" Enlar quickly moved to the window to peer out. Laydon joined him there. Still a bit disoriented, I stayed where I was on the couch, turning a curious face to the two men.

"There's some sort of party happening in the city," Enlar said, sounding confused. "I see a bunch of smoke, in a rainbow of colors. Is there a celebration of some sort that we didn't know about?"

"There are no kingdom holidays happening today," Laydon said grimly, studying the brightly colored smoke blotting out the afternoon sky. "That's not a celebration."

Another boom sounded, this time closer to the castle.

Taryn appeared at the workshop's entrance. A fine sheen of sweat beaded on her forehead, and her normally immaculately-styled blonde hair was disheveled. Several curls had escaped the hair ribbon tying them back from Taryn's face, and clung damply to her cheeks. She brushed them away impatiently as she tried to catch her breath. It sounded like she had been running.

"The capital city is under attack," she announced without preamble. "You'll have to leave your work and come with me."

Immediately we all sprang into action. Enlar hurried to my side and helped me stand, walking me briskly to the door. Laydon followed us out. Taryn shut the door and locked it, then started down the hallway, not quite at a run, but quickly enough that we were hard pressed to keep up.

"What's going on?" Laydon asked her. "Where are the king and queen? Where's Chandra?"

"I sent a page to get Chandra," Taryn said. "Chandra was supposed to be taken to the king and queen's private chambers, to meet us."

"That's where we're headed now?" Laydon asked.

"Yes. I'll explain what I know when we're all together."

Taryn fell silent, and soon the only thing we could hear were our footsteps echoing against the stone floors of the Calian palace, punctuated by the occasional thunderous boom from various locations in the capital. As we passed by the various windows set in the castle walls, random flashes of magical illumination from the spells being cast in the city lit our way. I cast a fleeting, longing look out the windows. We were too far away to see any of the action clearly, and had no way of knowing how well Calia was holding its own against the invading Rothschan forces.

It didn't take us long, and yet every step felt like an eternity. But we finally made it to the royal chambers, where King Beyan, Queen Jennica, and Chandra were waiting for us. I nearly didn't recognize the royals—they had exchanged their formal court clothing for something plainer. Jennica wore a linen tunic over pale brown homespun trousers, while Beyan had put on a tunic of light chainmail.

I was impressed at their foresight. Not only would it be easier for them to move around, but it would be harder for them to be spotted as the king and queen, making them less of a target.

Queen Jennica looked relieved when she spotted us. "Good, you're here."

Taryn motioned to a chair, and the queen instantly sank down into it. "You may have gotten adept at dressing yourself without help over the years, but you're still hopeless when it comes to dressing your own hair. I'll take care of this quickly, and then we'll go."

The queen smiled ruefully, pulling out her hair ribbon and shaking out the messy hairstyle she had obviously done herself. "Thank you, Taryn. Please give your report."

Taryn chuckled as she deftly brushed the queen's hair out. "So, here's what I know. While you were holding Petitioner's Court, there were some explosions in the town just outside the capital, where my brother Rufan lives." She began braiding the queen's hair. "Rufan came to tell me, and I sent our battle mages—of which we have precious few—back with him to protect the town. But it seems to have been a decoy. Once the mages were gone, more magical attacks started happening, here in the capital." She finished the braid, tying it off with the hair ribbon she plucked from the queen's hand.

"We wondered why Rothschan hadn't attacked sooner, when we knew they should have arrived already. They were just biding their time, lulling us into a false sense of security." Queen Jennica stood and strode over to a large, worn-looking wooden chest in the corner, and opened it. The chest was seemingly bottomless as she handed out various weapons to Chandra, Enlar, Laydon, and me. "I know these are not the same as using your own weapons, but it's better than being unarmed." The queen strapped her own sword to her belt, and then looked at Taryn. "Let's go."

Taryn nodded and turned to the fireplace, her fingers quickly finding the hidden latch that opened the secret passage we had used before. It had only been a few weeks, but it felt like a lifetime ago.

As we all filed into the secret passage—Taryn in the lead, the king and queen behind her, Enlar and me next, with Laydon and Chadra bringing up the rear—Taryn, Laydon, and Queen Jennica all chanted the same spell nearly simultaneously. The dark passageway lit up with three separate mage lights, feeling almost as bright as if the sun itself had been streaming into the tunnels.

Taryn led the way down the tunnels, her spell light bobbing ahead of her. The tunnels twisted and turned so much that I was thoroughly lost within a few moments.

"Where are we going?" Enlar whispered. "Are we headed for the Great Hall?"

"No," Taryn said in a low voice as she turned left and disappeared around a corner. Her voice echoed eerily off the stone walls back at us. "And hurry; don't worry about being quiet right now. I doubt anyone will notice some random muffled noises in the walls at this point, what with all the commotion going on outside."

Funny, that doesn't make me feel better about being in here.

"Why are we in here? Why not just go through the hallways?" Enlar cursed as he accidentally scraped his hand against a jagged rock jutting out from one of the walls.

"Hard to maneuver in a crowd," Taryn said practically. "And it's better to be in here, just in case any of the intruders made it into the castle. We'd rather they not know where the king and queen are."

"*I* don't even know where we are, how could anyone else know?" I whispered to Enlar. He chuckled in response.

Taryn stopped in front of a blank rock wall. Queen Jennica and Laydon both recalled their mage lights and clasped their hands together, making their lights wink out, leaving Taryn's sole light to cast random shadows on her face and the wall. In its glow, Taryn found what she was looking for, and ended her own light spell just as the rock wall slid open noiselessly.

The afternoon sunlight spilled through the open doorway. Taryn motioned us to step through, and soon we were all squinting into the light, peering around us to get our bearings.

"Where are we?" I wondered.

Taryn pointed behind us. The castle rose up a good distance away, shut up tightly against possible invaders. We had apparently traveled under and beyond the castle, to a secret entrance set in a small hill on the edge of the castle grounds.

The castle also looked kind of fuzzy to me. Odd. I looked around me, away from the castle. The trees in the distance looked normal. So did all my companions, standing nearby. But when I looked back at the castle again, its walls still rippled, looking hazy in my vision, as if I was recovering from a night of strong drinking. Was this a side effect of the mixed magic I had drunk earlier?

"There's a protection spell on the castle, which I am able to trigger at will," Queen Jennica said, following my no doubt puzzled look. "It provides an extra bit of physical, as well as magical, protection."

"It took quite a bit to set up, as I recall," King Beyan remarked. "The spell required a specially made potion to cover the entire surface of whatever it was she wanted to enchant. Not only did the castle smell like a sour distillery for a week, but it was also quite an ordeal coordinating our entire castle staff to—safely!—put all that magical liquid on the building."

"Fortunately, once I completed the spell, the potion just disappeared from the castle walls. Otherwise, can you imagine how much of a hassle cleaning up would have been?" The queen giggled. Then she sobered. "So the castle is safe for now. We need to focus on the most important thing—protecting our people."

We were standing in a somewhat open field, with the palace behind us. There were stables to our right. I guessed this must be where the royal horses were kept and trained. Beyond lay the capital, and flashes of magic illuminated the sky, punctuated by the occasional not-so-distant-anymore boom and crackle of magical explosions.

And screams.

Queen Jennica looked ready to take on the whole of the Rothschan army single-handedly. I almost felt sorry for Renton. It wasn't going to pretty if he had to face her wrath. "We can't wait any longer."

King Beyan put a steadying hand on her arm. "Be careful, love."

"You as well. If you want to stay at Fiala's after you bring Taryn there ..."

"Not a chance. I'll join you as soon as I can." The king eyed our little group. "Can ... can you carry everyone?"

"Watch me."

The queen stepped back a few paces away from our group. Her slim, dark-haired form shimmered before our eyes, and where a human queen had been, now stood a large, majestic dragon with glittering golden scales.

I screamed. Or at least, I'm certain I did. My paltry noises were swallowed by the roar of the dragon's fire, as she opened her mouth, displaying an impressive amount of sharp teeth, and spewed a stream of fire into the sky.

Somewhere in the back of my panicked mind, I recalled something Taryn had said: *With Queen Jennica and Royal Consort Joichan present, an army didn't really seem necessary.* If Calia's queen was able to do *this*, then it was no wonder the kingdom didn't bother to keep a standing army. I wondered if the royal consort was also able to transform into a dragon, or if he became a different creature.

"Jennica!" Taryn called up to her queen. The dragon stopped spewing fire and turned a very large eye to Taryn. I was amazed Taryn was able to keep her calm under such a scary beast's scrutiny, but then again, she probably had had a lot of practice. "King Beyan and I will make our way to Fiala's now, and contact you through Laydon if need be. Be well, all of you."

The huge dragon nodded, head bobbing up and down. I grabbed onto Enlar's arm to keep from blowing away from the wind that was created from the dragon's simple movement. I'd have to grab onto a tree or something when the dragon took off. I surreptitiously started looking around for something rooted to the ground.

Taryn and the king left us, running toward the Academy and Fiala's boardinghouse. If our situation hadn't been so serious, it might have been funny, to see the Royal Advisor hitching up her skirts and running headlong into the city, with the king of Calia looking equally undignified. But I didn't have too much time to ponder the sight, because suddenly I felt myself lifted off the ground.

41

—·—

Chapter Forty-One

My legs dangled awkwardly in the air, while my torso was securely—I hoped—held fast in the sharp, hard claws of a dragon. I mentally corrected myself. *Queen Jennica.*

I screamed again, hearing it echoed right by my ear. Turning my head slightly, I saw Enlar in a similar position, just as startled as I was. Somehow, knowing that I wasn't the only one who was alarmed made me feel better, and I relaxed.

In the dragon queen's other claw were my brother and Chandra. Laydon held himself stiffly, as if he was fighting desperately not to show his fear. Chandra was the only one in our group who looked thrilled at this unusual mode of transport.

Can you imagine? Flying a dragon into battle? That would be incredibly exciting. As we lifted into the sky, I had a momentary, wild vision of riding—well, flying—into battle on the back of a majestic dragon, much like the one carrying us in her claws. Except my dragon was a deep crimson, representative of my home country, Rothschan.

My dragon-riding fantasy was short-lived. First, because my heart sank as I realized I was, even now, on my way to fight my own countrymen. And second, because once we were airborne, it took hardly any time to reach the heart of the capital city. The queen flew low, her long serpentine shadow tracing her passage on the city's cobblestones.

Below us, most of the city was shut tight against the magical attacks. The Merchants' District was in near ruins, with various fires burning in stalls and threatening storefronts. Part of the city's central fountain's stonework had been ruined, and the surrounding streets were rapidly flooding. Even with the wind whipping all around us, I could hear the dragon's angry hiss. Her rage radiated off her. The fountain was for more than just aesthetics; it would be the lifeblood of the city, where the citizens would draw their water for the day.

The city streets were a wash of red, dotted with gray—the army of Rothschan. Remembering my conversation with Laydon and Enlar, I felt sick.

How much power would it take to overrun a magical kingdom?

As many you would need to accomplish your goals.

It wasn't a dozen soldiers, or even fifty. But at least two hundred, if my estimate of how many people could fit in Calia's city center was correct. Possibly more.

And, sadly, the red I saw littering the streets wasn't only from the Rothschan uniform. Here and there I saw several unmoving bodies lying in the street—Calians unfortunate to be caught off guard, too slow or stunned to make it to safety. The sick feeling in my stomach threatened to spill over.

The queen roared, letting out a big blast of flame. A warning to the soldiers on the ground. A few brave or curious Calians peered out of their windows, their awe at the dragon Jennica in their midst winning out over their fear of the invaders outside their warded homes.

For now those magical protections were holding, but even the best crafted wards would eventually fall to the onslaught of spells the Rothschan army was throwing at them.

Something felt off, but I didn't quite know what it was.

Dragon Jennica roared again, but the sea of red and gray didn't part.

Even as I cried out, "No!" the queen breathed a huge stream of fire once more, cutting a swath through the Rothschan soldiers. I closed my eyes, heartsick, as several of my countrymen burned up before my eyes instantly.

The queen gently placed Enlar, Laydon, Chandra, and me on the cobblestones, then landed with a heavy thud that shook the ground beneath us.

But the most horrifying thing of all was that none of the knights cried out, fled in terror, or turned to fight. Even though a very large, very angry dragon had just appeared in their midst. Even though their brother knights had just died horrifically.

They just kept casting their spells. Oblivious to the carnage around them.

Wait. Casting their spells?

That didn't make sense. Given what I knew of magic study and the relatively short time Renton had raised his magical army, plus my home country's deep cultural aversion to all things magical, I highly doubted that my countrymen suddenly had become skilled mages so quickly.

Looking closely, I realized that the knights were all casting the same exact spells. In unison. Strange. In fact, while each individual was mouthing the words and pointing their fingers and releasing the spells, they perfectly mimicked each other, in the timing of each phrase and gesture.

They held themselves rigidly, in perfect control like any knight of Rothschan should be.

But their eyes betrayed their terror.

Any ambivalence I had been feeling at fighting my countrymen disappeared as I realized: I wasn't fighting *them*.

The knights weren't oblivious. They were possessed.

The sick feeling in my stomach solidified into a grim resolution. The true enemy—mine, my family's, even my people's—was Renton. Who was nothing more than a puppet for the rulers of Rothschan. Once this battle was over, the real war would just be beginning.

"Don't harm any of the knights!" I yelled over Queen Jennica's roaring. Seeing that the knights weren't running, she had redoubled her efforts to intimidate them. I'm sure she wasn't used to being ignored, in either her human queen or dragon form.

One by one, my companions nodded in understanding as they, too, surveyed the scene. "We'll do our best," Laydon called back. "But where's Renton?"

I pondered that question as I quickly scanned the area. Renton would have to be somewhere nearby, to be able to control the people, unless he was able to see through their eyes. A frightening thought. And also something we hadn't tested for when I ingested my friends' magic—*although*, I thought, *when it came to my newfound magic, we hadn't tested anything*. Another frightening thought.

But no, I didn't think Renton would be in hiding. Perhaps he'd be somewhere protected, but definitely not far from the fray.

And then I spotted him. He was standing on the pedestal of a stone dragon statue, looking more like a conductor than a fearsome leader as he waved his arms about. I threw my head back and laughed. The man wasn't even *trying* to be subtle, obviously wanting Calia, Rothschan, and probably the entire Gifted Lands to know victory was his.

This would be so incredibly easy.

And then Renton spotted me. The queen-as-dragon's arrival—and impressive display of might—had drawn his attention, but now he focused on the humans she had brought with her. Seeing me standing there, he grinned. A hungry, manic, and downright triumphant look spread across his face. He pointed at me. As one, the entire Rothschan army turned toward me and my companions.

I gulped. Perhaps this wouldn't be so easy after all.

42

— · —

CHAPTER FORTY-TWO

THE SILENCE WAS DEAFENING.

Our little group, composed of one dragon and four humans—two of whom were just fledgling mages—stared down the entire military might of Rothschan. Two hundred knights stared back at us, unblinking, with Renton smugly looking on.

We should have come up with a better plan, I thought inanely. *Any plan at all.*

"We didn't think this through, did we?" Enlar's whisper echoed my own thoughts. Mutely, I shook my head.

Renton's voice echoed across the expanse.

"Lovely to see you again, Miss Taethen. I must confess, I'm not that surprised to find you here … although I must say, you keep rather, shall we say, *interesting* company."

Queen Jennica snarled, revealing large, sharp-looking teeth. A low growl sounded in her throat as she shifted restlessly, but she didn't attack. She had evidently heard my earlier entreaty to not harm any of the soldiers.

But she hadn't promised not to hurt Renton.

Lowering her head, she blasted Renton with a stream of fire, even as I screamed, "Wait, Your Majesty. Don't!" In the midst of the dragon queen's inferno, Renton laughed. He continued talking, unfazed by the angry dragon before him. Or the fire that engulfed him. "Do your worst. As you can see, I am much better prepared this time."

Nearby, some of the Rothschan knights cried out. Convulsing, they fell to the ground, where they twitched a few times, then lay unmoving.

"Stop, stop!" I tried to get Queen Jennica's attention. "You're not hurting *him*, you're hurting *them*!"

The queen stopped breathing fire. In addition to the fallen knights, some of the ones still standing looked ragged and weak. Renton, however, remained unaffected by the dragon's flame. Even his clothes looked clean and unburnt. When he saw our incredulous faces, he laughed again.

"It's rather obvious you and your friends are outnumbered, even if you do have that ... abomination ... with you. So I suggest you surrender now, before things get ... unpleasant."

"What are your terms?" I called out.

"You turn yourself over to me, and your friends and golden lizard pet there get to leave. And then we'll leave. Simple, really."

"I doubt it will be that simple," I muttered. Louder, I said, "You'll leave my friends unharmed?"

"Of course." Renton sounded bored. "Well?"

"And what if we say no?"

"Then we capture you, destroy your friends, destroy the dragon, and destroy all of Calia." He smiled snidely. "I'd almost prefer it if you said no. Total annihilation would be such fun."

"He's bluffing," Chandra snarled. "It's a coward's trick, to stand there posturing behind an entire army. We can take him."

She was right. Partly. We could get to him, but not without hurting a myriad of people to do so. And we would almost certainly be killed in the process. I understood the political enmity between the two kingdoms, but I couldn't condone the dishonorable way my country was going about it. Homeland loyalty practically demanded that I support Rothschan in its endeavor to wipe out Calia, but now that I had come to know this magical kingdom and its welcoming people, I couldn't condone that, either.

I put my hand on Chandra's arm to prevent her from rushing headlong into certain disaster. She calmed down somewhat, but I knew she was chafing for action. From the fierce expression on Queen Jennica's face, I could tell she agreed with Chandra. Or maybe dragons always looked fierce.

"I don't know what to do," I admitted quietly to my friends.

"You can't give in to him," Enlar said. "He'll hurt you, or worse, and you know he won't keep his word to let us leave alive."

"You're right," I agreed. "But if I can give you all a chance to get away, I have to take it. And this might be the best way to get to him. With minimum bloodshed."

"You know he'll be protected, somehow. You won't be able to pinch him, let alone stab him." Enlar shook his head. "No, Adalynn. The best thing for us to do is get out of here, and come up with a better plan."

"Innocent people will get hurt. Both Calian citizens, and Rothschan soldiers. No."

From where he stood watching us, Renton called, "This isn't that tough of a decision. I grow tired of waiting."

"We don't have time to argue." Frustrated, Enlar clenched and unclenched his fists. "Laydon, tell her we need to get out of here."

"I can't." Laydon's voice reflected the pain I saw in his face. "It's not my decision, nor anyone else's but Adalynn's. She has to do what she thinks is right."

Chandra exploded. "I can't believe it! Laydon, you're as much of a coward as that fool up on the pedestal over there! You'd let your sister go off with an absolute madman, just because of some sort of twisted code of honor—"

Renton shouted, "I'll give you until the count of three. One ..."

"Don't do it," Enlar said to me, grabbing my hand urgently.

"Two ..."

I gently withdrew my hand from Enlar's. "It will be okay."

Renton raised his arms. In unison, his puppet knights all readied themselves to cast a spell. "Thr—"

I waved my hands in the air, then held them out, palms up, in supplication. "I agree to your terms. I surrender."

Renton's smug smile appeared again. If he had been a different sort of man, I suspected he would have laughed in victory or clapped in glee. But he had more self-control than that. Instead, he merely lowered his arms and snapped his fingers. The knights parted, a human wave edging a clear pathway down the cobblestones straight to the statue where Renton was waiting.

For me.

My throat tightened. Laydon folded me in hug, and I clung to him tightly, not wanting to let go. Enlar embraced me next, then Chandra. I turned to the queen. "Thank you, Your Majesty, for—"

A pointed cough caught my attention. I jumped; the sound was so close I thought Renton was right behind me. But a quick glance over my shoulder told me he wasn't. Still, I knew it wasn't wise to keep him waiting any longer.

I turned away from my friends and started walking slowly toward Renton. The complete stillness of the surrounding knights unnerved me; even knowing it was magically induced didn't make me feel less uneasy.

A whisper to my right caused me to stumble. "Adalynn."

I slowed my steps even more, peering intently into the face of the whisperer as I passed. I recognized the speaker: Dhani, a classmate a few years older than me. We hadn't been close, but we had mutual friends. Dhani's whispered words followed me. "Adalynn, free us."

As I continued my walk, more whispers arose. "Free us. Free us, Adalynn ..."

But as I stared into the faces of the various knights hemming either side of me, I realized—not a single one of them had actually spoken aloud. The magic that bound them, that made them hold themselves so unnaturally still, didn't allow them to speak, either. I was hearing their whispered pleas in my mind. But I had never been able to hear a person's thoughts before....

I thought of how I had jumped when I heard Renton's cough, thinking he was right behind me when he had never moved from his spot at the statue. Possibly, he was a very loud cougher. Or using magic to project his voice—he had power to spare, right now, with the entirety of the Rothschan army's magic at his disposal.

But what was it Laydon had mentioned, about the shared magic? It allowed for access, from one to many. And the reversal was also true. If they had the skill, many people could tap into one person's power.

I was nearly at the dragon statue, where Renton still stood on the pedestal.

Waiting for me.

Seeing him brought back memories of our first meeting, and I found it hard to concentrate as I fought the fear and revulsion that instantly rose up from remembering.

But I had to think this through. Something told me it was very, very important that I understand it, and I was running out of time.

Renton was connected to all of Rothschan. And I, being a child of that kingdom, and with shared magic now flowing in my body, was also connected. To Renton. And to all of Rothschan.

My eyes widened in realization. That's why I had heard my countrymen's thoughts. That's why I had heard Renton so clearly.

I reached the base of the statue. The majestic dragon statue, frozen as it readied itself for flight, gave me a sense of comfort as I looked up at it. In the shadow of one of its wings stood Renton, with an unconcealed gloating expression.

"A pleasure to see you, my dear," he said mockingly. "Come join me." He held out his hand to me.

Unwillingly, I placed my palm, sweaty with nerves, into his cool hand. Renton helped me onto the pedestal, then made a show of wiping his hand on his trousers. "Ah, I can tell someone is nervous."

I wanted to say something defiant, or do something to threaten him and wipe that smirk off his face. But that would have been a waste of energy. Instead, I willed myself to remain calm, and concentrated on sensing the collective magical energy of the people before us.

"You can tell your friends they can go now," Renton said, drawing my focus.

"They won't go until they make sure you won't harm me," I said, gritting my teeth. My head hurt from trying to concentrate on both feeling the people's magic internally and paying attention to what was happening externally.

"Then I'm afraid they'll be rather disappointed," Renton said. He grabbed my arm and drew me in front of him as a flash of silver appeared in his other hand.

Brandishing his knife, he snarled in my ear, "You have been nothing but a nuisance since the day you first stepped foot into my office. I still need your blood, but it will be much easier—and more satisfying—to collect it from your corpse."

He raised the knife to slit my throat.

43

CHAPTER FORTY-THREE

ACROSS THE SQUARE, MY brother's voice rang out, echoing across the stones. "No!"

Queen Jennica roared, ready for a fight.

And from somewhere unknown, whispers on the wind reached me: *Adalynn, we are with you.*

I found myself staring at the sea of red and gray before me. *Adalynn, we are with you.*

Those whispers gave me strength. I grabbed Renton's wrist, in an attempt to either stop his weapon or free myself, I'm not sure which. Fighting through the massive ache that was building up in my head, I reached toward those whispers, toward my people. Toward my friends.

Enlar. Laydon. Soldiers of Rothschan. I called out to them, to their magic, and felt it well up inside me—a trickle, then a stream, then a tidal wave, as they poured their magic freely into me.

Renton dropped the knife and doubled over, now weak and unresisting in my grasp. Pale-faced, he rasped, "What are you doing? I won't let you take this victory away from me!"

The flow of shared magic suddenly ceased, as if it had been dammed up. The sudden stoppage left me breathless and panting. *What happened?*

Renton was standing upright again. Some color had come back to his face. He smiled at me unpleasantly. "Ah. That feels so much better. For me, at least."

My eyes widened. He had somehow stolen some of the people's magic away from me! I reached toward him with my magic, trying to compel the well of power to return to me. Sensing my presence, he pushed back and tried to force me out of his head.

Beyond us, screams and the clash of metal upon metal distracted me momentarily. In the city square, the unnatural stillness had broken, and the Rothschan soldiers were fighting.

Each other.

It didn't seem like the knights knew who their true enemy was, or if they did, they didn't care. Their crazed, frenzied actions were a reflection of the madman who was trying to gain complete magical control of them. Anyone who was nearby or in their way was considered an enemy, even if it was a fellow soldier.

In the midst of the fray, I saw my friends trying to retreat. But the fighting soldiers had surrounded them, forcing them to backtrack from the various paths they were trying to use.

Can't Queen Jennica just grab them all and take off? I thought. But the area was too crowded—she couldn't even unfurl her wings. She did her best to protect them, delicately lifting one serpentine paw and knocking aside part of the Rothschan army like a giant cat knocking a toy off a table. I felt a deranged giggle rise up inside me.

Enlar gave a shout, motioning to Chandra and Laydon to follow him. He had apparently found an unobstructed path. Laydon turned to run after him.

A Rothschan knight ran at his turned back, sword raised.

I screamed, despairing that I was too far away to help.

A pale blonde blur stepped in between my brother and the knight. Even as Laydon turned to see what was transpiring, Chandra blocked the knight's attack.

But she didn't see the other one.

Laydon screamed as the second knight thrust his sword deep into Chandra's stomach, with an almost casual, detached air. He hadn't even pulled his sword free when Laydon slashed his neck with his own weapon, yelling incoherently. The man fell to the ground, clutching his throat, even as Enlar grabbed my angry, grieving brother and pulled him away to safety.

Hot tears tracked down my cheeks as I turned my full attention back to Renton. My fear of how Renton could destroy my beloved homeland, combined with the anger I now felt at his senseless revenge, solidified into a hard, steely resolve.

I reached out, one last desperate time, and found the heart of Renton's magic, deep within him. It was a twisted, thorny mass of power, feeding off the depraved hunger that poisoned his mind and heart.

"You want magic? Power? Is that what you want?" I screamed at him. "Then have it!"

With all the strength I had, I grabbed at the well of combined magic within me, and pushed it from me and into Renton.

He cried out.

And then the world exploded.

44

CHAPTER FORTY-FOUR

TIME PASSED IN A blur. In between periods of dreamless sleep, I would be woken up at various times and given something to ingest—usually food or water, but occasionally some sort of foul-tasting medicine.

You'd think with all the magic in this kingdom, they could at least make their medicine taste better.

I was too exhausted to protest, and quickly downed whatever it was I was being offered so I could go back to sleep.

Eventually, I opened my eyes and actually wanted to stay awake. The crushing exhaustion that had plagued me was no longer present. I looked over and saw Enlar sitting by my bedside. When he saw that I was awake and alert, he smiled. "Ah, she's awake!" He jumped up, opening the door to my room as he called down the hall. "She's awake! Let the others know!"

I heard footsteps quickly shuffle away. He closed the door, resuming his seat by my bedside. "I spend much of my time waiting for you to wake up, it seems."

I smiled. "At least this bed is more comfortable than a stable. And to be fair, I've spent some time waiting for *you* to wake up, too."

His grin grew bigger. "Let's call it even, then."

"How long was I out?"

"About a day or so. We all took turns making sure you ate or took your medicine. The Royal Healer said the first few hours would be the most crucial, but after that, your body would mend itself, given time and rest."

"I don't remember much, but I do remember that medicine." I grimaced. "Where am I?"

"You're in one of the guest suites at the palace," Enlar said. "The queen thought you'd recover faster if you had some privacy—and the Royal Healer attending you—instead of being subjected to the curious eyes of the others recovering in the city infirmary. The rest of us are staying here, too."

Laydon, Taryn, and Queen Jennica entered the room. Enlar immediately stood and bowed, offering his seat to the queen. She thanked him and sank down in the empty chair. Laydon found another chair for Taryn, while he and Enlar stood nearby.

"How are you feeling?" Queen Jennica asked me.

"Much better, Your Majesty," I said.

"Good. Because we have much to discuss."

I swallowed nervously. The queen smiled. "Don't worry, you're not in trouble or anything."

"Ah, forgive me, Your Majesty, but when you put it like that ... now I *know* I'm in trouble." Everyone in the room laughed.

When the laughter died down, the queen asked me, "What do you remember? From the battle with Renton, or afterward?"

I frowned, thinking. "I just knew I wanted him to stop. If he wanted power, then I would give it to him. So I did. After that ... I must have blacked out."

The queen nodded, as if she had expected that answer.

"Excuse me, Your Majesty, but where is Renton?"

"He's no longer here."

"Is he in jail? Back in Rothschan? Or did he get away?"

Queen Jennica had a funny look on her face. "None of those. He exploded."

The queen's matter-of-fact manner unnerved me more than if she had delivered that statement dramatically. Were Calians really that used to people magically exploding?

"Oh."

Queen Jennica must have heard something in my voice, because she softened her tone. "It's hard to accept, knowing you're responsible for someone else's death. Even if it's in self defense. Believe me, I've been there myself."

I looked up at her, a question in my eyes. She didn't bother to answer it. "There will be time for you to sort through your feelings. But right now, there's something important that needs to be addressed. You heard the unspoken feelings of your people, correct?"

Thinking about those whispers in my mind, I said slowly, "Yes, I think so."

"And when you 'felt' everyone's magic, and gave it to Renton, what did it feel like?"

I paused, contemplating the queen's question. Finally, I said, "It was like hearing all the knights' thoughts, only more intense. Concentrated. If those pleas were whispers, their magical power was like shouting. I couldn't help but notice it. Gathering it all into me felt ... natural. Like they all wanted me to have it."

"Perhaps they did." The queen sat back, a thoughtful look on her face.

"Excuse me, Your Majesty, but what does this all mean?"

Queen Jennica looked at Laydon, who sank down carefully on the edge of my bed. "Remember when you ingested Enlar's and my magic?" I nodded. "You felt our magical presence in your self, didn't you?" I nodded again. "As we could feel you. We just chose not to tap into it."

"You can do that?"

"To an extent, yes. It's the principle of magical reciprocity. Enlar and I both have innate magical ability, and the training to know how to use that reciprocity." He smiled at Enlar. "Or, partial training. That knowledge seems to make the difference. For people who have magic, but no skill, there is no reciprocity."

"Which is why Hendon was able to wreak so much havoc, years ago," Queen Jennica put in. "And why Renton was able to control your country's army so easily."

"But you were able to counter that, and wrest control away from him," Laydon said. "We think that's why the knights went berserk; it was backlash from that sudden change of power. Also, they were willing to give you their power, unlike with Renton, who took it from them forcefully. That willingness made quite a difference. And, most telling of all: you were so intertwined with the people that you could hear their thoughts, feel their emotions."

"And Renton couldn't?" I asked.

"He might have. We'll never know, since he's gone now and we can't ask him. But even if he could, it would seem that he ignored or suppressed their feelings, in order to control their minds."

I felt there was something important I was supposed to understand, but wasn't quite grasping. "All right, wonderful, so Renton got his power through brute force, while somehow I got it because the knights were wiling to give it to me. But now that Renton's gone, what does it matter?"

Queen Jennica and Laydon exchanged a look loaded with some indecipherable meaning. Laydon said carefully, "You have all the same abilities Renton had."

I shrugged, uncomprehending. Everyone gave me looks of various incredulity.

"You have *all* the same abilities Renton had," Laydon restated.

And then I understood. I was not just able to access everyone's magic, and use it. But I could also sense their thoughts, their feelings … and influence them, for good or ill.

I nearly fell out of my bed in shock, and had to fight the wave of panic and nausea that rose up in me. It was a frightful responsibility.

One I didn't want.

My mouth went suddenly dry. "What do I do?" I whispered. "Is there a way I can get rid of this, somehow?"

The queen shook her head. "Not that we know of, yet. It would take more time and testing to do that. And magic has its own quirks, one being that when power has been awakened, it can be difficult, sometimes even impossible, to suppress it again."

"Meaning?"

"You might have this power forever."

"*Forever*?"

"Well, in time, you'd get used to it." The queen smiled wryly. "Most of the rulers in the Gifted Lands would give anything to have this ability."

"Think of the havoc it would wreak if they did." Enlar shuddered.

"Which is probably why it's best no one, in a leadership position or otherwise, has this power."

"Would you want it, Your Majesty?" I knew it was an impertinent question, but at that moment, still reeling from the shock, I didn't really care about impropriety.

But fortunately Queen Jennica wasn't the type of royal—or person—who would have focused on manners over compassion. Instead, she leveled a shrewd gaze on me. "No. I know that sounds hard to believe, but as a ruler who loves her people dearly—no, I would not want to have the ability to bend my subjects to my will against their own. My dear Adalynn, we had no idea that the magical power we gifted you with would also carry such a dreadful curse. I don't envy your position, and I hope you accept my sincerest apology for inflicting this change upon you."

"And my apologies as well," Laydon said. "We didn't think through the consequences when we did this to you."

I shrugged, uncomfortable with their earnest declarations. "I'm as much to blame as anyone else. I agreed to go through with it. So, I have to figure out—what do I do now?"

"What do you want to do?"

"I don't know. I want to go home, but how could I? Knowing that I could hear everyone's thoughts, knowing that I could take over their minds in an instant ... it would be hard to fight such a temptation."

"You'd have Mother, Father, and me to keep you in check," Laydon pointed out. "And since you don't *want* to wield that power, that already sets up several safeguards in your mind against it. Renton obviously had no such compunction."

"But that temptation would always be there, within easy reach. The knights would know it, too. And ..."

"Yes?"

"Renton was just a pawn in a much larger scheme. The true blame for everything that happened lies at the feet of the king and queen of Rothschan."

My brother whistled. "Are you saying you want to depose the royal family?"

"I'm not sure what I'm saying. I just know that somehow, eventually, they will have to pay for their crimes. Whether or not I'm the one to make that happen, I don't know. But now I have the means to do it, if I wanted to. And that scares me, more than anything."

Queen Jennica spoke up. "While I personally have no love for the Rothschan royals, I can't say for certain that removing them from power would help anything. Not without some plan to immediately stabilize the country, with some person or group to take their place."

"I'm *not* volunteering!"

"I don't blame you. I've been raised to rule my entire life, and there are still things about the job I find distasteful. I'm sure my husband Beyan would have a much longer list. But I agree with you. Someday they will have to pay, but today is not that day."

I opened my mouth to speak, but instead a huge yawn escaped. Everyone else laughed. The queen stood, signaling the visit was over. "But for now, you need to rest, and get better."

"Your Majesty, before you go, may I ask a few questions?"

"Of course, Adalynn."

"What happened to the Rothschan knights, after the battle was over?"

"We offered them a temporary truce. Beyan and I discussed it, and under the circumstances, we didn't think it wise to take them prisoner, let alone execute them or ransom them back to Rothschan. If we even wanted to, which we didn't. Perhaps our small act of good faith will cause Rothschan to cease any future plans of vengeance. Anyway, your countrymen were free to leave, provided if they stayed or returned to Calia, it would be in peace only, under penalty of death." She smirked slightly. "And I'm sure, once the story of how you defeated Renton gets back to the king and queen of Rothschan, your family will get a complete pardon, and they'll be interested in making our countries' temporary truce more ... permanent."

"Oh. That was ... extremely fair of you, Your Majesty." I knew my home country would not have made such a generous offer, if the situation had been the other way around.

"You said you had more questions?"

"Oh, yes. Ah, my eyes may have deceived me, but ... did I see you swipe away the soldiers during the battle? Like a giant cat?"

The queen laughed. "I didn't want to hurt any of them—too much—but we had to get them out of the way quickly. I did my best to be gentle and careful. Besides, they were all wearing heavy armor, so I'm sure none of them felt a thing. Honestly, hitting that armor hurt my paw." She shook out her right hand. "It still stings."

We all laughed as Queen Jennica left my room, followed by Taryn. Laydon gave me a brief hug, then also left, passing Enlar, who lingered in the doorway.

"What is it?" I asked him.

"It's nothing, really." He fidgeted, and I realized I had never seen calm, collected Enlar *fidget*. "I just hope you get better quickly, that's all."

"Oh, thank you. But I suspect there's something you're not saying?"

"Yes. Not only do I miss you, but I also don't want to be the only adult in a class full of young, fledgling magicians."

I laughed, realizing what he meant. "That's right! Magic classes should be starting soon at the Academy. And I forgot—we'll be in the beginner level classes."

Enlar laughed too. "Well, I know *I* will be, at least. They might let you skip a few levels. What with stopping a magical war and all that."

I plucked a pillow from my bed and threw it at him. He easily avoided it. It hit the doorframe as he ducked out the door, his laughter echoing down the hallway.

Epilogue

Sometimes the best action is inaction.

I recovered quickly, and within a week the Royal Healer declared me completely healed, both physically and magically. Just in time to start my classes at the Academy. Enlar's guess had been correct; since we were both novice magicians, we were in the beginner's group, and were the oldest students in the class. The other students ranged in age from as young as five to (not counting us) as old as fifteen. Students advanced based on skill, not age, but most students had already moved to at least journeyman status by the time they were young adults. Enlar and I were extremely aware—and rather self-conscious—of our status.

But the magical classes were fascinating enough to help take our minds off that—or, mine anyway. Knowing that we felt a bit awkward, Limande, Laydon, and, occasionally even Queen Jennica, were kind enough to give Enlar and me private instruction. Eventually the private tutoring grew more frequent, and our attendance in the group classes dwindled.

Which was fine with me. Not only did I learn better—and faster—in private study, but the flexible classes meant I would be able to leave the Academy whenever I needed to, without missing too many magical lessons.

After the aborted attack and Renton's demise, many of the knights had stayed in Calia and helped rebuild the capital city. Others had left, either to return to Rothschan or to find their fortune in another part of the Gifted Lands. After the capital had been restored, the Rothschan knights who had assisted either settled in Calia or returned home.

Chandra had a quiet burial in Calia, attended by the king and queen, Taryn, Enlar, the other refugees, Laydon, Fiala, and me. I hadn't known her long, or well, but I mourned her brief friendship. And her unrequited love for my brother. I wished her life had been happier for the short time she had walked the Gifted Lands. Seeing Fiala and Laydon growing closer in their grief for their beloved friend and sister, I knew that my brother had picked the best partner for him. And I knew I would never dishonor Chandra's memory by mentioning her secret to my brother. Telling him wouldn't do him any good, anyway.

I visited home as soon as I could take the time away from my classes. Laydon came with me. Mother and Father were delighted to have the entire family back together, even if it was only temporary. They had both completely recovered from their abuse at Renton's hands, and had settled back into my childhood home.

"Can we convince you to come to Calia to be with us?" I asked one night after dinner. "Laydon makes a good living, teaching at the academy. And the queen gave me such a generous reward. I have more than enough for all my expenses."

Mother shook her head. "We're so grateful to Queen Jennica for that—the money you've been sending home has been so helpful. But while Calia sounds like a lovely country, our place is here. Rothschan isn't a perfect place to live, but for us, it's home."

"Besides," Father said, patting my hand, "we can't change anything for the better if we're not even living here." I had told them about how Laydon and I had recreated Renton's magical experiments, and how those experiments had changed me.

"You're right," I conceded. "But you can't blame me for wanting you nearby. I'll be at the Academy for at least a year or two, depending on how fast I advance through my classes."

"You'll be a full-fledged magician in no time," Laydon assured me. "You're already way ahead of most of your peers in the beginner levels."

I snorted. "If by 'ahead' you mean I'm older than most of them by close to a decade, then you're right."

"I didn't mean it that way, but now that you mention it ..."

I stuck my tongue out at him. My brother laughed. "I take it back. Maturity-wise, you're definitely not ahead of them."

Our parents and I laughed too. Mother asked Laydon, "Adalynn may move back when she's done with her classes, but I don't suppose you'll be coming home too?"

Laydon shook his head. "It's been too long, Mother. I don't consider Rothschan home anymore. My heart is in Calia."

Something about the way he said that last bit made her look at Laydon sharply. "What do you mean?"

He grinned. "It's time and past I told you. Mother, Father, I know you won't move to Calia, but would you be up to traveling there in a few months' time? After all, I wouldn't want you to miss my wedding."

I hid my own broad grin behind my hands as Mother and Father both spoke at the same time.

"Your wedding?" Mother said, looking misty-eyed.

"Of course we'll come," Father said proudly.

"And of course, you'll be in the wedding," Laydon said, turning to me.

"Really?" I clapped my hands. "What would you want me to do? A magical display of some sort?"

"Possibly. You're getting much better at controlling your magic, although your emotions still have a tendency to take over if you're not careful."

Indignantly, I said, "I don't know what you mean—"

Down the hallway, a crash came from my bedroom.

Mother quickly stood up and headed toward my room. She returned shortly, some daisies in her hand. "I think this is the bouquet you picked this morning, Adalynn. The vase holding them shattered. There's water all over the floor."

Sheepishly, I looked at my brother. "Maybe we can find something non-magical for me to do at your wedding. For now."

He nodded, a smirk growing on his face. "We'll work on it. Maybe not blowing up my wedding could count as your final exam."

We spent the rest of the evening discussing the upcoming wedding, as well as Laydon and Fiala's future plans in Calia. Eventually, my family decided to retire for the night. I wasn't quite tired yet, so I offered to clean up the kitchen, thinking that might wear me out. But even after I was done, I still wasn't ready to sleep, so I went outside, closing the front door quietly behind me. I leaned against the house and looked up at the stars.

Next to me, the door opened and then shut. A tall figure crossed in front and then joined me, also looking up at the night sky.

"Can't sleep?" Father said.

"Just a lot to think about."

"I'll say. Your magic classes, your brother getting married ... there's much that is happening. But somehow, I don't think that's what's on your mind."

"No. I still ... I still haven't decided what's the best thing to do. Should I return to Rothschan? Stay in Calia? One feels like tempting fate. And one feels like running away from responsibility."

"You talk like you have only two options, when there's a world of possibility out there. You could choose a third thing: settle in a different kingdom that's not Rothschan or Calia. Or a fourth. Wander the Gifted Lands. There are even more choices beyond that."

"But what about changing things here in Rothschan? Possibly dismantling the monarchy? Maybe I'm being selfish, by staying at the Academy and taking classes. I should be back here, doing *something*. What if—"

"Those are two very powerful words, *what if*. And very paralyzing. Adaylnn, it's fine if you want to pursue your magic study, and it's fine that it might take a year or more to finish. A lot can happen in a year. Others might rise up, to force change. The current rulers might change, naturally. Or things might stay just as they are. But you should do what you need to do today, to be ready for the future."

I sighed. "You're right, of course."

He hugged me. "Trust me, that future is going to come faster than you think it will."

I leaned into my father, basking in his strength and his wisdom. I'd worry about Rothschan and all its troubles later. For now, I had my family, my friends, and my own bright future to look forward to. It would have to be enough.

I smiled.

It was more than enough.

Dear Reader: I appreciate you!

It means so, so much to me that you decided to read *Heir of Magic and Mischance*. I hope you enjoyed this third title in the Kingdom Legacy series as much as I enjoyed writing it.

If you have a moment, a short review on Goodreads or wherever you like to buy books and learn about new titles would be awesome.

Want to be the first to know about new adventures? Let's keep in touch!

Join the Newsletter and get a FREE TTRPG one-shot campaign set in the world of the Gifted Lands: http://www.rachanee.net/newsletter

Instagram: http://www.instagram.com/rachaneelumayno

TikTok: http://www.tiktok.com/@rachaneelumayno

YouTube: http://www.youtube.com/@rachaneelumayno

Twitter: http://www.twitter.com/rachaneelumayno

Join the community on Discord: Kingdom Legacy -(https://discord.com/invite/BRXcJJ3c6f)

—·—

TRAVEL BACK TO THE GIFTED
LANDS IN HEIR OF CROWNS AND
CURSES, THE FOURTH BOOK IN
THE KINGDOM LEGACY SERIES

CHAPTER ONE

"I CAN'T BELIEVE IT. They want me to be a what?"

I stared in dismay at the fancy script gracefully inscribed across the thick cream paper.

You are cordially invited to the dedication of Crown Prince Coran of Calia, to be held in our capital city on the third day of our annual Haerfest Celebration, in honor of the autumn season ...

And underneath, in the blocky handwriting I recognized as being from the hand of one of my best friends:

Dear Rhyss,

Jennica and I would be honored if you would stand as Coran's godfather. We can think of no finer person to be his future mentor.

The handwritten part of the note was signed by both my friend King Beyan and his wife, Queen Jennica.

The rulers of the northern kingdom of Calia.

"Did you get one of these too?" I held out the paper.

Across the table, Farrah reached over and plucked the ivory invitation from my unresisting fingers, narrowly avoiding her mostly full mug of mead. I grabbed mine up and took a drink.

Or tried to. It was empty. I turned it upside down, just to make sure. Yep, nothing there. Of course. Just my luck.

"Would you like some more mead, Rhyss?"

I looked up, sighing in relief. "You're an angel, Sylvie. That's why you're my favorite barmaid here at the Dragon's Tail."

Sylvie grinned as she refilled my mug. "I'm the only barmaid here at the Dragon's Tail. And you two—" she nodded at Farrah, who was reading the letter but looked up to give a brief nod of acknowledgement "—are in here often enough that I can tell when you're running low on drink even before you know."

"That's why you're the best barmaid in the best tavern in Orchwell."

Sylvie rolled her eyes. "It's the only tavern in Orchwell."

She topped off Farrah's cup, although it didn't really need it. "And I may be an angel, but don't think that flattery means I forgot your tab."

I groaned. Just add that to my already unlucky day. "I'll get it to you soon."

Sylvie snorted. "That's what they all say. You're lucky I like you. And that Farrah's been nice enough to pay down your bill from time to time." With that, the barmaid left to attend to another table.

Farrah, meanwhile, had finished reading the invitation, and was going over it again carefully, running her finger from word to word as if she needed to make sure she was really seeing what was written there. She burst out laughing. "Well, Rhyss. It looks like you've acquired yourself a baby."

I frowned as I ran a pale, freckled hand through my bright red hair. "Not like that, gods forbid."

"The chances of you actually becoming Coran's parent are slim. But that's not what gets me."

"What, then?"

Farrah laughed even harder. "The part about being his mentor."

Even if I was unsure about the whole godparent thing, her comment made me feel defensive. "Hey. I'd make an excellent mentor."

Farrah laughed so hard she couldn't speak for several moments. "Uh-huh, sure. You keep believing that."

I toyed briefly with the idea of pushing the issue, and then decided to drop it. This was Farrah, after all. She knew me too well, and was too often right about, well, everything.

"Well, what are you going to do about it?"

Farrah was waving the cream-colored paper in the air at me. I plucked it from her hands and stared at the fancy script again.

"Do I really have a choice?" I stared morosely at the invitation in one hand, and with the other, picked up my mug of mead and downed it one swallow. "I'm going to be the godparent to the heir of the Calian throne."

A few weeks later, Farrah and I traveled from our homes in the kingdom of Orchwell to its nearest neighbor, the kingdom of Calia. It was a trip we both knew well; as a Seeker, Beyan had been our former employer, and one of our dearest friends, before his marriage to the Calian princess, Jennica. He was still one of our dearest friends, as was Jennica. But instead of roaming the Gifted Lands Seeking out dragons, he now spent his time helping rule a kingdom.

Even after all this time, it still took some getting used to.

As if reading my thoughts, Farrah asked, "How long has it been since Beyan got married to Jennica and moved away from Orchwell?"

I scrunched my brow in thought. "Two years? Three? I lose track of time."

Farrah shook her head. Her violet hair, indicative of her half-Fae heritage, fell in front of her ebony face, and she tucked it behind her ear. I thought she was going to make a quip about time's not the only thing you lose track of, or something similar, but instead she was marveling about something else. "I honestly never thought I would have seen the day when Beyan got married, much less had a child. Never mind marrying into royalty. It had just been the three of us, for so long. I guess I never thought things would change."

"You've known him longer. I suppose it did come as a bit of a shock when it happened. But things can't stay the same forever."

"That's true." Farrah looked ... sad? Wistful? I couldn't quite read the expression on her face. For some reason, it worried me. Farrah was usually the calm, logical, competent one. Sentimental was not a word I'd ever use to describe her. She turned that indecipherable look on me. Now I was really worried. "One day the same thing might happen to you and me."

"I hardly doubt I'll go off and marry a princess."

Farrah shrugged. "You could. But that's not what I meant. Ever since Beyan left the field, it's been harder to find work. We were lucky with Kaernan's commissions, but it's not like he takes them all that often—"

"But he did recommend us to his other Seeker friends."

"Who had their own established teams and only hire us if their regular team can't do the job. It's not like it was before. We might end up working for different Seekers instead of being hired together. One of us could move away from Orchwell. Or maybe one of us decides to leave the help-for-hire business entirely. My point is, things are changing, but it feels like we're not choosing the changes, the changes are choosing us, and I hate feeling powerless about it all."

Farrah looked away. I was too stunned by her outburst—so unlike her—to have a response, and for a while the only sound was the clop clop clop of our horses' hooves as we traveled the well-worn road north to Calia.

Finally, I ventured, "Are you okay, Farrah?"

She sighed heavily. "Yes, I am. Or, I will be. Don't worry about it." Her tone told me the conversation was over. At least, for now. Quite possibly, permanently.

Farrah changed the subject. "What did you get as a dedication gift?"

Fine by me if she wanted to talk about something else. Dealing with emotions was never my strong suit, anyway.

I patted the satchel attached to my saddle. "Just a little token, really. Baby's first sword."

"Rhyss. You didn't."

"Well, he might need to go out in the world adventuring one day. Rescue princesses, stop evil sorcerers, slay dragons. Well, forget that last part. He'd be disowned by his parents if he did that."

"But what is a baby going to do with a sword? Is it a magic sword?"

"Um. No. It's just a regular sword. But really, what is a baby going to do with anything? It's not like he'll remember his dedication, anyway. Someday his godfather Rhyss will teach him how to use that sword, so really, I'm ensuring we'll have a strong bond in the future."

Farrah snorted. Miffed, I asked, "What did you get him?"

"I bought a simple necklace with a small golden sun for a pendant."

Now I snorted derisively. "Sounds impressive. I'm sure a newborn baby will love jewelry."

Farrah ignored my comment. "And then I enchanted it so when he wears it, it will mark him as a Friend of the Fae. It will keep him safe from the tricks and glamours of minor faeries, protect him from the Fae who might inhabit the woods and waters of the Gifted Lands, and its status will be recognized by the Faerie royals, King Finvarra and Queen Oona of the Seelie Court, should Prince Coran ever visit."

I swallowed the witty comeback I had been preparing, and instead repeated, "Sounds impressive."

This time I truly meant it. Farrah's gift would definitely be useful for a royal child and future ruler.

Farrah must have caught my changed demeanor, because her face changed from smug to sympathetic. "I'm sorry about my earlier comment. A sword is a great gift. He'll grow into it, and I'm sure he'll love training with you when he's old enough."

"It's really a silly thing to give him. I mean, Coran is the Crown Prince of Calia. He can have hundreds of swords made for him, much finer than the one I'm giving him. Magic to boot, if that's what he wanted. He doesn't need the absolutely worthless one I'm giving him."

Now it was Farrah's turn to ask, "Is everything okay?"

I laughed, but it wasn't a happy sound. "You're worried about things changing. I'm wondering ..."

"Wondering what?"

I sighed as the words came out in a rush. "Why Jennica and Beyan picked me to be the godparent for their child. For the heir to the throne, of all things! It should have been you—you have magic, after all. Or I'm sure Beyan has a Seeker cousin or knows someone in Orchwell who is still an active Seeker. But aside from being a friend of the royal couple, I don't have anything extraordinary to offer Coran. It just doesn't make sense to me, that's all."

We rode on in silence. I pretended to admire the scenery around us—the green of summer was beginning to give way to the reds and golds of the coming autumn.

Inwardly I chastised myself. Now who was being all emotional? But, I realized, it was a sentiment I had been harboring for a while, since we had gotten our invitations to the dedication. I just hadn't allowed myself to fully face my feelings about the situation until just now. But as long as Farrah and I were getting personal ...

When Farrah finally did say something, it was with her usual unflinching honesty, the trait that seemed so harsh and yet, over time, I had learned to appreciate. "You're right, Rhyss. At first blush, you do seem like a surprising choice. But Beyan and Jennica wouldn't have wanted you specifically without a good reason. And sometimes traits like bravery and honesty and trustworthiness are more important than having magical powers or an inherent ability like Seeking. You're important to the royal couple, and therefore you'll be important in the life of their child. And that's all that matters."

I hope so. I didn't say the words out loud, but Farrah gave me a gentle smile, as if she had heard what I'd been thinking.

"Is there anything else bothering you?" she asked.

"Yes, actually," I said, smirking. "Shouldn't it be godsfather, not godfather? Although godsfather is harder to say." I tried out each word. "Godsfather. Godfather. What do you think?"

Farrah groaned. "I think you should spare me your superstitious nonsense."

Talking about the gods never failed to get a rise out of Farrah. The religious beliefs in the Gifted Lands was as varied as its people—some believed in the old gods, as I did, that were rumored to have founded our kingdoms. Some worshipped the Fae, whose ancient magic permeated our human realm to varying degrees, depending on where you lived. And some people didn't believe in anything at all, unless it was something they could see with their own eyes and create with their own hands.

Farrah's half-Fae heritage made her uncomfortable with the idea of Faerie worship. "I believe in myself, but not like that," she would quip whenever the subject came up.

I grinned. "I haven't yet, and I don't plan to, ever."

Farrah grimaced and sighed. "Lucky me."

We fell into a companionable silence. We passed a few farms and single homes along the way, then reached the modest-sized town on the outskirts of the Calian capital city. From there, it wasn't much longer until we reached the open gates to Calia's capital, with its cool gray stone palace rising in the distance.

We passed through the city gates, which were, as usual, bustling with merchants, traders, visitors, and Calian citizens entering or leaving the city. Farrah scrutinized everything as we walked by—the city walls, the gates, the cobblestone streets, buildings, and even the majestic fountain in the city square.

"Would you stop gawking? You're acting like you've never been to Calia before, when we both know you've been here dozens of times."

Farrah stopped examining everything and gave me an exasperated look. "That's not why I'm looking, silly. I'm just impressed at how quickly the capital was repaired after the recent attack. You can hardly see any damage at all."

Oh, yes, that was right. Several months ago, Rothschan, a fellow Gifted Lands kingdom, had caught Calia off guard with a surprise magical attack. That Rothschan wanted revenge for the overthrow and subsequent death of King Hendon, who had been a beloved knight of Rothschan before becoming a not-so-loved king of Calia, was not a surprise. That the kingdom used magic—which they outright mocked, feared, and despised—to attempt that revenge was a surprise. One that had nearly succeeded in ruining Calia, and had definitely caused significant damage to her fair capital city.

Looking around, I saw that Farrah was right in her assessment. "Queen Jennica and King Beyan must know how to inspire their subjects. A generous treasury doesn't hurt, either."

"I wish we had been there to help," Farrah said. "Although it sounds like they had things under control. For the most part."

I chuckled. "I think that was the first time we missed all the action. Who would have thought going on a Seeker commission would be less exciting than staying home and going to visit friends?"

"Not only was I surprised when we came home to find out the news about the attack on Calia, we got a second surprise when Jennica and Beyan announced her pregnancy." Farrah chuckled as well, remembering. "Although, with everything that happened, it was smart of them to wait until they could be sure Rothschan wouldn't try to attack again."

I thought for a minute. "That's right; Beyan mentioned they were just about to announce it when all the chaos with Rothschan erupted. But are they sure Rothschan won't retaliate in some way? That's a kingdom with a long memory that holds even longer grudges."

"Didn't Beyan tell you?"

"Tell me what?"

"They have an ally from Rothschan now. Several, in fact, and some of them had been refugees living in Calia for a long time. But this new ally has the magical ability to overthrow the kingdom's current royal family and rule in their place, if she chose to. And the Rothschan royals know it. So there's a sort of stalemate between the two kingdoms right now. A rather reluctant truce, if you will."

"Really?"

"Honestly, Rhyss, don't you remember? It's pretty big news; Beyan had to have mentioned it."

I frowned, trying to recall my last conversation with my friend. I had been so surprised by his "Jennica and I are having a baby" announcement that I may have missed out on the rest of what he had been saying. I'm sure as King Beyan, his subjects hung on his every word, but my friend Beyan knew exactly what I—his longtime friend and former traveling companion—was like.

But I had always paid attention when it counted. Like if our group was under attack by bandits. Or we had to tread quietly because a dragon was near. Things like that.

Farrah shook her head at me, like she was annoyed, but it was more from force of habit than anything. After all the years of traveling together, she knew what I was like, too. She gave a heavy sigh of fond exasperation. "Well, at least you remembered that Rothschan attacked Calia, even if you didn't recall the details. That's something, at least."

"Don't worry, if Jennica and Beyan talk about it, I'll act like I know what they're talking about."

Farrah laughed. "Beyan will see right through that. Besides me, he's the only other person who knows you all too well."

Our conversation had taken us into the heart of the capital, past the Merchants' District, beyond the Academy of Magical Arts that Queen Jennica had founded a few years ago, and right to the palace gardens. Just beyond was the fountain-lined walkway leading to the Calian palace. The shimmering blue-and-green cobblestones in the palace courtyard always gave me the feeling I was underwater. No matter how many times I had been here, the palace never ceased to impress me.

Farrah giggled at me. "Now who's gawking?"

I playfully poked her—no easy feat, since we were both atop horses. "Still had to believe rough-and-tumble Beyan lives in this fancy place."

Her grin softened as she stared at the majestic building before us. "Changes," was all she said.

As we approached, the door to the palace flung open dramatically. A musical voice proclaimed, "Lord Rhyss and Lady Farrah have arrived! Welcome to Castle Calia!"

Continue Rhyss's story here:
HEIR OF CROWNS AND CURSES

—·—

ACKNOWLEDGEMENTS

DOES THIS WRITING THING get easier with time? I'm not sure about that, but I do know I have an amazing group of people in my life who help make this whole writing thing so much easier. I couldn't do it without any of you.

Thank you, again and as always, to my editor Tom. Not only are you incredibly generous with your time and expertise, I'm glad you actually look forward to reading the next book!

Special thanks to Erik, for helping me figure out "all that military stuff." It definitely made researching (not necessarily one of my favorite parts of writing) easier.

About the Author

Rachanee Lumayno is an actress, voiceover artist, screenwriter, avid gamer, and amateur dodgeball player. She grew up in Michigan, where she spent way too much of her free time reading fantasy novels. She still spends too much of her free time reading fantasy, although now she writes them as novels, narrates them as audiobooks, and creates them as improv for various roleplaying campaigns as well. *Heir of Magic and Mischance* is her third novel, and the third book in the Kingdom Legacy series. She is also a staff writer for two webcomics and an upcoming video game. You can find her online at her website, www.rachanee.net, or on Instagram, TikTok, or YouTube (@rachaneelumayno).

CRITICS ARE WILD FOR ROBERT J. RANDISI!

"Randisi always turns out a traditional Western with plenty of gunplay and interesting characters"

— *ROUNDUP*

"Each of Randisi's novels is better than its entertaining predecessor."

— *BOOKLIST*

"Everybody seems to be looking for the next Louis L'Amour. To me, they need look no further than Randisi."

— JAKE FOSTER, AUTHOR OF *THREE RODE SOUTH*

"Randisi knows his stuff and brings it to life."

— *PREVIEW MAGAZINE*

"Randisi has a definite ability to construct a believable plot around his characters."

— *BOOKLIST*